SOl

C000242639

J.S. Morton

Dystopic

An imprint of Duck and Cover Books.

Dystopic Publishing

An imprint of Duck and Cover Books

First published in the U.K. 2020 by Dystopic
Publishing.

An imprint of Duck and Cover Books.

71-75 Shelton Street

Covent Garden

WC2H 9JQ

www.duckandcoverbooks.com

ISBN 978-1-916065-77-2

Edition 2.

"The choice for mankind lies between freedom and happiness and for the great bulk of mankind, happiness is better."

George Orwell

The Dream.

Alone in the cosmos, thirty-three million miles from Earth, the S.S. Santa Maria approached Mars' atmosphere. He had done it! Bryant Fisher was the vessel's sole occupant. He was about to be the first human ever to reach the surface of Mars. The ships designed for Mars could only be piloted alone, driven by someone with skill, determination, courage, valour, good looks, a chiselled jaw and of course, a great sense of humour. Dozens had been selected for this mission. Most had backed out; some had undertaken this voyage in the past, only to fail. Not today, though, not for this man.

After 33.9 million miles, navigating the last two felt like billions more. As it approached Mars, the vessel pierced through the planet's muggy atmosphere like the sun through a dark pond. He activated the landing sequence with slight trepidation; he had logged thousands of Mars landing simulator hours. But the reality was, no one had ever done it for real. 'Hisss' came the sound of the landing stabilisers as he touched down on the surface. Safely down, landing checks completed, Bryant hit the live feed button on his apps. This was a historical moment and needed to be documented in the most scientific way possible, by social media and live streams, naturally. The twenty-seven billion inhabitants of Earth were ready, eager, waiting. They were about to watch him step foot on foreign soil. Not since the 16th of July 1969 had any human taken such a significant step. Bryant Fisher was about to join, nay lead the ranks of brave astronauts and physically plant his foot into the history books for eternity.

As he hit the button, the ship's door whistled open much like a porch curtain on a breezy summer day. The Sun's light beaming in, it permeated the dark corners of the ship, and he was ready, the world was ready, and notably, the live feed was ready. This was it! His connection was live. All he could hear was chorus upon chorus of one word. Bryant, Bryant, Bryant, chimed through the ship's speakers, music to his ears. Bryant, Bryant, Bryant, Bryant!

"BRYANT, god-damn it!" cried Mr Rubinat. "Daydreaming again, Bryant? If that isn't the third time this month? These cars certainly won't wash themselves. What on earth is the matter with you, son?"

Painfully awake, Bryant snapped to attention as though 5000 volts had just coursed through him as he spilt his now lukewarm bucket of water over the dry ground beneath him. His manager, Mr Rubinat, tutted typically, rolled his eyes, and walked back towards the showroom. Not before yelling, "Next time's the last time!" As he slammed the plate glass door behind him. Bryant's colleagues, who had been washing the other electric vehicles, chuckled and walked off—making the same startled bucket-dropping gesture to each other as they did.

"Why don't you try not sleeping at work? It can't be that difficult," echoed the voice over his shoulder. Bryant turned to see his friend Jimmy who had just rolled up and dismounted his e-board behind him.

"You try washing cars for a living! It's so dull," replied Bryant. "Seriously, though, it's these entry exams for the Academy. I've only got two more weeks. I just can't get my head around the practice questions."

Jimmy and Bryant had been through it all. They lived in the same District, went to school together, and usually spent every waking hour side by side. But as inseparable as they were, even Jimmy struggled to support Bryant's obsession with getting into the Academy.

"Dude, come on, you know as well as I do, only one person from each District makes the Academy every year. Those exams are impossible. It's a pipe dream. Focus on what's real."

"You might feel differently if you were eligible," replied a somewhat perturbed Bryant.

"Whatever," said Jimmy, "Your mum's making us dinner tonight? I'd take Pam's lasagne over the Academy, and it's ridiculous tests any day of the week." Jimmy crouched, grabbed a helmet, and then tossed it playfully at Bryant, "Come on genius, I'll race you there."

The year was 2369. The Space Academy had been the result of humanity pulling together in their darkest hour. World leaders had combined forces with one goal; colonising Mars. Life on Earth had become unsustainable. Living was now just to exist, fuelling the future. Joining the Academy had become the elitist, most exclusive, and highly coveted vocation on the planet. Entering it, however, was as elusive as finding the end of a rainbow. Should you join, you were part of the future! Entry, however, was challenging. Doctorates didn't matter; degrees, as they were, had fallen by the wayside, not even standard I.Q. mattered. Every year, each District across the globe held an examination. There were 300 questions, and the pass mark was 100%. Get one question wrong, score 299 out of 300, and you had failed. You weren't good enough. Despite the enormous improbability of getting all 300 correct, somebody would always manage. Each year one person from every District got to enter the hallowed Academy. They would join the ranks and become a hero. Once initiated, they were heralded the District over, going from zero to hero faster than the speed of light. Leaving light itself looking ahead, wondering what could possibly move more quickly than it did. That for Bryant was the dream, and it was all that mattered. He was like Ahab chasing his whale, Jason searching for the golden fleece. As far back as he could remember, he had dreamt of space, visualised being a purveyor of the future. He would then wake from those dreams to eat his 'Planet Rings' cereal, -the cereal that had won him a tour of the Academy when he was 9-. Bryant had watched all the Authority produced Space films; multiple times. He vexed friends and family alike with the recitation of lines, visual effects, and facts. The films themselves were dramatic, euphoric, but factual and scientific—more docudrama than fiction. The goal for him was space. The dream for everyone was space, given the dramatic lack of it. Yet now, after what felt like a thousand years of growing up, he was finally eighteen. He'd come of age, and that meant he was at last eligible to face the impossible head-on and sit the test for the Academy.

"Hi, Jimmy," came the gravelly yet cheery voice of Pam Fisher.

"Hi, Mrs Fisher," replied Jimmy.

Bryant's mother Pam had run the District cinema all of her life. Her family had owned it for as many generations as they could remember, and between them, they had kept it independent. This meant that for now, it was away from the clutches of the Authorities. Cinemas permitted alcohol. It was encouraged. But because of the sheer power of the special effects, sounds, and general experience. Cinemas like this, in Districts with little to do, often attracted teens with Blackmarket psychedelic drugs. So, poor Pam had spent a lifetime dealing with tripping teenagers rather than genuine moviegoers. Between that and the watchful eyes of the Authorities, it had given her a real steeliness. She was a pleasant lady, greying around the edges but elegant and hardy. She still had the voice of an angel, albeit one who had spent eternity gargling strong antiseptic mouthwash.

"Where's your other half?" Pam asked Jimmy as he entered the room. "He promised he'd help his sister with her science project…again!"

"Huh?" replied Jimmy, mildly confused.

"Your other half Jimmy, my son Bryant! You know, the one you're never separated from," she explained.

"Oh, I get it," said Jimmy, throwing his hands up into the air. "Dunno, he's about. I just came for the lasagne."

"Don't be cheeky, Jimmy Fletcher," she retorted, her tone upping suddenly.

"Sorry, Mrs Fisher," replied Jimmy politely, "I think he's just putting the e-boards on charge in the garage."

Bryant's family composed of himself, his mother Pam, and sister Julie. Pam was in her late fifties, and she'd had a hard life. Bryant was seven years his sister's senior, and his sister was a handful. Byrant was all about the books, space, his duties. But even at the tender age of eleven, it was clear Julie would rather watch the world burn. There was no male figure in their lives. Their father Bryan had simply disappeared in the middle of the night about six years ago, not even leaving so

7

much as a note. It had left Pam to bring up a five-year-old minx as well as a soon-to-be teenager all by herself. Her husband's disappearance was shrouded in mystery even to this day. But the world was overpopulated, people did disappear, and from the Authorities' point of view, it wasn't a bad thing. Pam had been distraught, but she'd never really had the time to show it. Her husband, the man she loved, was gone! He hadn't packed his bags, hadn't taken anything. She'd reported it, but Bryan wasn't a man of importance, so after a mere twenty-four hours, the case was written off.

The topic was still a sore one for Pam, and it hurt her dearly. Speculation, tattletales, and rumours within the District were that the man battled demons, alcohol, and drugs. He spent a lot of his time in the old part of the District, but no one knew much else about him. Stories ranged from him being fed up and leaving to him simply taking his own life!

Having caught up with Jimmy and finally finished putting the e-boards on charge, Bryant entered the house and made his way into the kitchen. To no surprise to anyone, Jimmy was already three-quarters of the way through his second plate of lasagne. Jimmy was an incredibly faithful friend, but food was usually at the forefront of his mind. Jimmy was enormous, so were all of his family. Square jawed with an equally square head. He could shovel food away for days and get more intimidating. As a pair, they were polar opposites. Bryant was lean, handsome in a baby-faced way, and mildly timid. Jimmy, on the other hand, had confidence beaming out of his ears. He was a full six inches taller than Bryant, and as people would often joke (not entirely inaccurately), he was near twice his size. During their time in school, Bryant was dubbed 'the scientist' and Jimmy as 'his bodyguard', and the truth was Jimmy had saved Bryant from many a scrape in their years of friendship. Still, at 6-foot 5, Jimmy was officially exempt from any space programmes due to his height and build. If you were tall, strong, with a solid frame and with the world in a state of emergency, you were predestined to be a miner. Schooling for Jimmy was just a formality. His destiny would be to join the rest of his family in the deep-sea mining business.

According to the limited new history, roughly three hundred years ago, scientists discovered a new, very precious mineral that existed at the previously unexplored depths of the oceans. Mining was essential, yet even with the technology that existed was a very dangerous, arduous, and physically demanding job. The miracle mineral was named 'Orbitium', something which to the layman made it sound scientific. But instead, it was a ham-fisted metaphor for what it might achieve. Aside from being a precious ore, it contained a power unlike anything seen before. One kilo of it claimed to harness more energy than a Nuclear power station, and it was clean. The Authorities' best scientists stated that it was a very stable element, environmentally friendly, and plentiful in supply. Its discovery had led to a man named 'Hector Rosario' being able to develop engines that could break the light speed barrier. Rosario was long dead, but his name would live on forever. There were statues of the man wherever you looked, outside every Authority building in every District; he was ubiquitous.

The planet's population grew exponentially by the end of the 21st century, unsustainably so. Jobs, living space, food, and natural resources started their decline in the early 22nd century. Economies and Governments the world over had been on the brink of collapse. The world had long been stuck in a capitalist, consumer culture. People wanted and took far more than they needed. Buying one house, but then yearning for another. As the population grew, the competition between the rich and the wealthy 1% became a much more significant number. Consumerism and the capitalist society had seen the world's assets and space become scarcer than ever. The population was too big to survive, and something had to change.

The inception of the Space Academy coincided with the division of the world into Districts. It hadn't breathed a new lease of life into the planet, but it had delayed the inevitable. The discovery of Orbitium came just at the right time, and the development of light-speed travel gave humanity another chance, a rebirth. But to achieve it, the public could have just enough. Make just enough and work hard for the sake of all their futures.

The Districts ensured that the people would keep to their specific areas. You could have a maximum of two children, and life was assigned. Adhering to the rules was imperative. No one went without, and everyone had a specific purpose. It was a miracle, the planet united, knowing that they were working, waiting, hoping for a new life. Nothing they did was in vain.

The Space Academy was a vast entity, and they worked tirelessly. Almost a city or government of its own. They had dominion over everything. Why would they not? They were working on new engines, on bio-domes, and they were almost ready. It was just a case of testing what they'd developed. Machines had been to Mars; work was in progress.

It was now just a case of getting the first person there. The ball would roll, people would be selected and transferred to Mars, life would go back to normal. No more Districts, no more restrictions. The Academy was training and readying people to go to Mars to begin the setup, start colonising the planet. It would be any day now, the Authorities assured them. It would be an arduous process, but the people working together as one was imperative. Following the rules and trusting the process would ensure the survival of humanity.

The physical job of mining the Orbitium had created millions of jobs for the Districts near the ocean. It was a whole new industry, all set up and run by the Authorities. The severity of the work and the dangers involved meant that many in the sector perished. It was perilous labour but an acceptable risk. After all, you were playing your part in the survival of the species. From the remuneration point, mining was a very safe business financially because you had no setup costs and a guaranteed sale to the Academy. All you had to do, was report to your assigned post. You and your crew would mine, retrieve and deliver to the Academy. Much like a fisherman who went straight to market. People who previously had no job or income now had a definite one. Yes, it was dangerous. But should you die while mining Orbitium, the Authorities would pay your family a full two years' salary, such was the gratitude for the difficult work you were doing for your planet. A tragic death, but you died for the ultimate cause. You did your part for the space programme, for the Earth. What could be more important than that?

Since the Orbitium was necessary and valuable, keeping any amount of it for yourself was forbidden. Should you be caught in the heinous act, your entire family would suffer the consequences in very 'Old Testament' style 'Sins of the Father' punishment. You would be enemies of the Authorities, traitors of the people. There was no set punishment, but whatever happened wouldn't be pleasant. It was a harsh but effective safeguard.

Having eating as much lasagne as he could physically fit into this body. Remains which included Bryant's leftovers and any the over-realistic e-dog 'Roger' was eyeing up. Jimmy gave his thanks to Pam and stood up to depart.

"Are you leaving already, Jimmy Fletcher?" asked Pam.

"I did say I was only here for the lasagne," replied Jimmy. His insolence brought a wry smile from Pam, who hugged his massive frame as best she could him before vacating the kitchen, tasks to be done.

"Good luck tomorrow, Jimmy," she called back as she disappeared with a wash basket in hand.

"Thanks, Mrs Fisher," he yelled back; this left the now-standing Jimmy and Bryant alone in the kitchen, Jimmy's figure filling the door frame. The two unaccompanied save for the sullen-looking Roger, the sulky e-dog who'd missed out on leftovers.

The robot dogs had been a household luxury initially, designed for the wealthy. But over the years, given the sometimes dangerous nature of the overcrowded planet, the Authorities had made them mandatory. They could monitor, maintain and protect. Given to every household by the Authorities, everyone was safe. Crime wouldn't need to be reported. The dog would alert the necessary service immediately. Every home now safe from intruders, secure in themselves, knowing that neither they nor anyone could say or do anything that might harm the greater good. The dogs were no longer optional, and they couldn't be switched off; deactivating it was not your choice.

"You can call her Pam, you know?" said Bryant

"Yeah, it just feels weird," Jimmy replied.

"Why are you going already? All you did was eat," Bryant asked glumly, "You could stay? Maybe go over some more questions with me."

"Narr, you're alright," replied Jimmy, "I mean as fun as that sounds! I've got an early start tomorrow. First day being a miner."

"Shit," said Bryant. "I forgot you started tomorrow."

Bryant and Jimmy were both now eighteen, it was early June, and they had just finished school forever. Everyone was given a week's break after completing education before going straight into their assigned employment.

"It's still kinda early," pleaded Bryant. "We could do something else then?"

"Oh, I would, I'd love to," said Jimmy. "But unlike you, my job doesn't involve sitting in the sun napping all day. I need an early night."

Despite being in education, as soon as you turned sixteen, it was mandatory to have a part-time job. If you were old enough to contribute, sitting about the house when the planet was dying wasn't an option. You had to subsidize society; much like Rome, Mars wouldn't be built in a day, but they had to work every day. For his part-time employment, Bryant worked weekends at the local electric car dealership, washing cars. It was a job he loathed. Despite his dreams of the Academy, nobody saw it as realistic. Pam has been redying him to work with her at the cinema as soon as he finished school. The cinema was one of a dying breed of independent establishments, and Pam was determined to keep it that way.

"That's fair," replied Bryant. "I should probably help Julie, anyway. Keep that terror out of mum's hair. I'll catch you at the weekend for the community B.B.Q. though, yeah?"

Bryant stood, and he and Jimmy shared an awkward adolescent male embrace before Jimmy departed. Alone now with only his thoughts, Bryant went in search of his sister.

Testing times.

Three weeks had passed since Jimmy had been at Bryant's house sucking in lasagne like a black hole devours everything in its path. He had seen Jimmy briefly. But the long hours involved in his training had wiped out the typically effervescent Jimmy. It secretly made Bryant very pleased he didn't have a physically demanding job. It mattered not; the two of them were always together in spirit. Plus, they traded an endless stream of messages via phone or the virtual messaging systems that all houses had.

Mulling over his thoughts, Bryant lay on his bed staring up at the virtual solar system he'd installed on his ceiling. It was crude but laid back with his eyes open. He could behold an existence beyond his comprehension. Exam day was almost upon him, and the trepidation was real. The following day at nine a.m. sharp, he was due at his District Community, Recreation, and Public Affairs Centre to sit the Academy entrance test.

"Will you still remember us after you become a famous nerdy astronaut?" came the inquisitive voice of his sister Julie. Bryant sat up quickly, snapping out of his daze. His younger sister, complete with her three uneven ponytails, was sitting cross-legged on the floor, hands on her chin just staring at him.

"How on earth could I forget someone as weird as you?" he replied, as he sprung up from his bed and chased her from his room. The years rolled back as they dashed down the hallway, giggling franticly. Catching up with her was nowhere near as easy as it used to be, nor was picking her up and swinging her about like a rocket, something which culminated in them both collapsing in a heap on the floor.

"I've got to pass the test first, anyway," he said rather sullenly.

Julie shrugged. "But you're the biggest geek I know," she said teasingly. "I don't think anyone else spends all their free time studying. You'll pass it for sure."

"Thanks, I guess," he said as he ruffled her mismatched ponytails. "You've always believed in me. Seriously though, you and mum mean the world to me. But I need you to behave for her if the impossible happens. You have to promise me that."

"Fine," she said reluctantly. "But only when you're not here."

Julie had always been mischievous, tenacious, wise beyond her years, and although she was only eleven, you could tell she would never change. The grain was something she would always go against. It troubled Bryant. He loved her dearly, but there was no place in society for lateral thinkers. He wasn't sure he even understood. She talked of protest and doing what you wanted to do. Pam said that she took after their father, but Bryant's memory of the man was thin. He didn't know what it meant to 'take after him.' But even at her tender age, Julie questioned everything, trusted nothing.

"Good luck for tomorrow," she said to him as they broke free from their chaotic embrace on the floor.

"Thanks, Jules," he replied. "I think I'm going to need it."

Bryant applauded as the presenter made his way to the stage, sitting expectantly in the audience, his supermodel wife by his side and their six immaculately presented and groomed children stationed all around them. He'd been nominated for a Nobel Prize this year, and he had a good feeling.

The orator opened his mouth to speak, and a deathly hush fell upon the audience.

"It gives me great pleasure to announce this year's awards," said the vaguely familiar but curiously unrecognisable presenter. "And what an occasion it is," he bellowed, "For we have six categories, but only one winner." A gasp of awe resonated from the crowd like the oxygen being physically sucked from an airlock. As he stared at the presenter, Bryant knew that he recognised the man but still couldn't quite place him. As the crowd silenced, the familiarly

unfamiliar man spoke again. "And the Nobel Prizes for Peace, Literature, Physics, Chemistry, Medicine, and Economics all go to the magnificent, wonderful Bryant Fisher."

The crowd roared like a lion defending its pride. Bryant's jaw dropped as he stood. He had been confident of winning one award, maybe even two, but all six were unheralded, ground-breaking, some might and should even say legendary. Moving gracefully like the proudest of peacocks, Bryant made his way to the stage, the adoring audience cheering his name as he walked...Bryant...Bryant...Bryant...Bryant. As he neared the stage, the noise reached a crescendo, the cheering growing louder, fiercer...Bryant...Bryant. The bellowing from the onlookers was shaking the stage with its ferocity, and they cheered his name louder and louder...Bryant...Bryant... Bryant.

"BRYANT."

Rudely awakened from his slumber, Bryant opened his eyes, wiped away the goo, and saw the weary-eyed figure of his mother shaking him furiously, like she was trying to get the stubborn dust out of an old car mat.

"Bryant, it's 8:30! Get up! You've got thirty minutes until your test starts."

Barely half awake and now with a sinking feeling of dread, Bryant met the gaze of his exhausted-looking mother head-on.

"Mum!" he shrieked, "Why on Earth didn't you wake me sooner?"

"Bryant Fisher, you are eighteen years old. I am certainly not your alarm clock!"

"Sorry, Mum," he said sincerely. "You look tired. Are you okay?"

"Oh, Bryant," she said gloomily. "You know it's a long night the day before the audit."

"That's right!" He remembered tomorrow was the much-feared, always dreaded quarterly audit. Every four months, the Authorities would go through every aspect of all independent businesses that still existed. In their minds, all business should be conducted by them. They didn't make mistakes, but people did. If it wasn't Authority run, they put you through the wringer four times a year to make sure you were doing things correctly. Every indie business would find itself firmly under the microscope. Any irregularity, even as far as a missing spoon, discrepancy in numbers, or a slightly unhappy customer, and you could find yourself losing it to them.

If you failed an audit, you lost it all, the District would take over, and you would be reassigned. Keeping up with the perpetual game of 'cat and mouse' was nearly impossible. It meant the independent businesses dropped like flies.

"I missed your help last night," said his mother. "That ever-ticking brain of yours never misses a detail."

Bryant had helped his mother with the audits for as long as he could remember. He was a stickler for details, and he was a real blessing. Lately, though he'd been so caught up in the Academy test, he'd forgotten all about it.

Feeling mildly guilty as Bryant bolted from the bed, he barked, "I'm so sorry, mum, but you've got this. You don't need my help. Wish me luck. I gotta go."

Bryant bent, grabbed his backpack and yesterday's clothes from the floor, dancing into them on his way out of the door.

"I made you lunch," Pam called after him. "Don't forget it."

But Bryant's mind had left the building long ago, and it was all noise to him. He shot down the stairs, grabbed his e-board that he'd left haphazardly in the lobby, and disappeared out of the door.

At this time of day, the e-board routes would be hectic since it was the approved and most affordable method of transport. He had twenty-five give or take. It would be a close call. Bryant had been riding e-boards his whole life, and he was more than adept at it. He carved through the traffic like a hot knife through butter. Despite the tricky navigation and the lack of time, he needed some music to prepare him. Reaching behind him into his bag as he rode, he removed the earbuds with one hand and placed them in his ears while the other simultaneously paired them to his phone. The sound of fast-paced rock filled his ears, amping him up for the day ahead. He glided through his fellow commuters with sweet melodies in his ears. It all became rather poetic, and a deep feeling of serenity swept over him. It was 8:45 a.m. He should be there in five minutes. He'd make it, he'd be sweaty and unkempt, but he'd get there.

Rounding the last corner of the designated e-board route, the site of his destination filled his gaze. He could see it. The familiar sight of the all-encompassing structure occupied his view. The building itself was where almost anything official happened, adorned with the District emblems and a star-studded cast of statues lined up outside. Each District had one, all a carbon copy of each other, the place filled him with a sense of pride, and it was almost in touching distance. "Phew," he thought to himself. Suddenly a shrill beep interrupted his music how he hated interruptions. He glanced down as he rode and looked at the source of his disruption, a light that accompanied the sound. It was his e-board battery warning light, "Bugger," he thought to himself. He hadn't put the thing on charge last night! Bending down as he rode, he managed to peer through the LCD to check the battery percentage. It had 15%. It would get him there; the test came first. He could worry about getting home later.

"Hey, watch out!"

Bryant barely made out the words through the noise in his ears. Standing back up, he looked up as fast as he could. But it was too late. A prominent figure was heading towards him more quickly than his brain could react. The two of them collided with a *SMACK,* and everything went dark.

As humanity had grown, Earth's population had swelled to oppressive numbers. There's a finite amount of space, and towers could only be built so high. Living space had become almost non-existent. The traditional borders that used to separate countries had become virtually impossible. All of the large cities had grown exponentially, and there was no longer a way to separate them from the neighbouring ones. Borders overlapped; landlocked countries and continents became one. There was just no keeping them apart. The traditional voting and election system became impossible because you were now eligible to vote in several constituencies, cities, and countries, depending on where you lived.

When the time came, the World's leaders had devised and approved the Mission to Mars. In reality, it was the only option the planet had to be annexed. The Space Academy now took precedence over everything. It and its members had free rein. The rules didn't apply to them because they were all that stood between life and death.

The heads of state would meet, have parties, and mingle. They convinced everybody that things had to change, truth's changed regularly, history was written and unwritten. The lines became blurry, and nobody really remembered the first official reason, but slowly and surely, walls went up around the globe. It was a method of protection, keep everyone in their areas. The planet divided up into Districts, each one fenced off from the next. They were all virtually identical, each District governed by its Authority or the Authority. However, you wanted to look at it. They were like a Hydra, many heads all belonging to the same creature. Nation-states were gone, the leaders of which all disappeared overnight; nobody questioning where they went or what they did. It was the Authorities in charge that was the absolute truth.

Your District, which was identical to its neighbour, would supply you with everything you would need. Work, shelter, food, entertainment, entertainment after a fashion at least. News from other Districts was limited, books, paintings and music rare. Possessing such items wasn't prohibited, but it was deemed unorthodox behaviour. The internet was limited, serving only to give you the required information. It wasn't the most fantastic way to live, but they were alive; the same couldn't be said were things not the way they were. Conserving the planet and allowing food and resources to remain were paramount. Councils, elections and voting became a thing of the past. It was superfluous.

The rule of the Authorities sustained life, rationed, food, water, and employment. Rules were in place and set in stone. Everything done was in the name of colonising Mars and keeping the human race going. The rules never changed unless they had to. Any changes made by Authorities were a last resort, actioned only in the name of preservation. You could move freely within your District, but crossing into another was rarely permitted unless you worked for the Academy. With such an enormous population, people needed equal distribution for everyone to cohabit.

Bryant lived in District F, which had been historically near Hamburg in Germany. But it had been decades since world maps existed. They were not illegal but being caught with one was a significant risk. They were considered confusing, outdated, and irrelevant. The same was true about most of history. History was what had caused the situation. Dwelling upon it was worthless. Looking forward, being progressive was all the mattered. It had also been decades since anyone had spoken any language other than the common tongue. If the planet was to prosper, then working and communicating together was vital.

The Academy examinations and just about any other District matter took place at the District Community, Recreation Center for public affairs. The District Bryant called home was physically the closest one to the Academy. He could always catch a glimpse of the famous clock tower when he was in the Centre. The goal of space combined with his proximity to the Academy had always exacerbated Bryant's love for it. Being the closest District geographically meant that the Academy had an enormous culture within it. Whoever passed the yearly exam became a genuine celebrity within it. (Something as much to do with the fact that 'Stardom' only really came with being in the Academy.) Film and music stars served only to provide information and hope and thus earned a regular wage. Everyone was equal to the task; however, some like those in the Academy were understandably slightly more equal than the rest.

Hannibal's voyage over the alps had been an easier one than Bryant's journey across the stage. Traversing the platform to accept these gleaming, golden coins had taken an eternity. He could see them now. All six calling out to him like a baby bird in need of its mother. Soon Bryant Fisher, the marvellous, remarkable genius that was Bryant Fisher, would collect all six Nobel Prizes.

He was now almost at the podium, expectant arms outstretched. So close he could feel their glow. Their radiance warmed his soul. But, suddenly, there was a tremor. What was happening? The stage was shivering, wobbling, quivering. Members of the audience moved from their seats and had started to mount the platform. He didn't recognise any of them, yet they were ruining his moment, climbing the stand like angry apes, grabbing at him, shaking, rattling. Shouting, physically shoving him. They shouted, "Hey, hey, hey!"

"HEY!"

"Are you alright, kid?"

He was startled, awake, confused. His head felt someone had buried an axe deep inside it. What had happened? Bryant opened his eyes and blinked like a child opening them for the very first time. Looking up, he saw six strangers stood above him. Flat on his back on the floor, Bryant sat up slowly.

"Oh no, oh no, oh no, you shouldn't be sitting up!" exclaimed a stranger. "The medi-bot is on its way."

"What time is it?" asked Bryant dazedly.

"It's time you looked where you were bloody going!" chirped the angry man in a suit with whom he had collided.

The kind-looking lady stood over him shot the man a deep look of scorn before saying, "Why it's 9:15, dear. But you need to be more careful. You could both have been seriously hurt."

"9:15?"

"It… it's 9:15?" he stuttered.

Dragging himself from the floor sent him into a spin. But the epinephrine kicked in, and he focussed. There was no time to waste. Bryant could make out the familiar triangle-shaped entrance hall of the District Community, Recreation Center for public affairs, his vision was blurry, but he could see the magnificent bust of Rosario, the flags, the emblems. He grabbed the loop of his backpack and, without a second thought, started to run.

"What about your board?" the kind lady called after him. The words fired past Bryant's ears. An off-target missile, missing his consciousness completely. His focus was on the building in front of him, and nothing was breaking his stride.

Bryant sped into the lobby like a storm bringing a dirty wind. He arrived at the reception desk, stopped, and bent over double in the middle. Clutching at the counter firmly with both hands, he sucked in wild gasps of air as though his life depended on it. Oxygen began to return to his brain, and he opened his mouth to speak.

"Huh-uh… Bryanhant FFishuh here for the Academy tests," he gasped frenetically. Taking her time to look up from the papers in hand. The hardy-looking lady with a neatly arranged, regulation Authority plait opened her mouth to speak.

"And how do I spell FFishuh?" she asked sardonically.

"F.. I.. S.. H.. E.. R!" he pleaded, "Please hurry."

Tap… tap. Tap… tap.

Came the sound from the old keyboard. All Authority buildings ran ancient computer systems. With the lack of history, old technology was as esoteric as it came. Everyone learns about new technology, but old systems with no manuals were complex. They claimed it was because they had always used it. But most suspected it was because it was so old-fashioned nobody could hack into it. As technology grew more advanced, hackers constantly advanced with it. If you ran systems only ever seen in the past, a past you controlled, then this system to the modern hacker was as complex as it came.

Tap… tap… tap. "Fisher, Bryant?" she inquired.

"Yes, sir, I mean ma'am. That's me," he exclaimed excitedly.

"The test started half an hour ago, Fisher! You're late," she asserted.

"Yes, and getting later by the minute," he bleated facetiously. The lady was neither impressed nor phased by this remark,

 "They don't take kindly to tardiness, Fisher," she said.

"Yes, I know," Bryant tried to explain. "But there are very good reas"-she cut him off before he burbled further-"Seat 101 Fisher, you can go through. But you only have half an hour to complete all 300 questions. So I suggest you get moving!"

Sneaking into the auditorium was no mean feat. There were hundreds of people hunched over desks, furiously scribbling away. Curiously, all exams were still on paper, and the answers completed in pencil. Something that was seldom questioned.

The noise of hundreds of pencils scratching away resonated through the auditorium like a million bees desperately making honey. Bryant finally forced his way through the myriad of tables to find his number, seat 101. But, before he had the chance to sit, there was one blast of a shrill siren that alerted everyone. A thousand eyes all looked up at the dishevelled stranger. Bryant glanced down at himself and realised he still had his bag with him. One of the service robot dogs bounded up to him like a silent assassin, snatching the bag from his hand and then departed as quickly as it arrived. A thousand eyes went back to their papers. Another close call for Bryant. Belongings were not permitted in the auditorium. Should he have taken a seat, he would be disqualified as a cheat. "Come on, Bryant," he told himself, "focus!"

HONNNNK came the noise of the klaxon.

The noise signalled that there were just five minutes of the exam remaining. The last five minutes became a desperate scramble. On the one hand, because you only had five minutes left. On the other, if you were still writing when the final klaxon went, you were disqualified for carrying on after time. When the penultimate bell rang out, you had a genuine test of wills on your hands. If you wanted to continue, you had to keep track of the minutes. However, since there were no clocks on the walls and no devices allowed in the auditorium, every second that ticked away after that sound was a real gamble. Put the pencil down too soon, and you lost valuable minutes. Keep on writing and run out of time, and your efforts were for nothing. For Bryant, time was a valuable commodity. He needed every second of this test. The following five minutes were going to be tense.

Sweat beaded from his brow. Three minutes had passed since the klaxon sounded…or was it four? The format of the test changed a lot as it progressed. Some questions were kind enough to give you a multiple-choice element. Bryant had tactically saved these until last. Problematically for him, the two minutes, one minute, however much time it was he had left, wasn't enough to attempt a rational answer. He had a real fight to the death that involved just ticking boxes as fast as he could. They would be wild stabs in the dark because even if he answered all the other 299 questions correctly. If just one was blank, it wouldn't be enough.

Bryant's pencil ticked away, A for this one, C for the next. He was ticking as fast as he could, but time ticked away faster—the clock and Bryant mano a mano. Simultaneously one ticked down, the other up. Ten questions left, B here, D there…tick…tick…tick. There wasn't an ounce of his body not drenched in sweat. He figured at this moment, disarming a bomb or taming a lion whilst disarming a bomb would be a less stressful activity. Tick…tick…tick, three questions, two, one time up, it was done. He dropped his pencil the moment the last tick successfully filled the box. The universe almost seemed to slow down as he watched the pencil fall to the desk, hovering in mid-air until finally, it fell. *Honkkk,* the sound of the klaxon engulfed the room, the pencil silent as it hit the desk. "Yesss," he shrieked audibly. Before covering his face with his hand and stifling the sound. The test was over, but noise (klaxons aside) was not yet permitted.

As he stood in line to vacate the hall, a rushing feeling of dread replaced his triumph, like a running tap no one had switched off. The water had reached the brim and now overflowed. His jubilation at finishing the test swiftly replaced by the realisation that he had essentially guessed a large chunk of the test. Sure, they were all four-question multiple-choice, but even with a hefty dose of luck, statistically, he probably only got five of them correct. No amount of hopeless optimism could convince him it would be good enough. He'd given it all just to get there on time, and now the reality of what happened was sinking in. He's lost his e-board, all of his belongings and was far from home. The Academy test pale in comparison to his next one! Make it home, unscathed and face an angry mother.

Back down to Earth.

The door swung shut behind Bryant like a guillotine swiftly sliding down, quiet and elegant until it hit its target, terminal. The door closing both physically and metaphorically. There were no re-retests! "Great," he thought to himself as the rain fell sideways from the sky. Looking up, he saw angry swathes of grey clouds. As his glance shifted to his feet, he saw that a puddle was already starting to form around them. Reality and anxiety came for him once more. Having a dream of the Academy had propped him up. All of his life, there had been a chance. His excitement at being able to take the test had substituted the truth. What if he failed? He'd never considered that. Now it was a life of working in the cinema, surviving audits, serving idiots. He had wanted to do his duty, be a pioneer. In his mind, he was unique, and one day he would prove it. Maybe he wasn't. Perhaps he was simply ordinary, regular Bryant. His mind raced, it was a unique mind, but it didn't know how to comprehend how he felt. Maybe because it wasn't, he tried to focus, but he had more significant problems right now. His e-board would have been scooped up by one of the accident teams. An unreported collision would have been logged. Mum would have to pay a fine. It would be a scorch on her record. Everything had to be reported. Taking his backpack into the test was a mistake. He would have to wait for the contents to be examined by the exam board. It had been empty save for his phone, a half-eaten sandwich, and some scrappy notes. But his phone was vital, and the way in which his stomach growled indicated that the half-eaten sandwich was also very much in demand.

Mobile phones had long since been genetically linked to each individual. It would only work for you. It served as a phone, a G.P.S. tracker, an e-wallet and even an identification card. Your whole life existed within that device. Without it, he couldn't use a pay screen, he couldn't get a taxi, and he couldn't use the monorail. Despite being an adult, and regardless of her ire, he desired very much to be able to call his mum. It was a long way back home, an arduous journey on foot, a cold, very wet walk of shame.

"Bryant Fisher, where have you been?" yelled his mother. Her words flicked between anger and concern, leaving Bryant desperately trying to figure out which was more important to her. He hoped it was the latter.

"It's 6 p.m., young man! I've been worried sick," she chastened. "I've tried ringing your phone. The G.P.S. location isn't working. Jimmy hasn't heard from you. Then I had a call from the Authorities about an accident this morning, you know I have had to pay a fine for that! You're lucky it wasn't worse! Then when you finally show up, you're sodden wet!"

"I'm hungry too," he added.

Pam shot him a cold, hard look. He was exhausted, freezing, wet, hungry, and in pain. But Bryant knew when his mother was in a mood like this. He daren't argue with her.

"I'm so sorry, mum," Bryant started. "It wasn't my fault… I…I just needed to get there. Some man knocked me off my board. It's just I was so close, and I didn't think! Mum, I just wanted to pass that test." Bryant tried to carry on, but the emotions got to him, and he broke.

"Oh sweetie, come here," she said. She was annoyed, worried, and annoyed that she had been so worried. But in a moment like this, she could see that her boy needed his mother.

"Oh, Bryant," she repeated as she held him.

"I'm so sorry," he uttered between snotty blubbers. "It was just so important, and now it's all over, mum. There's no way I passed the test! I had once chance."

"Oh, I know, bunny," she replied. "But look, sometimes things happen that we don't understand. Maybe we think we want something. But we don't always know what's best for us.

"This might be a genuine opportunity for you, sweetie. I mean, look at everything you have? You have a best friend that adores you, a sister that craves your attention, and a mother that needs you far more than you know."

Bryant looked up at his mother, then down at her shoulder. It looked as though someone had plucked a big grey rain cloud from the sky and rung it out all over her arm. He wiped his eyes, then his snot ridden nose on the back of his sleeve and righted himself.

"You're right, mum, you always are. I...I guess I just wanted it so badly."

"I know you did," she responded. "You might not have the Academy, but you have us! Now dry yourself, and we'll get some pizza. How does that sound?"

Bryant smiled. He turned and squelched off towards the bathroom. "Thanks, mum," he called back as he departed.

"And put those wet clothes straight in the machine," she grumbled. "I don't want to find them on the floor."

Two weeks had passed since the day he'd dubbed; 'Crash, late, angry mum, fail, wet, dream shattering day.' It still hurt knowing that if only he'd been there on time, if he had woken up earlier, he might have done it. Everyone told him that everything happened for a reason. He was doing his best, but he figured this one at most to be a crappy reason.

"You know there's no water in that bucket?" bellowed the voice over his shoulder. Startled, Bryant looked over to see the figure of Jimmy looming towards him. He looked down and checked the bucket. It was on its side, contents everywhere.

Bryant laughed a laugh he hadn't managed in a while. Wiped his eyes, stood, and said, "It's a good job you're not Mr Rubinat!" They both chuckled as they embraced each other.

"How are you doing, buddy? It's been basically forever," said Jimmy. It had felt like they hadn't seen each other in aeons. Jimmy eating all the lasagne at Bryant's house a few weeks ago was their last physical catch up. They had spoken often and at length about the test, much to Jimmy's delight. But this was the longest they had ever gone in their lifetimes without seeing each other. It was strange, perhaps a haunting glimpse into the future. Jimmy all at sea, Bryant on dry land. A change was imminent, not a pleasant one.

"Come on, dude," Jimmy effused. "I persuaded my mum to give me some credits. I can just about buy us some lunch."

They exchanged glances, knowing precisely what the other was thinking.

"Planet Pizza!"

Jimmy was a popular figure at Planet Pizza primarily due to his prodigious appetite. That's to say he was a popular figure any day except Tuesdays, which happened to be today. It was no coincidence as Tuesday was buffet day. The owner, Mr Goldstein, had jokingly considered devising a way to exclude him from the buffet or add some surcharge just to Jimmy. They would all chuckle, but it was only half in jest. The upside was he knew Jimmy would usually make up for it with the vast amount of takeaway he and his family ordered. Planet Pizza was still an independent restaurant. As a result, it had dominion over what it served. Food in the Districts was designed to be largely perfunctory. Pizza was a luxury, unnecessary. Food should sustain, nothing more. Being the only pizza place in the District meant its popularity was immense. The Authorities had it eyed for removal in time, but they were always cautious about easing things out. Knee jerk reactions could prompt unrest. It was far more effective to turn the screw, bit by bit, very slowly. If you lowered the temperature in tiny increments every day, would anyone even notice?

"How did you get your board back?" Jimmy mused. He nodded in the direction of the slightly battered board on charge outside next to his.

"Mum had to pay a fine," he murmured apologetically, "and I had to apologise to that dick."

"You did hit him," said Jimmy.

"So?" asked Bryant.

"Moving on then," replied Jimmy. "So, what are you going to do now? Surely your days of napping at the car wash are numbered?"

"Rubbish job anyway. Oh, let's wash a car and make it all clean and shiny so that they can drive through some mud, and I have to do it again a week later! We only serve the officials, fancy cars that always have to be clean." Bryant moaned. "What a pointless task and they never tip."

Jimmy laughed, "Tell me how you really feel."

"Pffft," said Bryant. "I've given notice anyway. Two weeks, and I'll be with mum full time at the cinema."

"When do you get your results?" Jimmy probed, switching the subject.

"Don't know, don't care," said Bryant shrugging his shoulders.

Jimmy stood plate in hand, "I'm still listening," he said, moving in the buffet's direction. He piled his plate high for the third time, catching the owner's eye as he did so.

"Hi, Mr Goldstein," Jimmy chirped. Mr Goldstein offered up a single grunt before Jimmy headed back to his friend.

"It's my first day at sea tomorrow," Jimmy said casually.

"Tomorrow?" mouthed Bryant. Almost choking on his food. "Really?"

"Yea," said Jimmy, "why do you think I'm filling up? Anyway, I did tell you last week on the phone."

"I'm sorry," replied Bryant, "I've been trapped in my head lately."

"You don't say," -Jimmy joshed. Punching him playfully on the arm across the table-, "Hey, at least now our families don't have to be mortal enemies?" Jimmy said with a wry smile, "Those Academy types are all dicks, anyway. Think they are all high and mighty because they go up instead of down."

Jimmy's family, extended family, family friends, and acquaintances were all miners. His household, much like most of the working classes, had a rather dim view of the Academy. The miners were risking their lives to provide for them and the way of life of those in it. There was no love lost between the groups. Despite the need to get to space, the miners saw their job to be just as, if not more important. The disparity irked more than a little. The difference of opinion between their families had never been of any real significance. But Jimmy's father had never been too pleased with Bryant's desires to join the Academy. A feeling he had made all too clear when he got drunk last year at a family B.B.Q.

After stashing away mountains of food between them, the pair finished and settled up. Thanked the relieved looking Mr Goldstein before heading outside.

"I'd better get back to work," Bryant said unenthusiastically. "Those cars won't wash themselves."

"They're unlikely to get washed with you there either," chuckled Jimmy. Who was so pleased with his comment, he punched Bryant playfully on the arm once more.

The force nearly sent Bryant tumbling to the floor. "Funny," he grimaced as he looked down at his arm, hoping that this punching thing wouldn't last.

"Good luck tomorrow, you lump, be careful."

"Nothing to it," Jimmy replied as casually as possible.

The boys high fived nodded to each other before jumping on their e-boards and going their separate ways.

It was 7:30 am, and Bryant was getting ready for his last day at the car wash. It was a month today since what he now considered to be his failed attempt to join the Academy. He was mentally preparing himself for his new life, trying to anyway. But, the disappointment still ate at him. There had been no results as yet. It was taking an excessive amount of time this year. As much as he knew that envelope would contain nothing but earth-shattering disappointment, he was also finding it hard to move on until he had confirmation. He still harboured the tiniest shred of hope, that maybe, just maybe, by some miracle, things might be different. This couldn't be his life!

Whirrr

He could hear the noise of the hairdryer coming from upstairs. Presumably, his mum was drying Julie's hair. It was hard enough to get the girl to wash, difficult to get her to do anything. Then once you'd completed that miracle, you had to get her to sit still long enough to dry it. The thought of his poor mum having to look after her alone had almost made him not want to go to the Academy at all.

He had until nine before he had to be at work; he had plenty of time, so he decided he would have that second bowl of cereal. Not washing cars still required plenty of energy. Halfway through the second bowl of 'Planet Rings' (the marshmallow ones), it became a genuine struggle. "Where does Jimmy even fit all this food?" he thought to himself. Suddenly, his thoughts were dashed by the ring of the doorbell. "Mum, Doorbell!" he shouted toward the stairs. No reply, nothing except for the continued noise of the hairdryer. "Eugh," he hated getting the door. He put his bowl down and reluctantly dragged himself from his chair.

"Are you Bryant Fisher?" was the greeting that came from the surly, impatient delivery man.

"Yeah," was Bryant's response. This was odd. Post was never for him.

"Sign here, please!"

Bryant spent thirty seconds perfecting his elaborate squiggly signature on the screen. Something which drew a sigh from the man. The man abruptly grabbed the screen back from Bryant's hands and thrust the letter against his chest. He was in his van and gone before Bryant even had time to blink. When he did, though, he looked down at the letter pinned to his chest. *The Academy* was the logo that emblazoned the top left corner of the envelope.

Bryant gulped. This was it; these were the results.

Shutting the door with one hand and heinously tearing through the top of the letter with the other. He got through the seal, tearing some contents in the process. He removed the letter and then unfolded it slowly, fold by fold, by fold.

The Academy.
Deliver by hand.

F.A.O. BRYANT FISHER.

Dear Mr Fisher,

We are pleased to inform you that you have obtained the required score to pass the entrance examinations for The Academy.
Your marks in each section are:
Section one: 50/50
Section two 100/100
Section three 50/50
Section four 100/100
Passing score 100%

Bryant read the first paragraph repeatedly. He read all thirteen lines on a loop until he was sure he wasn't misreading it. Should he pinch himself, ensure he wasn't dreaming? He was pretty confident he wasn't; it didn't make much sense, but he didn't care. What was happening? He simply couldn't contain his joy.

"Mum," he yelled, "Mummmmmmmm!"

"I'm just finishing your sister's hair, Bryant. I'm sure there's probably more milk in the fridge, honey. Have you looked at the back?" she replied. Naturally assuming there was some breakfast emergency.

As she descended the stairs, Pam arrived to see Bryant bounding towards her, paper in hand, cheeks flushed, eyes red. He wore the look of a dog that had just been told: "He could go for a ride in the car."

"What is it, Bryant?" she gasped. Unsure as yet whether to be happy, sad, angry, or disappointed.

"It'ss…it'ss…" he started. "It's the results from the exam, mum. I've passed, I've passed!" The mangled letter fell from his grasp and floated to the floor.

"Where's Jules?" he asked. Sprinting passed his mother up the stairs. "Jules, Julesss," he called as he ran, "Julie, where are you? I've passed the exam; I've passed the exam!"

Leaving his mother in a daze as he dashed past her. Pam bent and picked the letter from the floor.

The bottom section had folded back on itself during Bryant's jubilant exclamations. So she took it to the kitchen and flattened it out to give it a read.

The Academy.
Deliver by hand.
F.A.O. BRYANT FISHER

Dear Mr Fisher,

We are pleased to inform you that you have obtained the required score to pass the entrance examinations for The Academy.
Your marks in each section are:
Section one: 50/50
Section two 100/100
Section three 50/50
Section four 100/100
Passing score 100%

She then noticed that it continued onto the reverse, so she turned it over and began to read.

This year, however, heralded an unprecedented result. Amazingly, two people managed to obtain the pass mark of 100%.
Naturally, because the Academy can only accept one graduate per year, with this in mind, it is with regret that we must inform you that you have not been selected on this occasion.

Graduates to the Academy must conduct themselves with the highest standards. We were informed that you arrived thirty minutes late for the examinations.

We would like to take our time to remind you that tardiness is not an attribute we look for in Academy recruits.

We thank you for your interest in the Academy, and we appreciate the hard work that must have gone into your preparations.

For the stars
Yours sincerely.
Commander Steele

"Shit!"

Pam thought out loud. He clearly hadn't read the obverse. He was upstairs, jubilant. She felt sick! Everything around her became a blur. In the distance, she could still hear Bryant chasing Julie around the house. The two of them had collided in the living room in a pile of giggles.

"I knew you'd do it, nerd pants," taunted Julie. Was the noise Pam made out between her passing thoughts.

Each second that passed felt like decades. Stars were falling and crashing to the earth all around her. Every fading moment made opening her mouth to speak even more difficult. She knew she was about to do one of the hardest things she'd ever had to do as a mother. She had to tell him; why did she have to tell him? Her words were about to shatter her son's dreams.

"B... B... Bryant," she croaked. But the din in the living room was vast, and her words fell on deaf ears.

"BRYANT!" she snapped.

Silence fell as Bryant stopped tickling his sister and stood up, almost as if at attention.

"You read all of the letter, didn't you?" she asked. Knowing full well, he hadn't. The grin fell from Bryant's face and crashed to the floor. He could see the tears forming in the eyes of his mother. He knew that something was wrong.

She didn't need to utter a single word; Bryant moved towards her and grabbed the letter from her sullen hands, flipped it over and carried on reading.

Julie remained on the living room floor, eyes aghast as she watched all the colour drain from her brother's face. Like an hourglass losing sand. He took a step back and crashed against the wall wishing that it would just eat him up.

"No, No, No… It can't be," sobbed Bryant. "Why would they do this?"

For the first time in her life, Pam Fisher didn't know what to do. She grabbed Bryant and held him. He fought her off at first before conceding and falling hard into her arms, letting it all out.

Reality.

The initiation ceremony for new Academy recruits was always a televised event. Each District unknowingly receiving a tailored broadcast. The new member offered superstar status for that day—the next brave woman or man off to save humanity. Viewing wasn't strictly compulsory, but it was as close to it as it could be. Whatever you were watching, doing, or whichever device you were using at the time was commandeered—seized by the event. Any screen that could display it would. It was difficult to avoid, especially if watching it was going to be particularly painful.

Initiation was always swift. Just two days had passed since Bryant held that envelope in his hands. The Academy literally in his grasp. He'd been picturing himself in this moment all of his life. It nearly came true. For a moment, he thought it had. But yet, here he was watching someone else being presented with the award. He turned away. Watching this made him feel physically sick.

"Congratulations," he heard the presenter say. "The winner of the 2369 Space Academy entrance tests is Carlos DeVore."

"Eugh," Bryant thought out loud. The way they said 'winner' resonated through his brain. It was like winning a prize, the most fantastic prize that existed. Life on Earth was subservient, and people were cogs. He wanted to be more than that. Bryant watched 'DeVore' earn his wings. As he walked across the stage to the podium, he knew in his heart this should be his stage. DeVore was from further south in the District, unbeknownst to just about anyone, but historically close to the Mediterranean. It was much warmer there, and the man's skin was golden, his hair sandy. Bryant glared at him, his good looks, that glow. What a wretched man!

The presenter continued amid the passionate onlookers, many of whom were gathered outside.

"Welcome to your future, Mr DeVore, and welcome to the future of humanity." They shook hands, and a shiny ostentatious medal was adorned to the shoulders of the elated

37

looking DeVore. Expensive, luxury champagne bottles were opened before he was carried away, hoisted aloft by his peers.

"Unfortunately for Mr DeVore, there's no time to waste for the planet, but l know he'll get a hero's welcome at the Academy," said the presenter, "But just because the celebrations are over for him. It doesn't mean they should stop for the rest of us, so…let's…keep…this…party…going!"

Fireworks went off as triumphant music played. The mandatory, non-compulsory viewing period was now over, and Bryant could now switch the television set off abruptly.

Pam, who had been in attendance, opened her mouth to speak. Before deciding better of it, holding her tongue. Bryant stood up, grabbed his coat, and headed for the door.

"Bryant," Pam spoke, "where are you going?"

"Out," he replied moodily. "I'm going for a walk."

Pam thought about stopping him but knew that it was better to let morose teenagers be moody.

"Okay, well, don't be long," she replied as cheerily as possible. "Dinner is at seven." Bryant exited, the door crashing behind him, leaving Julie and his mother alone in the silence.

The next few weeks drifted hazily by; autopilot mode had well and truly kicked in. Bryant's last day at the car wash came and went. They all chipped in and bought him a mug that said, 'I'd rather be in space.'

He helped his sister with her science project with stifled enthusiasm. "This rocket will never get to space!" he'd yelled at one point. Storming out as he did so, only to realise he was yelling at his eleven-year-old sister, not an astrophysicist. He met with Jimmy briefly, and as per usual, they ate more dinner at Planet Pizza. Then finally, after weeks of avoiding the truth and living in utter denial, anger, grief and depression. He conceded that he wasn't going to the Academy and started work with his mum at the cinema.

Most of what occurred at the Academy was a closely kept secret, although the recruit would hold some 'Real World' style video updates for the first few months every year. These updates usually had Bryant glued to them. For obvious reasons, this year, Bryant had avoided as much of it as he could.

To make matters worse. It seemed this 'DeVore' was quite a hit with the ladies, the men, the children, essentially everyone except him. Whenever there was a recruit, especially one who cut such a popular figure, chatter and gossip was hard to avoid.

Since each District was, in essence, a world of its own, the idle talk was rife. Working at the cinema usually had its perks for a teenage boy. Given that most of the District's youths came through it at some point. It usually gave Bryant the chance to impress some girls who came in with his film knowledge or ability to dish out free popcorn. At present, however, the words that hung off the lips of most people that frequented were about the suave 'Mr DeVore'. He was a poster boy, and it was about how interesting or handsome he was, making Bryant unusually grumpy.

Stood at the front counter, staring into the space some girls he knew from school occupied, he caught a voice from behind him.

"Why do you find yourself a nice girl?" He heard his mother ask. Bryant turned to see his mum behind him, clipboard in hand, "Mum, eww!" he said.

"What?" Pam asked. "It might be a pleasant distraction?"

Bryant rolled his eyes, "Nothing," he sighed, "this just isn't the conversation I want to have with you!"

Undeterred, Pam continued. "What about her?" she motioned. "She's cute. Didn't you take a class one of them?" Bryant did a double-take. His mum was right. It was Kylie Williams; they'd taken Maths together for three years. She'd not spoken to him once.

"Yes," he replied pensively, "but mum, she'd never be interested in me."

"Nonsense," said Pam, "no one is too good for my Bry Bry."

"Excuse me, ladies," Pam continued. "Would either of you be interested in getting a drink with my handsome son here?"

Bryant looked at her, mortified. He tried to speak before turning ruby-red; at any rate, it would have been utter gibberish. He ducked down beneath the counter as though he had dropped something. The two girls looked over very briefly. Chuckled, glanced at each other awkwardly before walking out of the door. Once they had departed, Bryant stood up from his hiding place, "Mum", he yelled. Before storming off.

"Hey, what's the matter?" asked Pam as she went after him.

"Oh, how about you just embarrassed me in front of people I know," fumed Bryant.

"Sorry," she said. "I was only trying to help. I just thought it might be good for you to take your mind off things."

"I don't want to take my mind off things," he yelled passionately. "I want to work at the Academy! Not this stupid cinema. This here, this should be me!" He motioned to a 3D cardboard cutout of DeVore stood in the room's corner. Even as a cardboard cutout, he was arrogant. He glared at it, and the tanned, cheesy grin beamed back at him. Bryant snapped. He ran at the poster, tackling it to the ground, awkwardly wrestling it on the floor.

The cardboard version of DeVore was no match for an angry teenager, and it wasn't long before Bryant had mangled it severely. When he finally stopped, he rolled over and shuffled towards the wall. Curled forward, almost fetal with his arms over his knees, he began to sob.

Pam sat on the floor next to her son, putting her arm around him.

"Sometimes it's best just to get it all out," she said.

"I'm sorry, mum," he wept.

"It's okay, sweetie," she replied, holding his hand tenderly. "I understand."

"But I've ruined your poster."

"Oh, it's fine honey, if you don't like him, then neither do I!"

"But I just want to be him, mum. It's not fair. He has everything!" Pam moved his arms aside and pulled his face to her so they were eye to eye.

"Hey now," she said, "Don't you ever say that. Why would you want to be like this idiot? So, he's in the Academy? He's not Bryant Fisher! He's not the smart, kind, caring, wonderful man that I know." This made Bryant smile a little. "I'd take Bryant Fisher over him any day."

"Thanks, mum," he said.

Pam produced a tissue from nowhere, handing it to her son. "I know it's tough, honey, but look at what you have?"

Bryant nodded.

Pam stood, stooped, and patted her son on the back.

"Take a break," she advised. "But when you return, I'll be in the office. The next audit isn't far away, and I could use that brain of yours."

Blood, sweat, and stars.

Being brought back down to Earth is never easy for anyone. This is especially true if Earth is the last place you want to be. Bryant was sick of these Academy updates. This 'DeVore' character was an absolute cheese ball, and his popularity was flourishing. He'd just about accepted that he worked in a cinema, and he would not be a space pioneer or anything remotely exciting. But the Authorities were milking this guy's popularity. Billboards were popping up all over the District. His face adorned all of them. He was advertising new documentaries, mattresses. Even the newspapers had stories about how he overcame his adversities. A District gossip e-zine had even had him answer stupid questions like his favourite foods, colours and pastimes. They were using his face for everything, and it was intoxicating. He could avoid crappy internet blogs. He could ignore the electronic billboards. But what he couldn't deal with his face being on the back of his favourite cereal box. 'Planet Rings' cereal now had this smug face staring back at him.

Sitting eating breakfast, he casually turned the box over to read the space facts usually there. Today's box, however, had none of that. Instead, it was just facts about Carlos DeVore and how he had always dreamt of space. Bryant couldn't take it anymore. Born of frustration, he grabbed the open box and snapped, shaking it, convulsing it passionately. "Stupid DeVore!" When he was finally done, he snapped out of his trance to see the consequence of his actions. Planet rings were now scattered far and wide, covering most of the kitchen floor.

Clearing up the mess caused by DeVore wasn't top on his list of priorities. "Roger!" he commanded. The e-dog had been sitting dormant in his charging pod situated in the kitchen's corner. The shout of his name, accompanied by the sight of a floor covered in wholesome chocolate goodness, was all he needed. He dutifully set about the business of hoovering up the mess. Although the e-dogs were synthetic, they were programmed to be a real dog. Chocolate cereal loops were not part of his diet. But his programming told him otherwise.

The e-dogs were a curious invention. You could set them to 'Full dog mode', and it would act, look, and feel just like any genuine dog did. You could play fetch in the park. It would bound up to you the minute you entered the building and lick every inch of your face. It would eat all the important post, make a mess of the sofa's arms, and even leak coolant in corners of the room. But because they were mandated in every household, not everyone wanted a dog's full-time commitment. They could be tailored to a variety of settings. In the Fisher household, Roger primarily lived in 'monitor and maintain' mode. This rendered the dog essentially inactive, except it would always have that glow in its eye to say that it was on, and you could not turn it off or take it out and leave it somewhere.

The dog's supposed purpose was to record and monitor for any threats like a CCTV system would. If someone it didn't recognise entered the house, it would react. The truth was though it recorded constantly, watched, listened. Deviant behaviour would not go unnoticed. Despite significant public unrest at first, there had proved to be many incidents where the dogs had saved lives and livelihoods. Back in the days of referendums, a marginal vote had swayed in favour of them. Knowing every household was both protected and monitored had seen burglary rates become almost non-existent. The dogs had been such a mainstay for so long. Most people didn't even really give them a second thought. They were in people's best interests in terms of safety. Julie hated it. She droned on about them being remote activated or how the dogs had caused people's disappearance. It was essentially nonsense to him. She was eleven. But the notion that someone could remotely trigger it did make him a little uneasy.

Watching Roger make light work of the scattered planets, Bryant realised he could use someone to talk to. He'd been trying to convince himself he was fine. But the random outbursts would seem to suggest otherwise. He needed his friend. He had tried getting in touch with Jimmy several times this week. Since his training finished, he had joined the rest of the family and begun the unenviable task of mining. Jimmy and his family worked in the Northern Sea, it was a fair distance away, and the depths the miners sunk to meant that it was almost impossible to get a live call to them. It was possible to send messages, but the delay was horrible. He had tried many times to get word to him, all to no avail. He'd recorded and sent about a thousand messages but had yet to get one back. Lonely and isolated, he felt disconnected. This couldn't be life. He felt as though there just had to be more for him.

Throughout their life, Jimmy had been untouchable. He was solid, never really thought he just did. Bryant, in contrast, was the opposite. He depended on Jimmy but sometimes wished his friend would see things a little differently. On the upside, Jimmy had always had the broadest shoulders, both literally and figuratively. Bryant never worried about his friend; he took everything in his stride. But it was now they were apart, and he had some perspective the realisation set in that Jimmy was a deep-sea miner. According to the statistics, it wasn't that dangerous, but the numbers told one story, reality another.

A lot of deaths that occurred happened at the surface. In that instance, it automatically meant it wasn't linked to the mines. But there was severe stress, pressure, and the myriad of drugs involved in sustaining the body at such depths, and that was before the very physically demanding aspect of the work itself. Almost no deaths would ever be attributed to the mines. Now that he pondered and considered it, knowing that his friend would now go through this process repeatedly for the rest of his life filled him with dread. He'd never really thought about how perilous it was. The numbers were one thing, but everybody knew miners had a short life span. A chill ran over Bryant's body. In truth, he feared for his friend's life.

Deep-sea mining, and thus the retrieval of Orbitium, had become one of the World's primary occupations. It was fundamental. In the beginning, around the time the mines were created, the Authorities had undertaken them. But it was gradually outsourced to the general population. The official reason behind that being to provide jobs, income, and purpose to those who previously had none. It was a vital cog in the space race. Those who were of a specific size were predestined to be miners. If you were over six feet in height, then you were too tall for the Academy. Your disposition also meant it was a waste sitting you behind a desk, a till, or in a taxi. The technology existed to allow travel to the depths of the deepest oceans. But the training for it was intense and the actual task even more so. The human body could not naturally withstand the pressure at the ocean's vast depths.

Revolutionary machinery and drugs allowed it to be possible. But you needed to be strong. Those who were too weak would often perish just during the training process. The drugs changed frequently and always unofficially, and there was no liability assigned to the developers. It was life or death. The planet had to be saved. Experimental drugs were a necessary evil. Then there was the work itself. The labour was long and arduous; the mineral was abundant, but mining it was hard graft. Each trip to the seabed had to bring back enough ore to cover the expedition's costs and make a sustainable profit, the mines were there to be used, but you had to give back. A direct sale to the Academy was an odd process, but it meant none of the hard work was done by anyone in a position of power. The mining crews had to do it all themselves and live off the fruits of their labours until they could make their next trip. Even with the drug infusions, the human body could only handle so many hours at extreme depth. If you tried pushing through this limit to mine more, there were often fatal consequences.

There were hosts of other potential dangers, too. Machinery and equipment would often fail at that depth. There were accidents because of fatigue, hypoxia, or narcosis, and if you were ever severely hurt, there was no way to get help. After a trip, the body would always need to spend a minimum of two weeks on the surface before returning. This would push tired miners to their limits. Desperate attempts to mine just that bit more before surfacing often led to disastrous consequences, but people were desperate to make a living, in need of contributing so that life would change and go back to normal.

It was a legal requirement to report accidents or death or any incident ever for that matter. But if someone was crushed by machinery or had a heart, lung, or any other underlying condition. That would be the official cause of death. The same would be true if they spent too long at the bottom, resurfaced and had an aneurism whilst driving their car. A car crash would be the reason.

Some suspected that the reason behind the ill-reporting of figures was because the actual number was exponential. Still, figures supposedly didn't lie, and a convincing enough statistic is all it takes for some to ignore the evidence. Very few relied on what the eyes saw, and their ears heard anymore. The simple fact was, the miners retrieving the ore meant they were working for the future. It Provided for the Academy. If many died along the way, given the oppressive population figures, it was seen as a necessary sacrifice.

Ringgggg.
Chimed the doorbell.

The noise entered Bryant's thoughts, popping them like a pin violently stabbed through a balloon. "Muuummm!" he yelled. "Mummm." Before remembering, he was home alone.

After yesterday's outburst at the cinema, his mum had given him the morning off to 'get his head together'. He wasn't sure what that meant. Regardless it was time he'd frittered away in a bubble of his thoughts. He hated answering the door. It was after nine, so it was unlikely to be the post. He hoped that it wasn't the faith mongers. They droned on about "Faith, fate, and divine purpose." He never wanted to listen, they were seen as fanatics, and they were in short supply. They talked about how there was more to life, that there was a world beyond the Districts. But they had been ridiculed by the Authorities to the extent that they weren't even stopped. People thought they were a joke, so did Bryant, but he hated to be rude and just didn't have it in him to tell them to "Go away!"

Bryant put down his spoon, stood, gave the boxed picture of DeVore the middle finger and reluctantly, he headed for the door. When he opened it, he was greeted by a genuine surprise. In front of him was a man dressed in an oh so familiar uniform, the stylish black of the Academy, complete with armband and glittery hat. Their uniforms were not only impressive but wreaked with style, tailored to the last millimetre. The majestic man was flanked on either side by two others who were lesser in rank or stature but equally magnificent nonetheless.

"Are you Bryant Fisher?" barked the man with military precision.

Bryant just stood there. Mouth agape, looking around him, he couldn't comprehend it. This was a high ranking Academy officer with two others; it was like having royalty at this door.

"I'm looking for Bryant Fisher!" the man repeated. With a fast-growing sense of impatience.

Bryant raised his hand slightly, "Yeah, that's me," he managed.

"Sign here, please," the man commanded. Stretching his arm out, the device in hand.

Doing as ordered. Bryant nervously took the screen from the man's hand and hastily, shakily, squiggled his name. His knees had turned to jelly. They were trembling so hard that he was using most of his brainpower, focussing on stopping the wobbling. In his mind, they were breezing about like a hammock casually swaying in the wind. He wasn't sure how much longer he could cope before they gave way altogether.

Bryant finished his squiggle and handed the screen back to the man, managing a solitary "Thanks," as he did so.

"Fisher," the man barked. "This is an urgent communication from the Academy. We require a response within twenty-four hours, do you understand?" The man removed an A4 envelope and handed it to Bryant.

Bryant convinced his head to nod. The man took this as acceptance and turned about on the spot, his subordinates did that same, and he departed envoy in tow. None of this made any sense. Why were they here? What was in the letter? Bryant had a thousand questions; he needed the men to leave so he could return to the house. Dumbstruck, he wasn't sure how well his legs would serve him. So he waited rigidly for the three men to be out of sight before he moved from his spot. Crept back into the house and shut the door at the second attempt. He found the nearest wall fell against it and proceeded to slide down it onto the floor. Safe in his hallway, it was then he looked down at the envelope he had clutched within his quivering arms.

F.A.O: Bryant Fisher.
By Hand.

Was written on the left-hand side, on the right was the logo of the Academy, and that was it. He turned it over to see that the envelope had an official tamper-proof seal. What on earth was inside, what had made them hand-deliver a letter to him? Why take the trouble when they could email it? His brain ran wild. He went to tear at the seal on the reverse. But something in his head stopped him. He realised that as long as it was still sealed, the contents could be anything. The possibilities were endless. Life had recently turned sepia. He needed hope like a sailboat stranded without wind. Slipping the sealed envelope cautiously into his backpack, he went upstairs to ready himself for work.

The cinema opened for business at noon, with the first showing shortly after. The custom was usually sparse. Entertainment was a necessity; that was the only reason it remained, a small escape. Everybody worked, even more so at this time of day. Movies were more factual than entertaining. Films were usually about working together and or saving the planet, subversive brainwashing. There was the occasional blockbuster. But it was generally about a space mission or a true story about miraculous events of the past that led to a space mission. They were Films about the life and events of heroes, Hector Rosario or the Academy's great leader, Commander Steele himself. The early showings were children's content. Essentially, the same as the adult versions, only more superficial. Although few, the early showings probably attracted the most dedicated moviegoers they had. As it got later, adults and adolescents alike piled out of work, schools or institutions. That's when it got more complicated. The film's content bored most adolescents, but the experience was quite something if you mixed it with drugs and alcohol.

Having Bryant at the cinema full time was a godsend for Pam. It meant that she could start later in the day, or he could help her out by coming in to operate the front desk. He could marshal the limited staff or anything else she might otherwise have to do herself. It allowed her to focus on more pressing matters, which was usually an impending audit. The cinema had once used dozens of staff in its heyday. But with the changes in society, most people did little other than work in Authority positions, mine or watch the mandatory non-compulsory television programmes at home. Pam could only afford to employ a few part-time staff. Staff who were either older adults otherwise deemed obsolete for Authority jobs or teenage citizens. It was usually the latter. Older people, in general, were rarely seen. Such was the care extended by the Authorities; the senior citizens, as well as the sick, would be taken care of by the state, taken to some retreat but rarely heard of or seen again.

Pam had the bulk of her team at work during the evening. So having Bryant with her, especially in the daytime, was a real blessing.

"Hi, Mum," Bryant said somewhat cheerfully.

He opened the lift up counter and slid underneath to join his mother near the till.

"Hi, Bryant," she said with a smile on her face, "I'm just doing a stock take for the audit. Would you be able to monitor the desk for me?"

"Sure," replied Bryant, dumping his rucksack and coat underneath. Once in situ, his mother disappeared off, clipboard in hand armed and ready for the day ahead. Bryant flicked the switch that brought the heavy metal outer doors gliding up. As they moved, it allowed the patient sunlight to enter the building.

Bryant sat at the front desk, all alone with his thoughts. Sitting there motionless, bored, he could see the large envelope poking its corner out of his bag, like a beating heart that refused to be quiet—pounding louder, fiercer, asking, begging, desperate to be opened. Determined to ignore it, he tidied the desk, lined all the pens up in order, counted the tiles on the floor, counted the lines on the roof, watched the people walk by until he could stand it no longer. He knelt carefully, always keeping one eye on the front door, half under the counter. With his head poking up like a meerkat, Bryant endeavoured to rip through the seal. Fumbling around in the dark, he half got his thumb through the top of it. But as he tried to slide it open, the edge sliced at him, "Ouch," he said, "stupid envelope!" He crawled fully under the desk to nurse his thumb and sort this envelope out once and for all. Squeezing his thumb between the palm of his left hand. He carefully tore through the seal using his right. With one eye half on the door still and the other involved in his business underneath, he could just about sneak a look inside. Peeking in, he saw enough of the smug face of DeVore grinning back at him from inside the envelope. "Eugh," he thought, "he's even inside my mail."

"Excuse me!" came a sweet sound from above. "Is anyone there?"

Startled, Bryant jumped up, hitting his head on the underside of the counter with a thud. "Bugger!" he muttered to himself. With his left thumb-squeezing hand, he tried to rub the bump on his head. The other, half under the counter, tried desperately to zip his bag back up. Righting himself and finally back in view of the desk, he was face to face with a pretty brunette lady. The irritating backpack fell against his feet, still nagging at him, and he kicked out at it, sending its contents spilling out onto the floor.

"Yes, hi, sorry!" he started. Confident at first. "How can you help?"

She looked at him inquisitively. He chuckled, "Which naturally is what you'd like to know from me." he said awkwardly.

"Okay?" she replied, somewhat confused. "I have a gang of my nephew and his friends who are desperate to see the new 'E-Dog Patrol' film."

"Yes, of course. Who doesn't want to see it?" blurted Bryant.

"Have you seen it?" she asked politely.

"Gosh no," Bryant spluttered. "Who would want to watch that rubbish?" Having uttered the words, he peered over the counter to see four wide-eyed, expectant looking children staring glumly at him. "I mean, who wants to watch that rubbish space movie when E-dog Patrol is out." An awkward silence ensued. "So that's four children and one adult. That will be nine credits, please."

It had been centuries since anyone used cash. The District History Museum, a museum with a limited history, had a few 'Dollar' and 'Pound' coins on display. But their exhibition was to demonstrate the vulgarity and absurdness of cash. Not to celebrate it, more warning than nostalgia. Naturally, Bryant had never handled money in his lifetime. Viruses had ravaged the planet during the 21st century, and it was during that time that they came to realise how abnormal cash was. It was easily laundered, it spread germs, and was effortlessly stolen. Removing cash was simple, the screw turning incrementally once more, and people agreed. And that was it coins were gone, and it's anonymity along with it. Instead, everyone had a credit account linked to them. It was impossible to hack, steal, or lose credits. It also meant that all money on the planet was traceable down to each human. For most in the Districts, you got the credits you needed based on your circumstances, you couldn't exceed your limits, and you couldn't make any transactions that went unnoticed.

The lady removed her phone to pay for the expectant infant hoard surrounding her, but as she went to pay, Bryant spoke again.

"Can I offer you any sweets or popcorn?" he asked.

"Oh," she chuckled, "gosh no! This gang is hard enough to control with fuelling them. Just the tickets are fine, thanks."

He ushered them in the direction of their screen, and Bryant was alone once again. Exasperated, reliving his situational awkwardness Bryant ploughed his head into the counter in front of him, bent double and groaned away.

"Excuse me," boomed a male voice from beyond the counter. Bryant looked up from his slump to see a robust, well-presented gentleman stood before him. He carried an air into the building, less impressive than Academy officers, but this man was important.

"Hi, there, sir," Bryant said politely as he looked up.

"Everything okay there, son?" the man asked kindly.

"Yup, just fine! Everything's fine here, sir," Bryant replied.

"Strange, because it looked to me like you were sleeping." the man said as he whipped out a very official Authority ID.

"Oh gosh, no," said Bryant, now panicked. "It was just this girl, and I was…"

"Relax!" he said smoothly. Reaching out with his arm putting it comfortingly on Bryant's shoulder. "I won't tell anyone. But hey, since we're keeping secrets? I'm from the District safety team; why don't you give me a quick tour of the place, just you and me? It's nothing serious. I just want to make sure this old gal is structurally sound." he said, wrapping his knuckles on the counter.

"I can give you a tour," replied Bryant enthusiastically.

"Well, lead on, young man?" agreed the man from the Authorities.

"Sure," said Bryant happily. " Please follow me, sir."

"Popcorn, popcorn, popcorn, how much popcorn do we have?" Pam said to herself as she bustled out from her office. Still equipped with a clipboard in one hand, a pen in the other. The records had to be documented electronically, but there was no margin for error, not at all. So Pam would count it all on paper first before uploading it to the Authorities. She was in the process of measuring every morsel of stock in the building. As she reapproached the front desk, she looked around but couldn't see her son anywhere. It wouldn't be a surprise if he were in the toilet. She never understood how anyone could drink so much whilst doing so little.

Opening the hatch to transition from one side to the other, she scurried past the front counter, but she felt something tug at her feet as she did so. The mystery object caught the back of her heel, and she did her best to steady herself, but it was no use. She had been mid-power stride, and it had caught her unaware. Moreover, both her hands were occupied, leaving her at the mercy of the rucksack straps and their scattered contents.

"Eeep," Pam let out a tiny wail as she slipped and fell headfirst towards the floor. She managed to jettison the clipboard and, using her arms, grabbed the counter to soften her landing.

Having saved herself from serious harm, as well as most of her pride, Pam sat on the floor in a mild mess, giving her banged knee the traditional rub before beginning the task of scooping up and retrieving her scattered documents. Once composed, she looked across at her feet and immediately spotted her assailant an all too familiar blue backpack. The bag was half unzipped, and its contents scattered across the floor under the desk.

"Dammit, Bryant!" she cussed quietly to herself. Having righted herself, she set about picking up the debris caused by her son's rucksack trap. It was then, as she was carefully putting the items back in Bryant's backpack, Pam spotted the all too familiar logo of the Academy. She considered at first that it might be the same letter that contained the exam results. It wouldn't be the weirdest thing Bryant had ever carried about with him. So, she began stuffing all the random items back into his bag. She tried zipping it up, but the letter was so big. Holding the bag with one hand whilst operating the dodgy zip with the other, Pam began to pull it together. "Get Bryant a new bag for his birthday," she thought to herself as she did. In the middle of her thoughts, it occurred to her the original letter with the results had been folded, hence Bryant's misinterpretation. This one was much larger. Curious at this realisation, she removed it, noting that not only was it more prominent, but it was also hand-delivered. "Odd," she thought.

The top had the familiar tattered look that Bryant gave to most envelopes. But strangely, he hadn't opened it fully.

Curiosity got the Pam. So she carefully removed the contents and set them all down on the counter, spreading them all out. There were so many documents here, a pack that had multiple forms in it. A pamphlet about the Academy, the front page of which paid tribute to Carlos DeVore. Pam glanced at it for a second before spotting a cover letter in the corner of her eye.

The Academy.
F.A.O: Bryant Fisher.
By hand:

Dear Mr Fisher,

We write to you once more regarding your recent application to the Academy. Owing to unforeseen circumstances, a place in the Academy has now become available. With that in mind, we would like to offer you a place as the 2369 entrant to the Academy.

We understand that your circumstances might have since changed. But we would urge you to remember that this is a once in a lifetime opportunity. Should you wish to accept this place, RSVP to the contact number contained within this letter. The pack also includes some new starter forms, which we would suggest you complete as soon as possible.

As ever with the mission, time is of the essence, so if we do not hear from you within twenty-four hours, we will assume you do not want the place in the Academy and will have to retake the examination process.

We await your reply in earnest.

For the stars.

Yours sincerely.
Commander Steele.

"Holy crap!" Pam thought out loud. Coming full circle isn't the easiest of things to do. The last few weeks had been a rollercoaster even for someone as robust as her. Hearing noises coming from the direction of the screens. Pam quickly and efficiently put the contents of the letter back in the envelope, then in the bag, and set it neatly back under the counter.

"Ah, Mrs Fisher, I presume?" The words startled her, and Pam looked up to see the well-presented gentleman striding towards her, Bryant behind him eagerly bringing up the rear.

"And who might you be?" she asked sternly. The man's stride finally broke as he arrived at the counter; out came the arm once more, forcefully shaking Pam's hand whilst simultaneously Flashing his ID with the other.

"I'm just checking the structure, safety and security of the building," he said.

Pam paused, "And I see you've met my son?" she replied by motioning toward Bryant, who was now finally approaching.

"Yes," he said, "what a lovely lad he is too! Dedicated to the cause. He could make a substantial addition to your team here."

Pam nodded at the odd choice of words. She was standing attentively, waiting for what came next.

"Well," continued the man, "your premises look to be up to code. But I will need to go through all the safety records, maintenance logs, and staff training files, if I may?" The words "If I may" hung in the air like a foul odour. Being pestered constantly by the Authorities was all part of running your own business. They'd throw endless challenges at you and see how you would do without slipping up.

"Not a problem," Pam replied diplomatically and with a fractured smile. "Would you care to join me in my office?"

Bryant watched his mum usher the gentleman into her office. She shot him the universal look that meant 'behave' before closing the door—leaving Bryant alone once more at the front counter.

The rest of the day breezed by. Customers came and went. The part-time staff arrived mid-afternoon. He sold popcorn, nachos, big drinks, small drinks, organised cleaning, and even dealt with one spill. Time finally stopped its incessant march, and as soon as Bryant had a moment to think, it was 9 pm. He had shot the occasional glance towards the office throughout the day, but little changed in there. Every few hours, one or both of them had appeared to use the toilet or grab a coffee, but then it had been straight back to it. He certainly didn't envy his mother right now.

As closing time finally arrived, he finished his walk through the building. Everything was clean, all tasks complete. Switching lights off as he went, he thanked the staff for their work as he sent them on their way. Day one, running a cinema, hadn't been that hard. The rear doors were locked, and the only lights that remained came from the glow that permeated through the frosted glass of the office.

Knock knock.

The noise of his fists knocking the glass cut through the silence like a gunshot in an empty forest. He opened the office door and stuck his head around the corner.

"All done, mum," he said. "Can I go home?"

Pam looked up from her mountains of paperwork, "Of course you can, sweetie."

Bryant took his cue and nodded in the gentleman's direction. His head disappeared from the door like a snake recoiling into its basket. The door creaked to a close, almost clicking the catch before it opened, and his head appeared again.

"Oh, mum," he asked, "what's for dinner?"

Having a free rein to order anything from Planet Pizza was a rare treat. He wondered if he'd get this every day? It almost made up for the fact that he had been at work for nine hours; doing actual work versus daydreaming in the sun was tiring. He was exhausted, and his feet hurt. But the sight of this piping hot fifteen-inch pizza sat in front of him was a boost for even the reddest of eyes. He threw his body down on the sofa and his feet onto the coffee table simultaneously as he took a slice with one hand and the remote with the other. The television could be operated through voice command, but flicking through the channels only to find nothing worth watching was something you needed a remote for. Without looking down once, he got through half of the pizza sat between him and the television. He watched an episode of 'Space Explorers' as he let the food settle in his stomach. It was the Moon episode. They had taken a memorial to Neil Armstrong and planted it on the surface. He had seen this one about a dozen times. He liked to analyse every aspect. His mind began to wander once more, and his slovenly daze was only interrupted by the appearance of Roger, who for some reason was active and presently sniffing quietly about the living room. "Weird!" he thought to himself. Julie's comments about the dogs permeated his soul, and he shuddered slightly.

Sat deathly still in his food coma, Bryant watched Roger linger about the living room. The mode he was in meant there was little urgency or energy to what he did. The dog had at first made a slow jaunt towards the pizza before being told to "Shoo," it was uncanny how real it seemed. Having been told to go, Roger then made a sluggish last-minute course change. Bryant watched as the dog plodded slowly towards his bag. The mutt arrived at the rucksack, stuck his head inside and proceeded to gum at the contents. "No, bad dog!" Bryant shouted. Either the bag was hindering its hearing, or it ignored him because Roger continued to abuse the bag's contents.

Not wanting slobbery belongings or half-chewed remains, Bryant stood and grabbed Roger's rear. The dog came peacefully out of the bag, but when it did, it had the letter from the Academy firmly clamped within its teeth. "Hey!" Bryant yelled at Roger. Bryant knelt and carefully prised the envelope from the dog's mouth. It was then he noticed that it was now fully open at the top, and some of the paperwork was poking out. Assuming that Roger had done it, Bryant took the envelope, swatted the dog on the head with it and sat back down on the sofa. "Bad dog!" he said once more, a command which sent Roger skulking off slowly towards the kitchen.

It had been such a long day; in truth, the letter had completely slipped his mind. Everything had. Kicking back on the sofa once again, he grabbed a pen from the table and removed the contents. Settling back down, he removed the brochure that had DeVore plastered all over it. He detached the pen's cap and began to doodle over the man's face. It was then midway through drawing a thick black moustache and a crude phallus on the face of the chiselled jawed DeVore, he noticed a cover letter addressed to him hidden amongst the papers. What could it be? He paused his childish drawing, put the pamphlet down and took up the letter in both hands and began to read.

The Academy.
F.A.O: Bryant Fisher.
By hand:

Dear Mr Fisher,

We write to you once more regarding your recent application to the Academy. Owing to unforeseen circumstances. A place in the Academy has now become available. With that in mind, we would like to offer you a place as the 2369 entrant to the Academy.

We understand that your circumstances might have since changed, but we would urge you to remember that this is a once in a lifetime opportunity. Should you wish to accept this place? RSVP to the contact number contained within this letter. The pack also includes some new starter forms, which we would suggest you complete as soon as possible.

As ever with the mission, time is of the essence, so if we do not hear from you within twenty-four hours, we will assume you do not want the place in the Academy and will have to retake the examination process.

We await your reply in earnest.

For the stars.

Yours sincerely.
Commander Steele.

The letter fell from Bryant's hand the minute he read the final line. As it floated slowly to the floor, he wondered once more. Was he dreaming? I mean, this was exactly what he dreamt about. Did he misread it? Had he been drugged? He paused, pondered for a second, physically pinched his arm. The pinch hurt, so he bent, picked it back up, took a deep breath and reread it. He read it for the third time. Then even a fourth, just to be sure. It seemed to check out; it made little sense, but this was real, somehow he had a place in the Academy.

Bryant picked up his phone. He rang Jimmy for about the nine millionth time. He still didn't pick up. Looking at his watch, it was 10:30. Surely his mum would be home soon? He needed someone to talk to. His mind ticked it was a brilliant and terrible place all at once.

Alone in a room, with nothing but his thoughts. The weight and gravity of the situation broke on him. All his life, all he'd ever known was going to the Academy. He'd sacrificed everything for it, and for what? So, they could dangle the opportunity in front of him. It had been like that carrot he would never catch. The last few weeks had been awful, soul-sucking, purgatorial. But in that time, he'd accepted that the Academy was gone. He'd realised what he had. He'd seen what he'd never seen before, what he been in front of him all along. He was close to his mum, had time for his crazy sister, and cherished every moment he would spend with his friend Jimmy. If he went to the Academy, he would give all of that up. And for what?

For the first time in his short life, Bryant knew what he wanted. He'd realised what was important to him. It was a moment of clarity like he'd never known before; he knew the decision he needed to make. Bryant picked up the letter from the table, typed the number correctly at the third time of asking, and dialled.

"Blachh!" what a day that had been, Pam thought out loud!

Finally, she genuinely thought it might never end. The rigid, righteous man had left around 11:30, and it had been far from pleasant. She had survived (she hoped). She'd drunk a ridiculous amount of coffee, something which had made it even harder to stop herself from climbing across the desk and physically throttling the man. But after years of their nonsense, surprise calls, and cancelled plans. Pam was very adept at holding her tongue. She focussed on what was important and showed the man every single scrap of paper, record, file, video, and log he requested. Finally, alone, she began to put her office back together. She opened the lockable drawer atop her desk, dropping a flash drive inside. But it was as she did so, a golden glow caught her eye. Halting her arm in its tracks, she dragged the drawer open again. The fifty-year-old scotch sat there, beaming at her, a murky brown ray of sunshine. It had been a gift from the employees for her fiftieth birthday. Now it just lay there, unopened, almost grinning; come and get me, Pam. Oh, how she could use a drink! She grabbed the bottle from its resting place and grasped at the lid; she poured an ample amount of the amber nectar into her empty coffee cup. As she raised the mug to her face, the familiar scent wafted into her nostrils, and she took a long, deep sniff. God, it smelt good. Intoxicated by the smell, she went to take a sip, but it was as she did, so she glanced at the digital frame on her desk; it had just rotated onto a picture of her family. She smiled a splintered grin as she thought about how nice it was having her family just the way she wanted. It was then it hit her.

"Bryant," she remembered. "Gosh, what a crazy day!" The letter had completely slipped her mind. Pam hastily got her belongings together. Put the half-full cup and bottle back into her drawer and bolted out of the cinema. The taxi she ordered took less than a minute to arrive, and she jumped in, setting off for home.

Slipping into the house like a mouse, closing the door gently behind her. She removed her shoes and entered her home. The sight that greeted her was quite the mess, but it brought a tear to her eye. Bryant was sprawled out on the sofa, shoes still on with one leg on the coffee table. The half-eaten remains of the pizza were on the floor, and she could see visible grease on everything he had touched. The state of the place should and would usually rile her up. But it warmed her heart after a long day. For the briefest of moments, her family was exactly as she wanted it. The things you take for granted. Wiping her eye, Pam crept towards her heavily snoring son. She carefully, gently removed his shoes, grabbed a blanket and covered him. As she draped the cover over him, she noticed that his phone was still firmly in his grasp. "Teenagers," she thought. Stooping to detach his phone, she heard a noise as she did so. With the telephone successfully prised from its owner she realised she could hear the awful warble of hold music. Looking at the screen, she discovered that he had been on the call for forty minutes. Shocked, she disconnected the call. She was desperately hoping that he hadn't dialled one of the 'kinky hotlines' again. Forty minutes to one of those would cost the earth. She set the phone down on the table. She finished blanketing her son, switched out the lights and crept upstairs.

Second chances.

The light above the door of his ship clicked to green, and as everybody knows, green means go! Bryant hit the switch on the keypad. The doors hissed open, and he stepped out. His live stream to Earth was ready. He knew billion's of people were all glued to their screens. Wherever they were, whatever they were doing. Everyone had stopped and was watching this handsome hero take his first steps on Mars. Text comments flooded the screen in his visor. Each remark more complimentary than the last. What a hero! Planting his feet on the firm, red soil in front of him, he said,

"These tiny steps taken by me are far greater ones for humankind."

The adoration on Earth grew as he plagiarised the words of Armstrong. His feet implanted on new terra firma. The shuttle doors closed behind him as he strode forward triumphantly. But wait, he stopped. Something was wrong. He looked down at his wrist; suddenly, the feed was gone. He tried reconnecting it, but it was no use. Panicking now, he tried mission command; it dialled and dialled but didn't connect. No longer as intrepid. He looked up and saw nothing; looking down, he discovered the same. His ship and everything around him had vanished in the blink of an eye. He was just floating now in oblivion; he was naked, his suit, his clothes had all disappeared, everything was missing. Alone, bare, and drifting. He took a deep breath to ease his panic, but it was only nothingness that filled his lungs. This was it, and it was all over. He would leave this new world the way he entered the old. Alone, naked and fighting for breath. He missed his family; he missed his friends. The strange atmosphere made it impossible to cry! He couldn't even cry. Bryant closed his eyes and let himself drift away. It was all about to end...except he could smell bacon and hear a voice. It was faint but a voice.

"Bryant... Bryant...Bryant!"

He sat upright, bathed in his sweat. He looked all around in panic. Bryant rubbed his eyes. His blurriness shifted, and thankfully it greeted him with the familiar sight of his living room. Thank heavens! It was just a dream. The smell of bacon had been real. It drifted from the kitchen and permeated his nostrils.

"Rip Van Winkel's up," came the voice from behind him. Bryant turned to see his mother moving towards him.

"Rip Van what?" he replied, utterly confused. Armed with a massive cup of tea, Pam approached her son. She set the cup down on the coffee table and ruffled his hair.

"Morning, sleepyhead," she said.

"Eugh, mum," Bryant recoiled his head in disgust. He was eighteen. Why was she still ruffling his hair?

Waking up was always hard to do for Bryant. It took him a few minutes to get his vocal cords to cooperate. Once they did, what they offered was unusually monosyllabic.

"Thanks," he grunted. Bryant shifted and cleared his throat; "What time is it?" he asked.

"9:30," came the response from his mother, "you've just missed your sister."

"Wait," stammered Bryant, "Julie was here?"

"Tore through the place like a tornado. I'm amazed it didn't wake you. We were a little worried you might be dead at one point," she said jokingly.

The death reference sent a chill down his spine. He shuddered.

"Everything okay?" Pam asked.

"Bad dream is all," said Bryant, standing and stretching. "Mum, where's my phone?"

"I popped it on charge in the kitchen, sweetie," was her response.

"Mum," he moaned, "I was in the middle of a phone call."

"I know you can talk in your sleep, honey. But whoever it was. Unless they were fluent in gibberish, I don't think anyone was interested in what you had to say" —Bryant cut her off, moving briskly towards the kitchen— "Mum," he went on, "that was an important call to the Academy!"

Pam went after her son and caught him in a giant hug from behind. She squeezed him hard, "Oh, I'm so proud of you," she said. "Did you tell them you wanted the position?"

As devastated as she would be if her son went to the Academy, and as much as it was everything she didn't want to happen. Her son's happiness and dreams always came first. Bryant moved his hands down towards his waist, breaking the contact between him and his mother. He turned and met her gaze head-on.

"Wait," he said, "you read my letter?" His tone changed quickly from soft to angry.

"Oh, I'm sorry, bunny," she replied. "I tripped over your bag yesterday at work. I wanted to talk to you about it. But you know how busy yesterday was."

"So," he started, "you just happened to trip over my bag, and the letter magically fell out and read itself to you, did it?"

His eyes flashed, and an angry adolescent rage crept over Bryant.

"Bryant Fisher," said his mother, "don't you—"

"—No, mum," Bryant snapped angrily. "You can't go through my stuff anymore. I'm not a child! I mean, were you ever going to tell me? What if I missed the deadline because of you?"

"Yes Bryant, of course, I—"

"—No," he continued, maddening still, "you've never wanted me to go to the Academy. Have you mum? Just for once, why don't you think about what I want?"

Bryant seized his phone, pushed past his mother into the living room. Grabbed his neatly arranged shoes and stormed angrily out of the house, slamming the door behind him so hard that the whole place physically shook.

"Bryant," pleaded Pam, but it was no use. By the time she opened the door to go after him, Bryant was sprinting down the road, already nearly out of sight. Conceding that she would never catch up to an angry teenager, she re-entered the house and shut the door the opposite way just as hard. Pam let out a yell in anguish before slumping to the ground in agony. Once on the floor that she began to cry.

Bryant ran and ran, and ran until he could run no more, and he finally stopped. His heart beat so fast, his pulsed raged, and his vision contained a red tint. He took a glance over his shoulder to confirm that he was, in fact, alone. "Eugh, how could she?" he thought angrily to himself. He pulled his phone from his pocket and glanced down at it. The time was 10:40. The men who delivered the letter came just before eleven yesterday. If he was going to respond to the letter, he had to do it now.

There was an old abandoned football stadium on the outskirts of the District. It was a place his father had taken him as a child. They would kick around an old tin can and tear about what was once a field. Then afterwards, when it got dark, they would lie on their backs near to the bleachers and stare up at the night sky together. The spot held a special place in his heart. His father was often in absentia. Memories were sparse. So, to this day, whenever he needed time to be alone or a place to think, this was where he came. His deadline was looming fast; he had come within a breath of turning down the place last night. After he had placed the call, he found himself on hold for what seemed like eternities. At the time, it frustrated the hell out of him. But were it not for the horrendous hold music stalling him and ultimately sending him to sleep, he might have turned down the place.

"Eurgh, imagine!" He kicked out at the floor in frustration. The boot sent a carved-up bit of turf into orbit briefly. It spun in the air briefly before it came crashing back down to Earth again.

How had he been so stupid? That was precisely what she wanted! She didn't want him to accept the place. She just wanted him here with her at the cinema! Bryant shoved his hand forcefully into his pocket and removed his phone. He wiped away the layer of sweat that had accumulated during his run and with a decision conceived primarily out of anger. He hit the buttons and began to dial.

"Good morning, thank you for contacting the Academy," came the cheery voice. "How may I direct your call today?"

"Oh, thank heavens!" he thought. An automated voice greeted the call he made last night. One that read out a million different options very slowly and then listened to absolutely nothing you had to say. When he had finally got it to accept his command, it had put him straight on hold. "We can go to space," he had thought. "But we still can't make a decent voice recognition system."

"Hi," was his response, "my name is Bryant Fisher; I'm phoning about a place in the Academy."

"One moment, please."

A few clicks on the line later and his ears were greeted by the firm, confident, deep soothing tone of a male voice. It was a voice that filled you with confidence and fear simultaneously. As though angry angels lept from the mouth of the speaker with every word enunciated.

"Commander Steele," boomed the voice, "to whom am I speaking, please?"

Bryant went to reply. But when he did, he found that his voice box had packed up and disappeared. His vocal cords had frayed and withered. As though his entire throat had been filled with cement.

On the other end of this line was Commander Steele. The head of the Academy himself. Bryant had posters of this man adorning his walls. He'd owned action figures of him. He even had Commander Steele toothpaste growing up. The toothpaste that gave your teeth added steel.

"Hello," came the voice again, "is there anyone there?"

He couldn't keep the Commander waiting any longer. Bryant took a big gulp, cleared his throat, and began uttering the most important words of his life.

"Hello, Mr Steele, sir," he spoke. "My name is Bryant Fisher; I'm phoning about your letter. I'd like to accept your position in the Academy." The end of the word 'Academy' trailed off into more of a squeak.

"Ah, Mr Fisher," replied Steele. "We thought you'd never call. Talk about an eleventh-hour moment? Good to have you on board. I assume you are ready to undertake the opportunity of a lifetime?"

The Academy had many rules. In some ways, it was like joining what was once the armed forces. In essence, it had replaced them. A world at one with itself did not need armies. When you signed up for the Academy, you knew that you would likely join for life. There were ranks, a chain of command, and certain privileges that only came with tenure. The first six weeks meant you could only wear only your Academy clothing. Even in your spare time, you could only dress in the official tracksuit. During the six-week induction, you weren't allowed off base. You also surrendered your electronics. Communication with the outside world was limited to the communal screens during an allotted time frame. The training was gruelling, the rules strict. But they had to be. There was no room for error in this industry. To be the future of humanity, purveyors of tomorrow, you had to be the best.

"Yes, sir!" was Bryant's response. "Looking forward to serving my planet."

"Excellent, Mr Fisher," said Steele. "Take today and tomorrow to relax. Get your affairs in order, and we'll see you on Tuesday morning at 0900 hours."

"Yes, sir," Bryant repeated excitedly.

"Oh, and Mr Fisher," came the voice.

"Yes, Mr Steele?" replied Bryant.

"Don't be late!"

When you joined the Academy, you became a hero, a superstar. But it had one other big attraction. Signing up even as a fresh recruit, you started on a very generous monthly salary. There were bonus payments for specific exercises and flight pay for any space excursions. Unlike most people on the planet, Academy staff had money to burn. You also got the added bonus of being able to drink for free at any of the bars in your District.

Even on the phone, speaking to Commander Steele would go down as one of his favourite moments in life. But it mattered not. He was sure he would talk to the great man many more times. He would be an Academy recruit in a matter of days. He still couldn't quite believe it. Lying on his back in this once great stadium, he wished his dad was here with him. Side by side, as they had once done. He wanted to talk to him right now. The memories he had of his father were fond ones. His mum rarely spoke about his disappearance, and there were so many things he didn't understand. From what he heard, his father had quite the drinking problem and had got himself mixed up with some dangerous people. All the memories Bryant carried of the man, though, were fond ones.

Alone on the tattered remnants of the grass. Bryant stared up at the sky. He was going to the Academy! This had been his dream for as long as he could remember. It was an exciting time, but he was very nervous. In his mind, he'd made the right choice; surely he had? So why was there this nagging feeling in the back of his brain? Standing up, he rocked his head back and forth. As if trying to physically dislodge the evil thoughts, trying to embrace his reality! He was going to the Academy. This was it.

"Woohooo," he shouted. Arms aloft as he ran around the old stadium.

As he ran, he imagined the years rolling back. The grass re-growing with it, the giant adoring crowd watching on, cheering for him. He was an Academy man now, and he was damn sure going to make the most of it.

New beginnings.

At precisely 0717 hours on Tuesday morning, Bryant got out of bed. He'd been awake at 0650, then again at 0700, then 0710. He'd left it to the last moment possible before prising himself from his bed. He hated early starts. One of his biggest fears about the Academy wasn't leaving his family and friends. It wasn't the training; it wasn't even potentially dangerous space missions. His biggest challenge was going to be the early rises. He'd packed his bags the night before. It was making him look super organised, although he was just buying himself more time in bed. He packed light for the first six weeks. According to the message he'd received, he would collect most of what he needed upon arrival.

Bryant gradually stood from his bed, stretched, yawned and progressively moved towards the door. The shutters were still down, meaning light in the room was at a premium. Julie had demanded she sleep on his floor last night, "I am coming back," he kept telling her. But once Jules made her mind up, there was no stopping her from anything.

Julie was known for snoring. It was like sleeping next to a running motorbike all night. But in truth, he'd been happy not to spend his last night alone. Knowing she was sprawled out on his floor. He moved from the bed, treading very carefully. Standing on his sister would not be the best start to the day. He navigated the dark human assault course and her various scattered belongings, managing to make it out the far side unscathed. He slipped quietly out of the bedroom door and made his way to the bathroom.

"Can I have your room when you're gone?" came the voice of his sister from behind him. "You know because you won't be here using it and that?"

"But you have your own room, Jules," he called back.

"I like your room, though," she said. "Plus, it reminds me of you."

"Fine," he said tiredly, "as long as mum's okay with it. You can sleep wherever you want. But I want it back when I'm home."

"Deal," she said.

Reaching the bathroom, Bryant turned slightly and saw the figure of Julie emerge in his periphery. She was still half wrapped in a blanket that trailed behind her as she headed downstairs.

He paused on the landing. He could hear his mother bustling away below. They'd made peace, but it was stifled, and they tried to keep their feud away from Julie. He was still angry, though, and the air between them was a little fractious.

He stepped inside the bathroom, locking the door behind him. As he did so, he could hear footsteps ascending the stairs. They approached the bathroom door and then stopped. On the other side, Pam stood, head resting sadly against the door, quietly soaking in the moment.

Bryant turned the shower on and went to get it. "Dammit," he'd better shave! Leaving the shower running, he got out his regulation foam and razor kit and began the task of removing the collections of the fluffy, furry hair that set up camps in various spots on his face. The running shower made shaving very difficult. The mirror steamed up constantly, and no amount of wiping made it stop. Undeterred, he persevered until ultimately he put a small nick in his skin with the razor. Red blood oozed out of the cut, spurred on by the warm, damp conditions of the bathroom. He looked in the mirror, meeting his gaze. He stared at the minor blemish in a daze, in a trance as he watched it produce more and more blood. He pushed his finger hard against the wound to stem the flow, but it instantly widened, forcing the blood out like a waterfall. It cruised out of his face dripping into the sink, filling it up and up until the basin was now a blood-red pond. He wrapped a towel around the cut in panic, but it soaked straight through. Trapped in this frenzied blood bath, he looked at himself once more. His face was wizened and pale. His eyes were wide and stricken with panic. What was happening? The blood had filled the room, forcing its way into his lungs. There was no escape. He was drowning, drowning in his own blood!

Knock knock.

The sharp rap on the door shook him from his daydream. He glanced down at the sink, relieved to see just a few spots of blood.

"Are you in the shower, Bryant?" his mother's voice permeating through the door. "Please don't leave it running if you're not in it!"

"Err, sorry, mum," he said, "I only hopped out for a second."

"Okay, please don't get water all over the floor," she said before departing. Bryant looked at himself once more. He wiped the small patch of dried blood from under his chin and finally got into the shower.

The journey to the Academy was about forty-five minutes by taxi from Bryant's house. They had sent a car, but it was only for him. His mother and Julie had work and school, respectively. Meaning he would say goodbye at home and undertake the trip to the Academy alone.

The time was now 0750, and it was almost time for him to leave. The three of them sat pensively in the living room. The silence was eerie. Julie sat between Bryant and Pam, constantly switching her gaze from one to the other like a pendulum.

Briinng

Came the sound of Bryant's phone. The noise signifying that his ride was here, interrupting the silence like a cockerel sounding out the dawn. Bryant stood nervously; Julie leapt up with him, trapping him in a sideways hug

"Don't go," she pleaded.

"Oh, Jules," he said, "you know I'm coming back? Six weeks will pass in no time." He shrugged free from the sideways hug to kneel and meet her face on, "But I need you to behave for mum when I'm away."

"Oh, good," she answered sarcastically. "I mean, I would have totally been a nightmare if you hadn't reminded me." He chuckled, and he pulled her in tight for a hug.

"I mean it, Jules!" he said, holding her tight.

"Pffft, fine," she said. Releasing her, he moved across to his mother.

"Bryant…" she started with a tear in her eye. He hugged her, and she held on to him for as long as she could. "Look after yourself, mum," he said. He stepped back, grabbing his bags from beside the door.

"Better not keep them waiting, I guess."

He opened the front door. Waved his goodbyes before closing it behind him. Once outside, he put his forehead against the door for a split second, unaware that his mother did the same, not two inches away. He turned about on the spot, moved towards the waiting vehicle, opened the door, and stepped inside.

As the vehicle pulled away, Bryant twisted his neck and looked back through the rear window. His sister had slipped past their mother through the front door and was running towards the car. Her figure loomed larger and larger as she approached, but then as the automobile gained momentum. It peaked before gradually getting smaller and smaller. He watched on until the sight of his sister became a speck in the distance before disappearing from view altogether.

The sight of the Academy was always an impressive one. Sat in its own grounds, it was almost a District of its own. It had massive, heavily guarded walls surrounding it. Inside was everything it needed to self-sustain: recreation grounds, swimming pools, shops, living quarters, and even houses.

His car approached the gates to be greeted by two armed guards. Satisfied by the stories and ID's they let the taxi cross the checkpoint. The enormous gates swinging open, allowing the car to enter. Bryant had never seen inside this part of the Academy, and he watched on in awe as the taxi moved through the camp. It glided along slowly, passing by men and women in Academy uniforms, platoons running past the famed clock tower. It was everything he had ever imagined, everything and more.

The car finally pulled up outside a large, very official-looking building, which Bryant assumed to be the headquarters. Not a single word had been uttered during the journey. He'd wanted a clear head when he arrived, not one filled with idle chatter.

"What do I owe you?" Bryant asked the driver, breaking the silence.

"Nothing," replied the chauffeur, "they always use our firm for Academy travel. A great bit of business for us. I have to say, though; we rarely pick up two recruits in one month."

"Good month for business then?" came Bryant's reply.

"Yeah, good for us," said the driver. "Not good for the other guy, though."

"Wait," said Bryant, suddenly very interested in conversation, "what do you mean?"

"Jus what I hear," the driver replied. "Chatter I eard. Something about an accident."

Bryant was confused. He went to ask more before remembering that taxi drivers always talked nonsensical gossip. Bryant nodded politely towards the driver as he popped the door open.

"Hey," said the driver, "just be careful. You never know who's listening."

"Thanks, I guess! I'll bear that in mind?" Bryant said sarcastically as he stepped from the car.

Taking his first steps on hallowed Academy ground, Bryant lurched forward then stopped. The stones beneath him had the crunch of a fresh snowfall. The distance from the car to the door of the building was roughly ten meters. He took his time, taking it all in as he walked. He could see the famous clock tower in the distance. Behind him, platoons jogged with military precision. Everything was like clockwork. He took a deep breath and sucked it all in. Even the air tasted different. He finally reached the door, stretched out his arm, and grabbed the shiny brass handle, took another large breath and a big gulp before opening the cumbersome door and stepping inside.

Changes.

As the end of his first week approached, Jimmy had already had enough of the mines. His excitement wore off almost immediately. The training had been fun to an extent, but his initial enthusiasm dashed within hours. The reality of working seven-day twelve-hour back-to-back shifts was horrible. The living quarters were creaky and old. Water frequently leaked from the pipes, usually dripping on you in your sleep, and there was little to do here after work other than drink sour gin and then fall asleep only to be leaked on. There was even less to see, and the pressure at these depths made the structures creak and groan, emitting noises like tortured souls, the damned dead, roaming around trapped at sea for eternity. It was haunting. Every waking morning was precisely the same. Rise at 0500, take the myriad of pills, supplements, and liquids needed to sustain the body at these depths. Eat the same high carb, high protein porridge. Put on your protective gear, perform safety checks, and then straight to very hard, very labour-intensive work. Not two months ago, he had been craving adulthood, but right now, he would give anything to go back.

Leaving for their first expedition had been very exciting. He got to go on his first boat ride and first trip on a submarine lift. His entire family would get involved now that he had come of age and left home on a family boat trip. It had been lovely until they parted ways at the surface. He went down the mines with his father, older brother, and the other able bodies; his mother stayed on the boat with the others, who couldn't work the physical aspects of the job—coordinating the efforts below. Jimmy enjoyed working with his family, getting to spend some time with his dad and brother, who he normally saw precious little of. However, the other families contained some real knuckleheads, and the conversation was rare and stimulating conversation rarer still. Jimmy missed his friend. Of the two, Bryant had always been the smarter one. It was unusual for the miner children to mix with non-miner families, but he had always liked Bryant. He had learnt much from him and passed many exams thanks to his help. At school, nobody trifled with Jimmy, but being the new boy here at the depths of the ocean meant he was at the bottom of the food chain. He had joked that there was no one lower than him in the world due to the depth, but it had fallen either on deaf, tired, or dumb ears.

They still had another week until they would surface. Jimmy thought boredom or routine might be what killed him, but he had to persevere. There was no room for weakness, not down here. Once a mining trip finished, they would go straight into depressurisation and spend forty-eight gruelling hours sweating, vomiting, retching, and writhing as their tortured bodies rid themselves of the drugs and acclimatised to the surface.

Two days into the mission, he had been lucky enough for his phone to get a tiny bit of signal. Unsurprisingly he had about nine million missed calls from his friend. It connected for just long enough to download six video messages. Jimmy speculated that there were probably many more to come, but six would keep him occupied for now. Jimmy had watched all six very long, chaotic videos in order. It had been like watching an epic biopic. He was documenting a retrospective rise and fall. It had made for tense viewing and was far from pithy. His friend had been through so much since he had been away. As pleased as he was to hear from Bryant, the large chunks of time spent at the depths of the ocean made him feel alone, disconnected. The takeaway fact was that somehow, inexplicably, Bryant had passed the exams for the Academy. Jimmy was speechless. He didn't know what to make of it, couldn't stop thinking about it, and felt so helpless, utterly detached.

"Jimmy, pass me that wrench," came the gruff voice of his father, Burt.

"Hey Jimmy," he continued, "you in there?"

Jimmy snapped out of his daze. Startled, he managed a "Sure dad." Before bending for the wrench and knocking a pipe loose from the wall with the top of his helmet.

Steam billowed out of the pipe and dancing about like a powerful hose tossed on a lawn. Jimmy stood just watching before his father grabbed the tube, tamed the dancing snake, and reattached it to the other end.

"Pay attention, damn it, Jimmy!" Burt growled.

"Sorry, dad," replied Jimmy, suddenly knowing how it felt to be Bryant. "I think I'm just tired."

"Mistakes can't happen, Jimmy! Down here, they cost lives," Burt said. "Take a break, clear your head, then get your ass back here."

Jimmy trudged off back to the mess area, annoyed at himself, angry at the situation, and frustrated at the world. He wasn't used to this. He stepped into the mess hall, closed the bulkhead door, and removed his helmet. He was rarely alone here, and in the silence, he thought about his friend; he contemplated how much he hated the reality of life, working for a future that probably wouldn't be theirs. Bryant would know what to do. He always did. He pictured him sitting about the Academy, people laughing, eating grapes and legs of meat. Stories told on silk rugs, people listening to Bryant, and all the brilliant ideas that flew from his mind. When they were young, Bryant spent hours filling Jimmy's head with talk of the Academy, how all that joined were heralded, heroes that worked on the planet's future, the parties, the camaraderie. He painted a wonderful picture, and for once, Jimmy wished he could trade places with his friend. Until now, he could talk to him any time of day or night. He'd see him every morning. They'd hang out most weekends. He'd never even had the slightest notion that was something he could take for granted.

Streamers and champagne.

Bryant had pictured how he might arrive at the Academy over a thousand times. Each time was slightly different, but always variations of a theme. There was a fanfare. People would be sat intently listening to the broadcast wherever they were. Spontaneous parties kicked off in the streets, a limousine picked him up from his house, and he was swept away. Fans lined the streets, eager to get even the slightest glimpse of him. His entrance to the academy would be an event, like an arriving dignitary. There would be red carpets and champagne on arrival. He would perform his acceptance, and then it would be straight to space since there was no time to lose.

Reality, however, had other ideas. Since stepping through the insanely heavy door, the only words uttered to him were, "Wait there, please!" Words that came from a lady who was frankly terrifying. As he sat in silence, waiting, he pondered as he analysed her. The only way he figured she could be scarier was if she was actually a crocodile. One that was wearing a white frilled blouse, fat rimmed spectacles and the curliest of grey wigs. Twenty minutes passed by, watching, waiting. Was it a wig? The chair he sat upon must have initially been used as a torture device. It was solid wood with a back so straight it could not have been designed with sitting comfortably in mind. He kept having to shuffle for comfort, but every time he did, the crocodile looked up, snarling.

Finally, the odd, awkward silence broke. A door at the end of the corridor opened, a man emerged and strode confidently down it towards him.

"Fisher!" he barked upon arrival.
Bryant stood just in time and stretched out his hand.

"Congratulations, young man." Bryant returned the gesture and gave the man his hand. They embraced for too long until finally, the vice grip his hand found itself in loosened, letting Bryant's crushed fingers fall back to his side.

"I'm Colonel Brooks," continued the man, "follow me, please."

"Okay," Bryant thought, "it had been a rocky start, but surely cameras were waiting on the other side of the door. Perhaps it was a surprise? They'd open the door to a sizeable crowd, adoring fans, or at very least just streamers and champagne?"

Having successfully crushed his hand. The man turned and sped off back down the long corridor. Bryant set off hot on his heels, thinking that jogging was the only way he could keep up with this inhuman pace.

"Sit, please," ordered Brooks. Bryant had finally caught up and made it through the door. It was just an office, nothing special here.

Disappointed, but doing as ordered. Bryant sat and met the gaze of the officer across the desk.

"Welcome to your new life," greeted Brooks. "I'm short on time. So I'll keep this as brief as possible. I will be your commanding officer. Any issues you have, feel free to come to me."

"Yesss, sir," replied Bryant. "But what about the ceremony? Where is Commander Steele?"

Brooks chuckled, "Don't be daft. Commander Steele is far too busy for initiations! The man's a hero Bryant. He has a planet to save." Bryant nodded, somewhat crestfallen.

"Now, about your initiation."

Bryant's eyes lit up once more, "Now we're talking!" he thought.

"I know you expect a big show today," said Brooks. "But the public can't handle a big deviation from the norm. We've recently had a ceremony. We need to wait for the dust to settle first before having another. Now, do you have any questions?"

"Well yeah, just a few, I" –

"Okay fine," said Brooks, "you deserve the truth. Look, we found evidence that your predecessor DeVore cheated on his test. Naturally, we can't have the public losing faith in our work or the system. All will be sorted in good time. Surely you understand?"

"Well, I" – Bryant started.

Brooks carried on belligerently, "In the coming months, we will release a statement to the public that DeVore could not fulfil his duties because of a medical condition and was honourably discharged. At which point we confirm that you graciously stepped into the void. It will be better than the normal ceremonies, Bryant. The same ceremony happens every year. Yes, it's exciting but ultimately forgettable. Not for you though, yours will be different. Bryant Fisher, the man who stepped up in his planet's hour of need. See, it has a ring to it."

Brooks did paint a picture, but he was still disappointed about today, though.

"Now," continued the officer. "I need you to sign these documents to say that I have explained all of that to you, and you understand."

Bryant picked up the dossier in front of him. It was several pages thick; he flipped it back to the beginning and started to read.

"Oh no, there's no time for that," came the voice from the other side of the document.

Bryant lowered the pages from his eyes to be greeted by the sight of Brooks holding a pen out inches from his nose.

"As I said, it's just everything I have explained to you. But I tell you what. We'll have a copy of it shipped over to your quarters later, and you read it as many times as you like then."

Bryant took the shiny blue pen that was dangled before his eyes. He swallowed, lowered the paper to the desk, and signed on the dotted line.

"Be sure to date it too," came the command from Brooks.
No sooner was it signed and dated, the document was whisked away. The pen almost scoring a blue line across the page as it went. Brooks stuffed the paper into his desk drawer and pulled out about a hundred other bits before thrusting all of them in front of him. Bryant picked up the first and signed. In the background of his mind, Bryant could hear Brooks warbling on.

"So here we have your contract, terms of service, pension agreement, liability waiver, insurance agreement, accidental death waiver, and signing away your freedom forever."

Bryant stopped. That was weird. Looking up, he said, "What was the last one?"

"Signing up to protect the freedom of the planet forever," said Brooks.

Bryant shook his head. He needed to pay more attention. He filled in all the forms hesitantly before they were all removed and disappeared as though they never existed.

"Okay, all done," said Books, "here is your ID. Make sure you have it with you on base at all times. Sleep with it, shower, eat with it, take it to the toilet with you."

"What happens if I don't have it with me?" asked Bryant.

"Why you'll be shot, of course!" replied Brooks.

Bryant's face went white. He looked up at Brooks, mortified.

"Joking," he said. Laughter bellowing from his lungs as he slapped Bryant hard on the arm. Bryant decided to join in the laughter and chuckled along awkwardly with Brooks. The mirth finally subsided, and Brooks spoke once more.

"But seriously, keep it on you at all times."

Reaching across the desk, Bryant grabbed the ID card. It had the Academy logo alongside his name and photograph. He smiled as he hung it around his neck.

"Now, here's your map of the camp," Brooks said, handing out a physical bit of paper. "I suspect you're going to need this rather soon."

Brooks then stood and thrust out his hand once more. Bryant raised himself from the chair and pushed his hand towards the man, bracing himself for the terror grip vice that would ensue. Crushing his hand once more as he spoke. Brooks said, "On behalf of your planet, let me thank you for your upcoming service to the Academy."

"Thank you, sir," replied Bryant. "I won't let you down."

Ushering him to the door. Brooks opened it as he almost chased him out into the hallway, "Your quarters are in block S. You must report to Sergeant Himinez upon arrival."

The door slammed behind him. And like that, Bryant was in the Academy. It was far from the inception had pictured, but in truth, he was now living in his dream. Bryant took a large breath. He then skipped excitedly back down the long corridor like a careless child. What adventures would wait for him on the other side? He opened the heavy door once more and stepped out into the sunlight.

The light blinded him at first, causing him to blink, squinting under the striking rays. His eyes focussed, and he saw an enormous figure looming before him.

"Excuse me, do you know where I can find block S?" Bryant asked politely.

"Why aren't you in uniform?" the man barked.

"Uh," stammered Bryant, "well, I only just got here."

"You only just got here, sir!" replied the officer.

"Er yes sir, sorry, sir. I just arrived. It's my first day." Bryant beamed.

"Well, son," replied the officer, "that badge around your neck says that you're an Academy recruit. And recruits wear uniform at all times."

"Yes, but you see…" –Bryant tried to explain.

"No buts, recruit! I'd suggest you get over to the Quartermaster and get yourself in uniform."

"Yes, sir!" Bryant replied, utterly terrified. He glanced down nervously at his map. His eyes were desperately scanning for answers. He found what he thought he needed and set off in what he hoped was the right direction.

"Double time recruit," barked the man. "If I catch you out of uniform again, you'll be up on a charge."

Bryant picked up the pace, doing his best to yell, "Yes sir," as he went.

After jogging about the campus for what seemed like forever, he found himself outside the stores. The map was hard to decipher. Even more so when you were running about in terror, he'd thought he'd found the place twice, and both times turned out to be wrong. Hoping desperately that this was the right building, he opened the door and stepped inside.

The smell of leather and starch greeted his nostrils upon entry. He looked around and saw an elderly, kind-looking, grey-haired man scribbling away behind the counter. The front area was tiny, and it appeared everything took place behind the desk. There were rows upon rows of clothes, boots, berets, backpacks. You name it. If it was Academy branded, it was there. Bryant stood and soaked it in. The place was just like heaven.

"Can I help you there, fella?" came a soft voice from behind the counter. "You look a little lost."

"Yes, sir, I hope so," said Bryant. Surveying the room before him. "Are you the quartermaster?"

As the words fell from his mouth, Bryant braced himself just in case someone tore into him once more. The grey-haired man chuckled and adjusted his spectacles on his face,

"You must be new?" he scoffed. "No need for yes sirs in here."

Still desperately trying to regain his breath. Bryant was relieved to talk to someone who wasn't terrifying.

The man behind the counter went on, "You need not fear me. I never get angry. Not unless you lose your gear, that is. As long as you bring something back when you want a new one, I'm as happy as Larry."

The door burst open, and another cadet bustled in, setting a tattered pair of boots down on the counter, "Same again, please QT," said the cadet. He looked over at Bryant, nodded, and said,

"Alright?"

The quartermaster took the boots from the counter, made sure they were both the same size and for opposing feet, departed, and then returned with a fresh pair. "Cheers, QT," said the cadet. Who then departed as quickly as he arrived.

The quartermaster then turned back towards Bryant. He looked at him up and down, "So from the looks of it, it's uniform you need? I'm guessing size small."

Bryant nodded and sighed a deep sigh of relief. The quartermaster opened up the gap in the counter and gestured to him.

"Well, come on in then," he said with a smile.

Contact.

Sitting in her office at the cinema, Pam scratched at her head. The summer holidays were upon them, and the front counter was at its busiest. It had forced her to get one of her evening staff to work the day shift while she went through everything for the upcoming audit. As helpful as it was during the day, it meant she was short-staffed later on. She'd run these numbers over and over. There was no way she could afford to employ another staff member and continue to turn a profit. She had always relied on Bryant's help. The strange thing was, as much as she continually believed in her son. She had never imagined he would get into the Academy. She had always supported and even enabled his dreams. But in her mind, he would be here working with her once he finished school. The magnitude of what had happened was something she was still coming to terms with. Pam regretted the way they had parted. It had left a small hole in her heart; yes, she would have been happier if he stayed with her. But she would never have done anything to jeopardise his dreams. He'd grown up so fast. The fact that she never imagined him leaving made her rue not appreciating him being around more. He was off on the adventure of a lifetime; her boy was an Academy man now. Something which made her immensely proud. She wondered desperately how he was. Being able to speak to her son regularly was something she never thought she would take for granted. She hoped he was okay; she hoped he'd forgiven her. Of all the things she could lose in life, her son wasn't one of them.

The first six weeks at the Academy were notoriously tricky. It was a make or break time for recruits; the rules were hard, and the training was tough. How you took to the initiation would determine how your career in the Academy would pan out. For six weeks, he wasn't allowed off base. He had no access to his phone or any other electronic device. He'd wear some form of uniform at all times. For forty-two days, you had to jump through every hoop, be the butt of every joke, and do absolutely everything asked of you. It was exhausting.

The first week had been the most challenging. Having never left home for more than a night or two, separating himself from everyone he knew and loved was an enormous test. His squad leader Sergeant Himinez was authoritarian, but she was at least fair. The less said about his fellow recruits, the better. The Academy entrance tests were notoriously difficult. So you would expect everyone in the Academy to be the bright leaders of tomorrow, the diligent heroes of the planet. That was true to a degree, but it didn't stop the asinine pranks within the barracks. He'd had his bed moved in the middle of the night and woken up in the middle of the parade ground. His toothpaste was emptied and swapped with body wash, and he'd even had his towel stolen when he was in the shower. It wasn't personal. All the recruits suffered the same fate, but how he wished he could speed up time.

The other disappointing news Bryant realised was that being in the Academy didn't guarantee that you would go to space. The Rangers were the only ones selected for space missions. But to be a Ranger, you had to pass the gruelling training. It wasn't for the faint-hearted. The completion rate was low, but he was determined to give it his best shot. For now, Bryant just had to focus. Get through the first six weeks, take whatever came his way, and then enrol for Ranger training. It seemed almost impossible, and he felt like quitting some days, but he never would. Bryant Fisher would get to space or die trying.

"Hey, Cryant," came the voice from the head that poked itself through his open door. "There's some hot bird on the video chat for you."

"That's my mum," Bryant snapped back.

"Alright," cooled Murphy, "just saying I would, technically it's a compliment."

Murphy lived in Bryant's barracks. He had been in the Academy for two years now, and unlike Bryant, he wasn't going anywhere. His time in the Academy would play out as a 'grunt'. Still, it was a better life than most had. Murphy wasn't all bad. Bryant kind of liked him. He just had this annoying habit of saying something thoughtless or vulgar most of the time he opened his mouth.

"Leave it out, Murphy," Bryant said, standing and shoulder checking him as he made his way out of the room.

Today was the first day Bryant had video access. Contact with the outside world, "Hallelujah!" He barged past Murphy and sprinted down the corridor to the room with the video screens. This was the first opportunity he had to speak to anyone he cared for or knew since he stepped foot in that taxi. Never before had speaking to his mum or his sister been such a privilege.

"Fisher, screen two." said the corporal who stood in the doorway. Bryant found his screen, pulled out the chair, and sat excitedly.

The images of Julie and his mother filled the cubicle in front of him.

"Hi, mum," he shrieked, "hey, Jules."

As he immersed himself in the booth, the images of his mother and sister appeared. The pair of them had been sat patiently on the sofa at home, waiting for him to join the conversation. He had another five weeks until he would see them in the flesh, so this call was special.

"Hey, Sweetie," said Pam, "how are you doing?"

"Oh, it's great, mum, the best!" effused Bryant. He was doing his best to convey affection for everything that had happened thus far.

"Are they feeding you enough," questioned his mother, "and what have they done to your hair?"

Questions like this would usually drive him bonkers. Not today, though.

"Oh, it's the regulation cut," Bryant said. "Do you like it?"

"You look like a microphone!" came the words from his sister.

Bryant chuckled, "Thanks Jules, it's good to see you too. Are you being good for mum?"

"I'm always good," said Julie.

"Ha-ha sure, of course, you are," Bryant laughed.

The next twenty minutes drifted. They reminisced, Bryant explained all about the Academy, the clock tower, the mess hall, the push-ups, the Ranger program.

They limited communal video screen time to thirty minutes. It would give you an audible warning with five minutes remaining, but at the thirty-minute mark, your connection would end. It was the only way they had ensured arguments didn't erupt over people stealing too much time. After the first six weeks, you could make a call in your room. But most still preferred the fully immersive experience the booths offered.

"Bryant, before you go, we have a surprise," Pam said, keen not to bring up their feud. Doing whatever she could to make amends.

"Ooh, what is it?" Bryant asked, intrigued.

"Just be patient."

Patience wasn't a virtue gifted to most eighteen-year-olds. So, he shifted the conversation to move his thoughts. Looking at the tired eyes of his mum, he asked, "When's the next audit?"

"Sometime next week, sweetie," she replied.

"What do you mean sometime?" Bryant quizzed.

"Well, it's a fun additional measure they've added," she said sarcastically. "They give you a time frame, but not an exact day. All I know is it will be someday next week."

"Well, that's shit!" fumed Bryant.

"I'll be fine, honey, don't worry about me. Just focus on being a space ranger," Pam replied. She was letting slide her son's choice of vocabulary. Bryant rolled his eyes at the term 'Space Ranger'.

"Mum, they're not called Space Ran-"

-"Baammmm!" the noise of the front door bursting open and almost deafened Bryant through the ear pods, nearly making him physically fall from his seat.

"Is he still there?" yelled a familiar voice.

"Yes, Jimmy, calm down," chuckled Pam. Jimmy hadn't long been back on dry land, and his depressurisation had finished just an hour ago. Despite his mother's fierce protests, he had jumped straight on his e-board and shot over to Bryant's house, desperate to get a glimpse of his buddy.

"Jimmmmmy, is that you?" Bryant called excitedly, raising himself from his chair.

Jimmy powered from the door across the room and threw himself onto the sofa. He squeezed himself between Pam and Julie in the process. Squashed awkwardly between the two of them, Jimmy spoke,

"Hey Spaceman, whasssup, buddy?"

Bryant's face illuminated. He had wanted to talk to his friend about everything in the world and had a million things to discuss with him.

"Yeah, I'm great," effused Bryant casually. "How's the deep sea?"

"Ah, walk in the park. Or should I say swim in the sea," the slightly unconvincing words almost dribbled from the pale and sweaty Jimmy. "Probably not as great as being a big-time space hero! How was your initiation? Did I miss it?"

Bryant went to speak, but then the screen went black.

"Noooo!" lamented Bryant as he fiddled furtively at the buttons in the booth in a futile attempt to restore the video screen. But it was no use. He sunk his head into the desk and sat there bent over, groaning.

"Um, excuse me."

Something had broken Bryant's gloomy silence. The sweetest of sounds filled his ears, his head still unmoving. He opened his eyes and looked hard to the side to see where this voice was coming from. He saw a uniform behind him but remained in his slump. But the noise was then followed by a gentle tap on his shoulder, and the scent of a beautiful perfume filled his nostrils. He breathed it in deep.

Bryant sat up mildly irritated and turned his head. The source of the voice revealed itself to be an attractive blonde female cadet. He studied the figure behind him; she was beautiful, the voice and smell of an angel.

"Sorry," she said to Bryant, who was sat there gawking. "But you're using my time."

Bryant shifted his attention back to the booth and found himself immersed in the video of someone else. Four strangers sat gazing back at him awkwardly.

"Sorry, so sorry," he said. He stood and awkwardly turned the chair back to its original position before trying to pull it out for her to sit on it. He then thought better of it and just left it in a weird diagonal position.

"Thanks," she said, chuckling gently at his awkwardness. "You're cute."

"Cheers," he jabbered. "Hey, do you want to?" Bryant started.

"I'm sorry," the girl apologised, gesturing to the booth. "But my time is running."

She sat, inserted her ear pods, and disappeared into the conversation in front of her.

Thoughts of this angel instantly replaced his disappointment at the call being cut short. He could still smell her perfume, and he couldn't stop thinking about her. He was certain she'd smiled at him. She smiled at him. She said he was 'Cute,' that meant something, surely? Eager to escape thoughts of what might have been, Bryant shifted his brain back to his friend. He was desperate to talk to him still. This latest encounter now at the forefront of the list of topics. He considered he could sneak out later and hitch a ride back to Jimmy's. They could hang out all night, and he'd return before anyone would notice; he dreamt the scenario out in his head, knowing full well that it was impossible. Back in reality, he arrived outside his room. He noticed someone had crudely drawn a phallus on his door. Ignoring it completely, he stepped inside, slumped on his bed, and stared out of the window up to the sky. He thought of his family and friends and how far he was from home, feeling all alone, a small tear formed on his cheek as he drifted off into a world of dreams.

The Inspector.

The surprise change in the format of the audits meant Pam was none the wiser as to which day it might befall her. She had spent the whole week so far on edge. Panicking every time even a remotely well-dressed person entered the building, leaving her drained. The man who called himself 'The Inspector' had finally appeared on Wednesday afternoon that week. The first she knew of it was hearing distressed calls from Mohammed.

Pam was prepared as well as she could be. But not knowing when an audit would happen meant you couldn't plan for it in the way you might want. Because you had to follow the inspector around like an unpleasant odour, answering all their questions, appeasing their every demand, given that she was understaffed and had a business to run, it meant they might catch you at an awkward moment. Fortunately for Pam, the weather was particularly pleasant this week, and business was slower than usual. She was rarely glad not to have custom. Today was an exception. This was her second audit without Bryant's help. Over the years, he'd been a real addition with it. Like his father, he had a mind that was always ticking and when it came to bureaucracy, overthinking was usually a good thing. She'd survived the last one without his help, and she was confident she would do it again.

The inspector's always had a team who came and went with them, like evil little minions. It was, as per usual, about as pleasant as a rectal examination. Dates inspected, stock poked and prodded, invoices scrutinised. Not even the seating was safe, rigorously checked for rips, tears, and even comfort. The entire process was probably more anal than a rectal exam. The day turned into torture as everything you thought you knew about your job, about life in general, was turned upside down, judged, and questioned. But finally, after a long gruelling day, it was all over.

After his team finished, the man known as 'The Inspector' escorted Pam into her office. The process was all but complete. She'd survived. It was just now the trivial matter of reviewing the action plan. There would always be suggestions on 'how to improve' that they gave you and a plethora of documents to sign.

"Can I offer you a drink?" Pam asked, summoning the remains of her manners. "Tea, coffee perhaps?"

"No, I'm fine," replied the Inspector. "This shouldn't take long."

"Who doesn't want a cup of tea?" Pam thought to herself.

Having invited himself into the office. Pam pulled out the chair opposite her desk for him to sit on. He ignored her gesture and made his way straight for hers, which was behind the desk. With his back to her still, she rolled her eyes, flipping the birds at the man's back briefly. As he turned, Pam dropped her hands to her sides swiftly. He placed himself regally in her chair, and with the air of someone who owned the place, he said, "Please have a seat, Mrs Fisher."

With him sat comfortably at her desk, Pam closed the door and took a seat in her office. It was unusual to be on the wrong side. It felt odd sitting here. She looked around and surveyed it from another angle, taking it all in. Blissfully unaware that it would be one of the last times she did so.

New normal.

Bryant was finally getting into the swing at life at the Academy. The rules were softening, or maybe it just seemed that way. It all started to become very ordinary. He was used to cold showers, eating en masse in the mess hall. He was getting better at running; he improved at press-ups, assault courses, remembering to salute superiors. He was even getting up early. The days rolled by, and he was now halfway through his induction. The thing he had found to be the most difficult was the lack of contact he had with those whom he loved—sitting on his bed in his very plain, fundamental room, surrounded by just a few belongings and the whitest of walls. He wondered how his mother was coping? He'd never hated working at the cinema.

On the contrary, he rather enjoyed it sometimes (not that he would admit it). But in his mind, it was always just a step for him. He'd never stopped and considered how difficult it would be for his mum without him there. He realised now that she was probably banking on him working with her. He thought about his family, and he wondered how long his friend had before he had to go back under the sea? What was his miscreant sister doing, what chaos had she created in his bedroom?

Bryant knew that his mother would be facing the audit sometime this week. It could even be today. He felt so out of the loop; he hated not knowing. A pang hit his stomach, almost like guilt. He suddenly really wished he was there. Looking after Julie solo and working full tilt must be hard work. Sat in front of the backdrop of the four white walls, Bryant regretted how they had parted. His mother was a hard worker, and she always did her best. He decided to book the time off for the next audit and help her just like old times. Everything would be alright.

"Fisher," barked a voice from beyond his door, chasing away his momentary peace. "Get your butt up. You're on patrol!"

He heard the now-familiar footsteps of Sgt Himinez depart back down the corridor. He jumped up, grabbed his hat, fixing it in the mirror. In it, he caught his uniformed gaze and gave himself the 'finger guns,' and smiled before departing his room.

"You run a tight ship here, Mrs Fisher," muttered the Inspector. "It looks like everything is in order."

"It looks like?" Pam thought to herself. She considered that there must be a manual for everyone who worked in a regulatory role for the Authorities—training them to speak in some form of riddle—a muddled talk of contradicting sentences and ambiguities.

The 'Inspector' sat at her desk, looking imperious. As though he owned the place and a dozen others like it. His hands scribbled away furiously, form after form. Until he stopped, right before the final one, looking up, he spoke, "It seems my pen has stopped working," he grumbled.

Pam looked over at her desk and what he was doing. It appeared to be just the matter of one more signature.

"You must get someone to audit those pens," she joked.

"Do you have another I can borrow?" he replied.

"Yes, there should be some in the top draw."

The Inspector glanced down from his perch. Spotting the drawer, he grabbed the shiny metal handle, giving it a firm tug. But nothing happened; it was stubborn. Mildly frustrated, he returned with a second, much more forceful yank. The old wooden runners fought back as though desperately trying to repel his advances before finally relenting. The drawer came shooting out like a rocket. It halted when it reached the end of its runners, applying the brakes. The contents shook everywhere, sending objects colliding with each other. There was the unmistakable *clink* associated with the sound of a glass bottle colliding with another container. The old coffee mug toppled onto its side, sending its liquid coursing out and filling the contents of the drawer like a burst dam.

"Oh, I am sorry," fretted the Inspector.

From her position, Pam watched on with horror. The moment his arm flexed the second time to dislodge the tenacious drawer, it all came flooding back to her. She wanted to stand and stop him, stand and run, throw something at him! Think Pam, think, think.

As the cup spilt, a familiar smell filled the air in the room. Pam sat motionless, her face ghost white. The inspector looked down at the drawer and noticed the stricken cup. He dipped his fingertip in the liquid and brought it to his nose for clarification. Time slowed as he raised his hand. Hand met nose and nose obliged, inhaling a long, deep, torturous sniff. The snort confirming what he already knew. He reached inside, removing both the cup and bottle from the drawer, placing both on the desk. Side by side. He inhaled almost with satisfaction. The air filled his lungs, and he smirked.

"Mrs Fisher, have you been drinking whiskey?"

Homecoming.

Bryant stood patiently outside his barrack blocks. The sun was high in the sky, and a cool breeze filled the air. He had ten minutes until his taxi arrived, but he wasn't taking any chances. He could now choose what he did next. In one hour, he could be back home. He could evict the squatter from his room. He could sit in his back garden. He could sit in the front room, make phone calls, watch TV, eat ice cream. He could see Jimmy. They could go to Planet Pizza. He might even take Roger for a walk. Whatever he wanted, he could do!

The last six weeks had been a burden, almost impossible. He cried a lot, questioned his decisions, cried some more, pondered running away, contemplated hiding. Before finally, day on day, he began to love every minute. The rules were no longer harsh. They made perfect sense, every one of them. Push-ups, assault courses, running all came easy. He even started looking forward to bettering his efforts. Surrounded by all these rules and routines, he suddenly felt a euphoric sense of freedom. He found liberty in order. He was more confident in his body, and his physique had even improved. He'd even managed to talk to some girls without completely burbling.

The sight of his taxi moving up the road burst his thought bubble. His two weeks' leave started now. He would make the most of every second. He could barely contain his excitement. But as he watched the taxi draw nearer, he couldn't help but feel like he would miss this place. It was bittersweet.

The taxi finally drew to a halt. Stopping just before his feet, he loaded his solitary bag into the back and climbed inside.

"Take me to Planet Pizza," he commanded. "And step on it." The taxi driver shot him an infuriated look in the rear-view mirror. "Worth it," he thought to himself. He'd waited years to say that. The car pulled away, speeding past the clock tower, through the quad, past the mess halls, beyond the parade ground, and then out of the main gate.

As it passed through the walls, the car steadily put distance between them and the Academy, looking back through the taxi window. The hum of the electric motor filling his ears. He smiled to himself before turning back around. He had passed basic training; he was now officially a member of the Academy! Filled with vim, he reached into his bag. His phone now back in his possession. He hit the first button on speed dial, placing the device to his ear.

Bryant was a member of the Academy. A fully-fledged adult destined to safeguard the future of humanity. But he was also still a teenager. Meaning the first and most important thing he would do with his leave would be see his friend, drink, and eat pizza.

Ten minutes had elapsed since the taxi dropped him off. Bryant had now peered through the glass window too many times. Jimmy wasn't in there, but he kept looking regardless. Deciding not to enter alone, he figured he would wait outside for his friend. That way, they could enter together as per tradition. His stomach rumbled, urged on by the glorious smell of pizza that wafted into his nostrils every time the door swung open. Today wasn't buffet day. So he looked through the electric menu that now filled his phone screen. If he pre-decided what he wanted, then hopefully, his hunger would dissipate sooner. Planet Pizza was expensive if the buffet wasn't on. But Bryant would have been paid, so lunch would be on him.

Bryant studied the menu for all of thirty seconds before deciding he would still have a pepperoni pizza. Decision made, he realised he hadn't checked his credit account yet.

He'd worked a part-time job for the last two years of school. But he had never seen many credits in his account. The car wash job paid a very basic minimum wage. There was a bonus commission based on how many cars you washed. Since Bryant worked part-time and spent most of it daydreaming, it was rare he got any commission, if at all. So, this was an exciting moment for him. It would be his first actual paycheque. He looked down at his phone, then back up briefly, no sign of Jimmy still. He logged in to his account, his spine-tingling with anticipation. His finger hovering above the button, anxious. He placed it on the scanner for authorisation, but it wouldn't work, typical. So he entered all the required details, date of birth, passcode, pin code, shoe size, height, mom's favourite TV show. Until finally, it authorised him. Bryant closed both eyes. Opening them slowly, he couldn't handle the disappointment if it hadn't gone in yet. Like a child hiding behind a cushion during a scary film, Bryant opened his eyes slowly and glanced down at the screen. Millions of numbers befell his eyes. He couldn't comprehend what he saw. His mouth sinking open in shock, he just stood there motionless.

"Is this some new greeting they taught you at space camp?" Jimmy's voice breaking through his trance.

Bryant looked up from his screen to see his best friend stood in front of him. "Jimmy," he shrieked. He shoved his phone awkwardly into his pocket and hugged the bear that stood before him.

"Nice outfit," Jimmy said to him.

Bryant looked down at himself, "Not been home yet, have I," he said. "Anyway, what took you?"

"Sorry, dude," Jimmy replied, "these drugs are a killer. I've been throwing up all morning. The house is a mess, I went to leave, but mum made me clean up before I came out."

"It was your puke!" grimaced Bryant.

"So," replied Jimmy. "She's just going to clean when I'm out anyway."

Bryant surveyed his friend. He was still an impending figure. But he appeared gaunt, pale, and somewhat sweaty.

"We can do something else if you'd rather?" a famished Bryant said somewhat disappointingly.

"Don't be silly," Jimmy said, patting his stomach. "More room for food now." They hugged once more, giving each other a long pat on the back before entering the restaurant.

As they sat, Mr Goldstein looked up from his chair. His eyes flashing in panic before realising that today wasn't a buffet day. Calm once more, he settled back down to his paper.

"Full disclaimer," Jimmy whispered to Bryant. "I don't have any credit! If you don't either, we need to go."

"Don't worry," said Bryant, "foods on me." He reached into his pocket and removed his phone. The credit app was still open, and he thrust it under the nose of Jimmy.

"Holy crap," exclaimed Jimmy. "I reckon we could buy Planet Pizza with that."

Bryant was still in disbelief. His first month's pay, along with the training completion and various bonuses, was more than most people made in six months. The fact of the matter was, neither Bryant nor Jimmy had ever even seen that amount of credit in their lives.

"So, what'll you have?" Bryant said confidently.

"Er, one of everything!" Jimmy replied only half in jest.

They ordered, and the pair talked endlessly, aside from Bryant's video omnibus. They hadn't properly spoken since Bryant had joined the Academy, so; naturally, he did most of the talking, with Jimmy having only grim tales of the mines. They devoured as much food and drink as they physically could before deciding that three hours in a pizza place was more than enough.

Jimmy stood to leave first, "I'd best be off," he said, "got another round of treatment later. Then probably more vomit to clean."

Bryant nodded grimly, "I'll see you tomorrow at yours, though, yeah?"

"Sure thing, buddy," said Jimmy. He got as far as the door before he stopped and turned back towards his friend, "Oh, Bryant. Don't come around mine in any Academy gear. It'll only set dad off."

Jimmy nodded towards Mr Goldstein, disappearing in a flash.

Bryant paid up, thanked Mr Goldstein, who looked at Bryant's uniform with a slight expression of disappointment before he left. As he walked, the look Goldstein has given him lingered momentarily; why would people not be happy he was in the Academy? He shook his head, dislodging the thought. He'd probably misread the moment.

It was a long walk back to his house, but for some reason, the fact he could happily afford a taxi made him want one even less. So, he walked. Six weeks was the longest amount of time he had ever been away from his District. In his mind, it would surely all of changed.

As he strode, he walked past his old school, past the carwash (keeping his head down), by the old bus shelters the kids used to make out in, past the park he played in as a child, past the strip with a few independent shops. So many places, hundreds of fond memories. He walked and walked and walked until finally, he found himself outside his house. It had been over a month since the taxi drove him away from this very spot. It was a Friday, so his mum and Julie would both be out for a few hours yet giving him time to do something nice. He reckoned he would give the house a clean, or some of it anyway.

As he opened the front door and stepped inside, the first thing he noticed was the smell. He paused and breathed in the aroma. He'd never noticed the smell his house had. He stood there frozen for a moment, just taking it all in. He finally closed the door and set his bag down on the floor.

"Bryant, is that you?" Pam's voice drifted from the kitchen.

"Mum?" Bryant yelled.

Dashing towards the sound of the other. They met in the living room and collided in an enormous hug.

"Oh, Bryant," she whispered as she held him, "it's so good to see you."

Bryant removed himself from the embrace. Pam placed both hands on his shoulders, sniffed him, and spoke, "Let's get everything you're wearing into the wash, shall we? And Bryant, maybe a shower."

Pam had jumped straight into 'mum' mode, and for the first time in his life, Bryant wouldn't change a thing. Grabbing his bag, he knelt and started unloading its contents onto the kitchen floor. It was then a thought entered his brain, and he paused before looking up at his mother.

"Mum," he asked, "why aren't you at work?"

They sat on the sofa, Bryant listening on as his mother explained the sordid affair to him.

"That's horseshit!" he groused.

"Bryant!" scolded Pam.

"No, mum, it's utter bollocks!" Bryant spoke defiantly.

"I see they've improved your vocabulary at the Academy," Pam said wistfully.

Bryant looked at her, "There's got to be something we can do? We can't just let them take the cinema!"

"I wish there was," Pam replied ruefully. "But it's out of my hands now. We just have to wait for them to finish making their decision. Until then, the cinema is closed until further notice."

"Eurgggghhhh!" Bryant yelled as he stood and paced around the room. "What were you doing drinking whiskey at work," he raged. "You've played right into their hands.

"Bryant," she said, "I know you're frustrated, and so am I. It had been a long day, and I didn't drink any. Anyway, it's done now. There's no use for 'ifs' and 'butts.' Remember what your father used to say? We just have to deal with what we have."

Bryant cooled his rage and sat back down on the sofa. It was nice to hear his mum mention his father.

"I have said nothing of this to your sister yet. Not until I know what's happening."

Bryant nodded. He sat on the sofa, putting his head in his hands. This wasn't quite the homecoming he had pictured.

The two weeks at home came and went in a flash. He'd used each passing day as a safety net between him and his return. At first, it was fourteen days of safety. Then it was seven, and that was okay. Then suddenly, he only had two more days between him and going back to the Academy. As it loomed forward, he welcomed the idea of going back. But he'd cherished each day he had in his old life. He'd spent plenty of time at home with both mum and sister. He'd seen Jimmy a few times, he'd eaten ice cream, stayed up late, and he had even taken Roger to the park.

Life in the Academy moved fast, and if you wanted to progress, so did you. Before he left, he had committed to Ranger training. He was excited but anxious. Ranger training was notoriously tricky. There were physical exams, plenty to learn, more to prove, and finally, your body had to be medically up for the forces and medications involved in going to space. There was almost no margin for error. If he failed, then there would be no space missions.

The harsh reality of life in the Districts was that nobody who worked either in the mines or in independent business could ever afford a house in their lifetime. Everyone was provided accommodation that suited their needs by the Authorities—one of the many exceptions to this being Academy members. The house provided was essentially yours, but you had to make payments for it to them. Despite the large population numbers, homelessness and poverty were non-existent. The new way of life had solved famine. Everyone got what they needed, shared and worked together. Making payment on your house would never affect you financially if you worked for the Authorities in one of the many establishments owned or run by them. The cost was automatically deducted from your salary. You were paid the amount you needed based on family and circumstance. You got exactly what you needed. Academy staff and Authority officials aside, no one had too much, and no one had too little.

If you did manage to run an independent business, you had to be making enough money to cover your payments, which was a genuine struggle because the independent companies just couldn't compete financially with District-owned ones. This meant if you had this life and fell behind on payments. Your ability to run it would be deemed inept. The Authorities would take over the business, and you would be placed into a job of their choosing. Between the quarterly audits and the struggle to turn a profit, independent companies dropped like flies. It was a brilliant way to give the people the illusion of freedom whilst showing everyone that they were better off following the rule of the Authority. The impression of freedom, being just that, an illusion.

The cinema was one of less than one hundred independent businesses that remained within the District, and it was a big District. There was a real kinship between the owners of said businesses. It was a true source of pride keeping them running. Pam's family had owned the cinema for centuries. It had been a grade two listed building, so it had always been well preserved. It was a stunning structure: stone brickwork, a large open foyer, marble roof, and elegant spiral staircases. Pam had worked incredibly hard at keeping ownership of it. She'd always known that life would most likely be easier working for the Authorities. Swallow their pill, get paid exactly enough. Just as she'd always known that keeping hold of it would likely be a futile battle, this day was always going to be inevitable, and she knew one day it would come. But knowing and realising are far from the same thing, and that knowledge didn't take away the hurt. She'd visited the cinema as a child, with her family, and was even the place where she'd met her husband.

With the uncertainty about the cinema lurking, plus the fact that Pam was making no money. Bryant made the subsequent two payments on the house. He tried tirelessly to convince his mother that he could just pay the bills for her, but she was too proud to live at her son's graces. She wanted him to live his own life. He'd need the credits for himself one day.

Training.

Reintegrating himself into the Academy after his leave had been tough. The running, assault courses and early starts had all been much harder than he remembered, and somehow, he'd gained some unwanted weight. He was slower and heavier, he missed home dearly, but at least he hadn't cried this time. It was of comfort that he knew he would soon start the Ranger training. He had been back five days now, and he was shattered. Tomorrow was the day it all began, so he'd turned in early to get plenty of rest. Sitting alone on his bed, he had in his hands a copy of a book his mother had given him. Books scarce in their nature. Just about everything was digital. This book was a simple volume about a ferocious beast called a 'tiger.' Bryant read the whole thing intently. They had been hunted to the point of extinction. However magnificent these creatures were terrifying. Big teeth, giant claws. It almost made him glad that they had long since been extinct.

The book had belonged to his father. It was one of many the man collected. One thing he did know about him was that he spent his early years gathering as many physical books as he could. Bryant recalled him reading some of them to him when he was younger. Despite his tender years, what always confused Bryant was why he collected such random books. Some would be about science, others about learning the basics of an old computer system. It didn't matter to his father. If it were a physical book, he would take it. He remembered him explaining to him that if you had the text in your hand, then they couldn't change it. What was written couldn't be unwritten, and that the same couldn't be said of the internet. It came across as fanatic rambling and made little sense to Bryant at the time.

The tiger book was fascinating, interesting facts and pictures about these beautiful creatures. He finished it quickly. It was still early, and he had a thirst for knowledge. His mother had bestowed two on him when he left. So he reached for the other. This one was a history book. They were taught little history that wasn't recent as a school subject. It was minimal. The Authorities wanted the world to move forward, not backwards. They denied the notion that history could be learnt from. Instead, decreeing that it just gave people bad ideas that needn't be replicated. So if it wasn't recent or relevant, it would simply be omitted.

He flicked through the first few chapters; it made for complicated reading at this hour. Turning over the corner of one page, Bryant closed the book and tucked it under the bed. Commanding the lights to turn off, he rolled over and drifted into a deep slumber.

This was it! Today was the day. Bryant Fisher was finally going to space. He sat in the rocket, his finger hovering, aching over the button, just itching to press the ignition switch. Space training had been a breeze, naturally. On his second day, the instructors kept him behind after training, keeping him back to ask him questions. How did someone so handsome and young know so much about space? He was fast-tracked through the programme, promoted, and before long, he was ready to go.

Sat here in the craft, raring to drive, setting off on the solo mission of a lifetime. He was off to Mars, the youngest recruit in history to pass space training. The youngest, most handsome to be selected to lead a solo space mission ever. Destiny. Final checks were complete, and he was a go for launch. He glanced out of the window. There was an adoring crowd watching on. He winked at the girls in the front row as he flicked the ignition switch. One furious roar later, the rockets were powering his ship up into the skies, through the clouds, past the Earth's atmosphere, and finally into space. Forced back into his chair by the might of the engines, Bryant mustered all of his strength and balled his hand for a single fist pump. He turned his head so he could look out of the window; he wanted to see space for the first time, with the excitement of a child entering the living room on Christmas morn. He opened the shutter, closing his eyes at first. He would open them gradually to survey the magnitude in front of him. One eye open, then the other, "Wait," he blinked. Rubbed his eyes and looked again. This wasn't space. Out of the window in front of him, he saw nothing, zero. He turned and looked back at what should be Earth and again was greeted by oblivion. Confusion turned to panic. He tried his radio, silence, what was wrong, what was happening? He was alone, isolated in solitude. Suddenly a colossal bang interrupted the silence. The noise was from the side of the spacecraft. What was that? Bang, it happened again Bang, bang, bang the noises grew, continued until it became a steady stream of knocking.

"Fisher," a voice entered his dreams, "don't make me come in there!"

Bryant sat bolt upright in bed; his body coursed with beads of sweat.

"Alright, I'm coming in. You'd better not be naked!" came the voice of Sgt Himinez.

The door opened before Bryant had time to gather his thoughts to speak. The face of Sgt Himinez appeared around his bedroom door. She wore a look that was both kindly and terrifying, like she might rip your arm off but help with the wound afterwards.

"I'm awake," Bryant managed.

"Damn it, Fisher, get your ass out of bed," barked Himinez. "I'm not your alarm clock."

"Yes, ma'am," he replied.

"Don't ma'am me," she snapped back. "Just get your butt out of bed." Her head then disappeared back around the door frame.

"Sergeant," Bryant pleaded, "what time is it?"

Himinez paused, looking back at Bryant. "What am I, your damn mother?" she said as she disappeared.

Bryant hopped out of bed, grabbing his phone as he did. It was 0840. He was due to report for training at 0900. There was no time for a shower, no time to eat. He shoved some toothpaste on a brush and thrust it into his mouth. He then did the dance that all tardy teenagers know, pulling on a pair of trousers with one hand while brushing his teeth with the other. Spitting the toothpaste out, he rinsed whilst pulling on his t-shirt. He then grabbed his hat and jacket and looked at himself in the mirror; no time for finger guns today. He smiled at himself, "You got this, Bryant," he said. Before departing down the corridor, out the door before sprinting across the quad. Fifteen minutes, he would make it...just.

Bryant arrived at hanger four at 0900 exactly. There were thirty other cadets already stood in line, waiting, watching.

"Good of you to join us, Fisher," came the voice of the instructor. "May I ask why you think you can show up late to my training?"

"Late, sir?" enquired Bryant. "But it's 0900. I made it. I'm on time."

"Yes, Fisher," replied the instructor, "but by the time you put your t-shirt on the right way around. It will be 0901, and you'll be late. Be here on time correctly, dressed Fisher. They were your instructions."

Stood firmly at attention, Bryant shifted his gaze down his body. Stifled laughter rang out from those around him. "Damn!" His shirt was, in fact, on back to front.

"Mr Fisher," the instructor spoke again, "can you dress yourself, or do you need one of us to do it for you?"

Bryant removed his arms from the sleeves and shifted the shirt around his chest awkwardly. Keenly aware that he was in the presence of others.

"Okay, class, it's a miracle. Mr Fisher has dressed himself," the instructor spoke. "Now get down and give me fifty. Keeping in mind, we don't start until you're finished. Don't keep us waiting."

Groans rang out around him from the thirty cadets who had spent the better part of twenty minutes stood rigidly to attention.

Bryant got down on the floor. Fifty push-ups was a big ask first thing on an empty stomach. He assumed the position, pushing out the first twenty as fast as he could.

As he approached thirty, fatigue set in hard, he couldn't do it.

"If you quit Fisher, you start all over again!" came the voice of the instructor.

More groans rang out.

"Don't bottle this, Fisher."

"Don't screw us, Fisher."

"Hurry up, Fisher."

The voices got less and less inspiring as he pushed on. Until one broke through the negativity. The softest, smallest voice having the grandest impact.

"You can do it, Bryant. I believe in you."

Bryant glanced as far as he could to the edge of his vision. The voice came from a familiar figure. The lack of oxygen getting back to his brain was probably making him hear and see things. But he was pretty confident the voice belonged to the girl from the video room. The one who said he was 'Cute.' With newfound vigour, he dug in deep to finish the last twenty. He couldn't give up knowing she was watching. Bryant finished. He let out a "Woohoo!" before collapsing into a sweaty, shaky mess on the floor.

"Get up, Fisher," ordered the instructor, "we have a long day ahead."

The rest of the day composed of classroom sessions, something which for Bryant was a little tedious. Most of what was being taught today was nothing he hadn't learnt a thousand times. Still, its format reminded him of school, and it filled his brain with beautiful nostalgia. The girl whose name he still didn't know sat three tables in front of him, the one he couldn't stop thinking about. He'd wondered how he would get her attention, strike up a conversation. What would he even say? Time was on his side. He'd figure it out.

The first week of training came and went in a flash. The theory side of it was easy and something Bryant immensely enjoyed. But the second week would involve practical tests, something he'd heard would be a great deal more complicated. They would simulate launches, spacewalks using equipment in the zero-gravity simulators. All the while, people would watch on, judging, analysing. Their facial expressions, heart rate, even breathing would be under scrutiny. It would be a long, complex process for sure. Still, as the weekend rolled around, he had more pressing matters at hand. His sister's twelfth birthday was fast approaching, and he'd promised he would take her shopping.

The school year now ran from mid-September until late August. The summer break lasted just a few weeks. There was no time to relax, and parents couldn't be expected to find care for endless weeks of summer. Children had so much to learn before going straight to work. In the meantime, they couldn't be a burden. The final school year finished in May. It was now late August. Just three months ago, Jimmy and Bryant sat together in Mrs North's geography class doing anything but geography. It felt like a thousand years ago now. So much had changed in such a short time.

Bryant's taxi arrived at the District centre. Each one had a small concentrated area for shopping. Everything you could ever need all in one place. It was rare you went shopping other than for grocery items; people couldn't be frivolous with money. You shopped if you needed something.

Bryant removed himself from the taxi. Thanking the man as he hauled himself out. As planned, he was roughly thirty minutes early. Mum was busy, so Julie had stayed the night with her friend as she often did, giving him just enough time to get a large cup of something heavily caffeinated. Space training would be a breeze compared with today's task. He was shopping with an eleven-year-old.

Large coffee purchase in hand, Bryant sat and nursed the piping hot beverage. He'd given his name when he ordered. Glancing down now, he noticed that they'd written 'Bryan' instead. "Huh," he thought to himself as he reminisced—the mistake forcing his father to the forefront of his brain.

Returning to reality, he blew on his coffee. The drink was still a million degrees. Bryant found a seat and sat to enjoy ten minutes doing nothing as he watched the crowds bustle by.

In his trance, he watched people scurry about desperately. Each one frantic, trying to get the cheapest items in the shortest amount of time. His new position of privilege hit him. For once, he wasn't desperate to get back to work. He could sit about leisurely. Safe in the knowledge, he could probably afford to pay for the shopping of just about everyone here. It was a delightful feeling but bittersweet as he felt the guilt. Why was he now suddenly so different from the others?

Suddenly, a familiar face appeared through his daze. A friendly grey-haired man met his gaze through the crowds, gave him a welcome nod before making his way over. Finally, he got it. It was the Quartermaster from the Academy.

'Fisher?' enquired the man.

Bryant stood automatically as if on cue. His brain scrambled, greeting the man as he arrived.

"Hello, sir."

The old man chuckled before replying. "Bryant, can I call you Bryant?" he asked. He didn't wait for a reply before continuing. "I thought I told you about the yes sirs, no sirs. Please, just Phil is fine." Bryant nodded uncertainly.

"What are you doing in town, Phil?" Bryant asked, still not sure how he felt about saying 'Phil.'

"Well, I'm following you, Bryant," Phil replied.

The grin on Bryant's face dropped. He panicked. Had he done something wrong? Phil wore the stern look for as long as possible before finally cracking and breaking into laughter.

"Bryant," he chuckled, "that look on your face."

Bryant relaxed at the sound of the laughter, mildly annoyed at how easily he'd fallen for it.

"Oh, Bryant," Phil winced, "can't an old man do some shopping on a Saturday?" Bryant looked down at the bags in the man's hands.

"Somewhat ironic," Bryant said, desperate to scrape back some of his pride. "The man who has everything out shopping."

They shared a laugh before the man spoke again.

"So, what brings you to town, Bryant?" Phil asked kindly.

"Oh," said Bryant, "I'm meeting my sister Julie. It's her birthday soon, so I basically have to buy her the world."

"And how old will she be?"

"She turns twelve next week."

"Ooft, good luck with that," Phil chuckled. "I'd imagine she's quite the live wire."

"You have no idea," replied Bryant.

Phil gathered his belongings to leave before saying, "Well, I'd best be off. You don't need an old man cramping your style."

Bryant stood, and they shook hands again. As he departed, Phil turned back and said,

"Say, Bryant, I could always use at hand as the stores, you know, if things get tough. I know how life at the Academy can be, so if you ever want to talk. I can make a mean cup of tea."

"Thanks," said Bryant, genuinely pleased. "I'll bear that in mind."

Phil disappeared back into the crowd, leaving Bryant alone again. The encounter distracted him from his thoughts, and he took a big sip from the coffee in his hand, completely forgetting that it was still a thousand degrees. He immediately regretted his decision as the molten coffee filled his mouth.

"Hot, hot, hot," he mumbled as he opened his mouth and let the liquid drain out of his mouth back into the cup.

"What are you doing, you weirdo?"

Bryant looked back up from his cup and saw his sister Julie stood expectantly before him. She wore a blue jacket that was incorrectly fastened. A hat adorned her head, squashing her pigtails.

"So much for the tough Space Ranger," came the words from his sister. "I mean, if I were an assassin, you'd be dead. Never have seen it coming.".

"Jules," Bryant uttered painfully through his burnt mouth, "where's Emma's mother?"

"Probably with Emma," she answered as she shrugged.

"Julie," Bryant scolded, "you shouldn't be wandering about on your own. It's not safe."

"Pfft," she said, "they let you wander around alone. People be more likely to get the idiot talking to his coffee."

Bryant smiled a wry grin, "What did I do to poor mum, leaving her with you?" he groaned. "At any rate, at least I can do my coat up properly." Bryant motioned to her mismatched jacket. Julie blew him a raspberry before taking a pew next to him.

Bryant's thoughts shifted to his mother; he'd been so busy since he left.

"How is mum?" he asked.

"I think she's sad," replied Julie.

"What about the cinema?" Bryant enquired.

"Dunno," said Julie, "she's at home all the time. It's all super clean. I hate it. It's like living in a museum."

"Don't worry about its Jules," Bryant said unconvincingly. "Everything will work out," he said, standing and adjusting her hat. "Anyway, come on. Let's take you shopping."

Smile for the camera.

The investigation, rather the decision making about what to do with the cinema, had predictably taken forever. Pam was no fool. She knew that writing was on the wall, but it would be the waiting that killed her.

It was likely they had decided what they would do within hours. Or, more probable, they already knew. Because they had been watching, waiting for the day that she slipped up. She knew the cinema had long since been on the list of businesses they wanted under their control.

The day the reckoning came, a summons appeared for noon. Pam considered taking a taxi, but time was hers at the moment. It was unusual, so she walked. As she approached the cinema, she stopped outside and took it all in. It was rare that she had time just to pause and think like this. There were decades of memories here. She hoped that it wouldn't be repurposed.

Opening the grand old doors, she took a big gulp before stepping inside. "Let's have it," she thought.

"Mrs Fisher," spoke the Inspector. "Thank you for coming."

Pam nodded, thinking to herself that she had no real choice.

"I appreciate that the last few weeks must have been difficult for you, so I'll keep this short."

Pam swallowed, then inhaled a large gulp of air.

"Considering the serious breach of rules, you have forced our hand. Your actions must have consequences," he continued. "The rules are there for everyone's protection. They are not to be challenged, Mrs Fisher. You might see it as a simple indiscretion. But I can assure you the guidelines are there to protect you, to protect others. You have been a patron of this establishment for more than twenty years, I understand. So you more than anyone should appreciate that employees cannot have or consume alcohol on site."

Pam nodded, knowing anything other than contrition was useless, "I understand."

"However," he furthered, "we aren't monsters. We understand that everyone is human. We all make mistakes. Considering your exemplary service, until now that is, and the fact that your family has been running this business for years. We feel that it would be unjust to remove you from it entirely."

Pam smiled uncertainly, "So, you aren't going to take the cinema?"

"Oh no, Mrs Fisher, we are. The cinema is now the property of the District."

"Oh, I see," she nodded, crestfallen.

"But what we would like is to offer you the opportunity to be the 'Deputy Manager' of the new District-owned cinema."

Pam's heart sank, "There it is, she thought."

"I mean, honestly, Mrs Fisher, this is a great opportunity for you. We will take care of all the nitty-gritty work. No longer will you need to worry about making a profit. You won't have to stress over finances, profitability, staff. I mean, this surely is welcome news for a woman of your age. The cinema will continue under your leadership. You'll get a competitive monthly payment that covers all of your needs. We'll give you staff. We'll give you fun. You simply have to turn up and do your job."

Pam gritted her teeth, "Careful now, Pam," she told herself. The age comment rankled her. This was far from what she wanted. Being a glorified puppet in her own theatre, but it was probably better than the alternatives, so she nodded sullenly. That was all the contrition they could have.

"Now," spoke the inspector, "we just need you to sign your new contract."

Pam glanced at the document. She picked it up to read it over.

"Oh, there's no time for that," he said. "But don't you worry. We'll have a copy sent to your house in due course so you can read it as many times as you like."

Pam paused and studied the paper in her hand, hesitant about signing away her life.

"If you don't feel up to the challenge Mrs Fisher, we can always find you a nice office job. I hear we have vacancies for customer service in rubbish disposal," he said rather menacingly.

Pam nodded in repentance, breathed in, and signed on the dotted line.

"Okay," he said as she signed the papers, "there is just one last thing we need."

"And that is?" Pam asked expectantly.

"A picture," he exclaimed, "we need a picture, Mrs Fisher. The people need to know about the new 'District run' cinema."

He moved and stood awkwardly alongside Pam, pulling a small camera from his pocket as he did so, "Smile for the camera, please."

A click and a flash, and just like that, it was done.

"Don't worry, Mrs Fisher, we'll ease you into the changes. Now," he said, standing and opening the door.

Taking the hint, Pam stepped out of her office. He followed her out, locking the door behind him.

They shook hands before he vanished, leaving Pam alone in the empty lobby, staring at the locked door that used to be her office, unsure about what was to come.

Flying colours.

Four weeks had come and gone since his expensive foray into town with Julie. He'd celebrated her birthday with them via video chat, and he'd even seen his mother in her new work uniform. They had spoken briefly, but his brain was elsewhere. He felt for her. He did. But she was lucky. The cinema wasn't gone altogether. What did she expect? The rules stood for a reason: he understood that now more than ever. She needed to own her mistakes. The common goal was all that mattered.

Bryant still missed his old life, but the more he invested at the Academy, the less it mattered. He made new friends and embraced new challenges. He helped Phil out in the storeroom, and they drank tea whilst putting the world to rights. Seeing everything from this side, life made sense. Those who were neither in the Academy nor working down the mines had a simple life. They had it all given to them; they got just enough to survive. But that was all they needed to do, survive. The real work was done elsewhere. They were just pawns in a much larger scheme. In a way, he envied them, even though he was glad he wasn't one.

The weeks of Ranger training flew by, and he felt at home. He trained hard in the range of simulators. It was incredible. He felt as though he had walked on alien soil, that he had blasted through the skies at light speed, floated in zero gravity. The equipment was unbelievable, and it was taken very seriously. You had to act and speak like you were on a space mission, getting tips and pointers for how it could be improved after every attempt. He rarely thought about what was happening at home. He seldom thought about anything outside of the Academy. Why should he? This was his life now.

The last week of training included passing a medical, something Bryant had learned wasn't as simple as it sounded. He had already had a medical as part of his induction, but that was a walk on the moon compared to the one coming. It was far from a 'cough here' job. Your whole body was put under scrutiny. Suppose your heart made even one unusual murmur. Should your hearing or eyesight be less than perfect, or if you had one slightly creaky knee joint. Then you weren't a suitable candidate for space. It was near impossible, and it made sense. You couldn't send someone who wasn't in perfect health on such an expedition. Only the best could be selected.

When Bryant's medical finally came around, he was anxious. He knew how high the stakes were. Orders told to report to a dedicated medical facility at 1000 hours, which was fantastic news. It meant a late start. He could rise at 0900, ready himself gently before taking a casual stroll across the camp. The instructions said the place wasn't far from his quarters, yet curiously it was a building he had never laid eyes upon before.

The medical centre was set slightly back from the other buildings. It was oddly alone on campus. He opened the creaky metal gate and walked down the path towards the building. He glanced up, stopped, and took in the stark grey gothic building that stared back at him. It was grey stone complete with gargoyles; what even were gargoyles? A chill shot through his body. It was like an old-fashioned haunted house.

Shuddering as he walked towards the door, picturing rooms filled with leather straps, sharp blades, creaky trolleys, and creepy staff dressed all in white, he entered with trepidation. With his eyes half shut, he stood there with his back to the closed door, grimacing. But when he took it all in, the sight that greeted his senses was in stark comparison to his expectations. The inside was bright, bold, and cheerfully modern. The walls were colourful and filled with inspirational pictures and slogans. A buzzer sounded as he entered the building, and it wasn't long before a pleasant, attentive male receptionist appeared.

"Hello," said the receptionist cheerfully, "how may I help you today?"

Still somewhat stunned, Bryant replied. "Hi, my name is Bryant Fisher. I'm here for my medical."

"Fisher… Fisher… Fisher…Fisher," spoke the man, scanning the list in front of him. "Ah, got it," he said, "you're pleasantly early. Go on through and take a seat outside room number one."

Bryant nodded in acknowledgement, "Thank you…?"

"Prashant," said the man, "and you're welcome. However, there is someone before you. So you may have a bit of a wait."

Life at the Academy moved quickly, so having to wait at this time of day sounded like heaven. Bryant departed the lobby and ascended the stairs. There were numerous rooms, and the place was eerily deserted. Climbing the steps to the first floor, he departed the staircase and opened the door. A sign on the wall pointed to room one, so he followed it and rounded the corner. As he navigated the mildly confusing signs, he finally found what he was after. With room one in sight, he noticed someone sat patiently on one of the chairs outside. The company filled him with both excitement and panic simultaneously. Bryant realised that the person waiting was the girl from the video room. The girl from Ranger training, the girl he couldn't stop thinking about.

There were just four chairs outside room one as Bryant approached them, his heartbeat so fast he was confident the doctor would hear it from here and instantly fail his medical. With the chairs in sight as he arrived, he deliberated for far too long as to how close he should sit to her. Sit too near, and it might be awkward; what would he say? Sit too far away, and he would give off the wrong message. Bryant stood there, deliberating until finally, he realised he had been stood looking at seats for far too long. He picked the chair on the end, leaving a gap of two between them. The still silence of the corridor was broken for a moment as he sat, and the chair let out a slight creak. He glanced in her direction briefly before turning back and staring at the wall.

"Do I smell?" she asked, breaking the ghostly silence once more.

"Um," Bryant replied. Unsure how to answer that question.

"I've been sat here alone, waiting for about forty minutes. There's no one to talk to! Then the one person who does appear sits as far away as possible."

"I think you smell nice," he managed.

"So, you've been smelling me?"

"No," he replied in a panic. "I mean, you look like you probably smell nice."

Flustered now, Bryant tried to engage his brain properly. "Why did he keep saying nice?"

"I mean…" he continued.

"I'm joking," she said, smiling. "It's fun to wind you up, though."

She bounced herself over the chairs that separated them until she was inches from him. He breathed it in, her scent filling his nostrils.

"I'm Mia," she said, holding out her hand, "Mia Evans."

"Bryant Fisher," he replied as confidently as possible.

"Did you say Fisher?" she quizzed.

"Uh, huh."

"Geez, man, the Doctor called your name ages ago!"

"What," said Bryant, "they did?"

In a total fluster, he went to stand.

"Woah, hold on, there cowboy," she said, putting her hand on his leg to cool his motion. "I'm just messing with you."

Bryant sat back in his chair, relieved. He could still feel the warmth of her touch on his leg. Pausing momentarily, he relished the moment. Breaking the silence once more, she said, "Fisher, oh so you're the replacement, huh?"

"Replacement," asked Bryant, "hey, I passed the test without cheating."

"Calm down," she chuckled, "you're too easy to mess with. For what it's worth, DeVore was an arrogant so and so. I'm glad you're here instead."

"Thanks," Bryant said, grinning, "so you met him?"

"Yeah, briefly, he was very cocksure, kind of a dick. Especially for someone who cheated to get here. Weird, though, right? That he cheated the test. I mean, he can't have done it without help."

Bryant pondered; he'd never stopped to think about it.

"I mean," Mia continued, "if you think about it. They must have known he cheated and that he had help to do so. It's odd that they let him into the Academy at all."

"That is weird," said Bryant, deep in thought. "Maybe they thought he would lead them to the people that helped him. But why would anyone want to cheat their way into the Academy knowing that they would probably get caught?"

They paused and gazed at each other for the briefest of moments.

Buzzzz.

The sound breaking through the moment, a wedding cake split in half by a knife, bride and groom now on opposing sides.

"Evans to room two, the doctor will see you now."

"That's my cue," Mia said, standing. "It was nice to meet you, Bryant Fisher. I guess I'll see you around."

She stepped towards the room, the door opened and shut, and she disappeared inside. A blanket of silence fell over the corridor once more, leaving Bryant alone with his thoughts. In his head now, he replayed the moment her hand touched his leg over and over. Irritatingly though, his thoughts were dashed by her talk of DeVore. "Stupid Devore." He'd almost forgotten about that man. Yet here he was in his head, even today. Why had he never questioned this before? Passing the exams was impossible. Cheating, getting the answers would involve quite some operation. It would likely require someone on the inside. But the bigger question that niggled at him was why?

His thoughts burst, interrupted by the sound of another buzzer.

"Fisher, to room one, the doctor will see you now."

Bryant swallowed. Shelved his thoughts, stood, and made his way to the door. Once there, he opened it and stepped inside.

Rangers.

Successful completion of Ranger training was accompanied by a passing out parade. An event that had since come and gone. Bryant had thought about inviting his family, but they were busy. Plus, they would only make a fuss. He was now officially a Ranger, and life gradually changed in the weeks and months that followed. He moved to the Rangers' block. He got a bigger room, and it was en suite! His peers treated him with great respect, and he no longer had to deal with stolen towels or sabotaged toiletries. He dived headfirst into everything asked of him and even earned a promotion to lance corporal. He used his time off at the weekends to go drinking in town with his fellow Rangers. Life for Bryant at the Academy was everything he had ever fantasised. He worked hard during the week and partied with his colleagues at the weekend. The camaraderie grew, his confidence raised. He rarely thought of or ventured home. It would always be there. He did all that was asked of him, questioning nothing.

As fantastic as it was, some things were a little odd about the inner sanctuary of Ranger's life. They operated out of a separate part of the base, and their jobs were very secretive. Everything they did revolved around the space missions, but they rarely spoke about them. They were always busy, but there seemed to be a real lack of real action. They trained endlessly in simulators. They operated at high G-force, practised using equipment and machinery, utilising the space rovers, even rehearsed suit depressurisation. It was great, but they never seemed to be a real mission. He'd asked, but no one answered.

Everywhere you looked, there were posters of Commander Steele. Each one was the man's portrait, just staring back at you. It was slightly unnerving. Wherever you went, another poster, just staring, almost watching you. Here he was observing, looking on in picture form, but no one ever seemed to meet him. He never appeared. Every morning when you reported for work, there was a minute's silence in remembrance of the brilliant engineer 'Hector Rosario', the man whose pioneering research had given way to the creation of light-speed travel. His work had led to the creation of the engines and thus further space exploration; so desperate was his research that he'd died in the pursuit of it. It was a solemn event, but no sooner had it finished. It was followed immediately by a minute's thanks, gratitude for the work that enabled humanity to continue. The solemnness would turn to clapping, whistling, and looking around at your fellow Ranger, smiling, jostling, shrieking. He understood the gravity of the man's work, but to do this every morning was weird. Yet with each passing day, it became more and more typical for him. It became euphoric and something he deeply looked forward to, the kinship, the jubilant celebrations, were intoxicating. The same was true of the posters. They went from creepy to uplifting. Like Commander Steele was everywhere, looking out for everyone, comforting, caring, watching.

When they were in town, talk from the Rangers would often end up on either Rosario or Steele. About which one was greater, braver, or who would win in a fight. Bryant listened on while his peers talked endlessly about people they had never met, almost as though they were family. How could they discuss people who seemed little more than the talk of legend?

Bryant had a few conversations with Jimmy, as much as he adored him. Talk of the mines was depressing, boring even. He had learnt that one of Jimmy's crew had died at sea, which meant they were also now a man light, forcing them to work even harder to break even. Bryant was sympathetic to a degree but was keen to remind Jimmy of the importance of the mines, how he had to keep going. Mum was busy and or tired, so he rarely talked to her. He had spoken to his sister a few times on the video chat. He loved his sister dearly, but she was always such an oddball. Asking such left-field questions, it was almost as though she didn't realise how important the work was that everyone was doing.

It was cute at first, but the conversations panicked Bryant. She was every bit like dad and questioned everything. She spoke with such reckless abandon, and it scared him in case someone overheard. Questioning the Authorities just wasn't done.

Days drifted by, more training, more simulations, until finally, an actual assignment. His joy was short-lived. He assumed, hoped, longed for a space mission, but this was far from that. He'd been assigned to a Ranger detail charged with receiving the Orbitium from the miners. Bryant knew that something happened to the ore after it was mined. He just never knew it was this. It was far from the high octane excitement he sought.

Once the miners returned with the Orbitium, they brought it to the Academy. It was weighed and processed before a Ranger team would exchange the ore for credits. A simple trade, two vital cogs working together. It made sense to a degree, but they were Rangers, not market traders.

The blur of weeks finally ended as he was ordered to report to hanger six for 1100 hours. Keen to impress and despite his reservations, Bryant arrived early and stood dutifully to attention outside.

"Fisher, you're with me," barked his new Sergeant. "Evans, you too."

Looking up, he couldn't believe his luck. Things had improved significantly. His new task did at least include the magnificent Mia.

The sergeant, whose name was 'Grimes,' assembled his team outside the hanger.

"Right, listen up," Grimes spoke, "most of you know the drill. It's a simple drop-and-pay. Tasers armed but strictly non-lethal force. They are no good to us dead."

A small chuckle rang out from the assembled crew. Why were they laughing? He looked around as all eight of them were issued with a taser. He'd used them in simulation, but never for real. These things had several modes, ranging from an inconvenient sting to frying every organ in your body. He grabbed the weapon handed to him and nervously attached it to his belt.

"Fisher, Evans," the sergeant spoke once more, "you're both here for the experience. Follow our lead and do nothing stupid. The situation is unlikely to get nasty, but be prepared just in case."

They both nodded. Bryant glanced at Mia, then back down at the shiny black taser clipped to his belt. He was confused, playing the words, "Unlikely to get nasty," over in his mind. Why would it be anything other than pleasant? Humanity was a team, working together for the greater good? Surely that was all that mattered? Were the tasers unnecessary?

Hanger six was a vast open space. A secure metal door at one end entered back into the Academy. Opposite it stood a huge metal shutter that could accommodate even the largest of objects. The rest of the place was vacant, save for some empty crates dotted about the area, and there was a large metal pad in the middle of the room. The gathered Rangers stood expectantly in a semi-circle. The distant hum of machinery the only source of noise.

A radio squawked.

"They're here, sir."

"Send them in," ordered Grimes.

The shutter burst into life, opening upwards slowly. The incoming sunlight parading in, blinding momentarily. Bryant squinted and made out the headlights of two ancient, rather beaten-up pickup trucks. The two cars pulled trailers filled with boxes and people who were sat haphazardly atop of them. As the trucks pulled forward slowly into the hanger, the clunky roller door shut swiftly behind them. They halted, and a lone man jumped out of the first vehicle. He made his way towards the semicircle, approached them and stopped.

"Grimes," he said, nodding at the Sergeant.

"Just the two today?"

"Leave it out, Grimes," the man replied angrily. "That was as much as we could get! You want more. Go dig it up yourself!"

"Alright," cooled Grimes, "no need for hostilities. Unload the trucks. Let's see what you have."

The man whistled, signalling to others. Five men hopped out of the trucks, and another nine joined them who had been riding behind. They quickly unloaded the boxes onto the metal pad that stood between the two groups getting straight to work. As he watched them work, Bryant noticed how big and strong all the miners were. Man for man in a fistfight, the Rangers would be no match for them.

Watching the miners go diligently about their task, Bryant spotted a familiar face. Unsure at first, but on reflection, it was Butch, Jimmy's dad!

"What are the odds?" he thought to himself.

He quickly scanned the other dirty faces. If Butch was here, then surely Jimmy would be too. He blinked at first, not believing his eyes. But he wasn't dreaming. One of the men unloading the boxes was Jimmy. Bryant stepped forward slightly out of rank and opened his mouth, "Jimmy, Jimmy," he called.

On the opposing side, Jimmy looked up from the boxes. It was Bryant. As unbelievable as this was, he'd hoped this wouldn't happen. As happy as he was to see his friend and as much as he wanted to run up to hug him. This wasn't the place for them to be seen together, for either of their sakes. He did his best to shoot him a smile. He was shaking his head all the while as if to say, "Bryant, no!".

Undeterred, Bryant persisted, stepping further forward. "Jimmy," he called again.

"Is there a problem, Fisher?" Grimes said, turning his head towards Bryant.

"No, sir," chirped Bryant.

"Then get back in line, Ranger."

Bryant stepped back into his formation. He looked across and saw some miners who were chuckling. One of them grabbed Jimmy by the shoulder, "Friend of yours, Jimmy?". Jimmy shook the hand off him, continuing with his duties.

A voice sneered from the gathered miners, "Better listen to your master."

Slightly confused, marginally hurt, Bryant just wanted to talk to his friend. He knew there were tensions between the groups, but he never dreamt it to be to this extent.

The miners continued to unload their goods, unaided by any of the Rangers until finally, the trucks laid bare, and all boxes sat on the pad. Grimes pulled a device from his pocket before speaking, "Six hundred Kilos, that's half what we were expecting."

The man who had led the miners stopped and strolled up to Grimes, so they were face to face. He was several inches taller than him and was an imposing figure.

"As I said, that was all we could get. Are you gonna pay us or not?"

"We'll pay you," said Grimes. "We'll give you forty per box."

"It's usually fifty!" said the man

"Yes," grunted Grimes, "and there's usually more."

The man stood there unwavering, fists clenched by his side.

"Fine," he said through gritted teeth.

"So, do we have a deal?"

The foreman nodded. Grimes opened his device once more, tapping it with the one held by the miner. A *bleep* signified that the transfer was complete. The foreman turned and headed back towards the trucks.

As he walked back to his crew, one miner picked up a wrench from the truck's cab and started towards them. He had a tattoo of a snake that ran up his neck and a frenzied look in his eyes.

Grimes put his hand on his taser.

As the foreman returned, he grabbed the man with the snake tattoo firmly by the arm.

"Leave it," he said to him, "it's not worth it."

The foreman nodded at his team, and the assembled miners started loading back into their trucks.

"Wait!" yelled Grimes.

The miners halted in their tracks as Grimes approached. The man with the snake tattoo had his back to him as he

125

arrived. "Hey, you, what's in the bag?" Grimes asked, motioning to the sack around the man's neck. Grimes put his arm out to take the bag, but the man was steadfast and unmoving.

"Give it to him," commanded the foreman. "We don't want any trouble."

The man with the snake tattoo reluctantly removed the bag from his shoulders, placing it into the outstretched arm of Grimes.

He knelt, placed the bag on the floor, and gently started unzipping it to see what was inside. With the bag finally, open. Grimes stretched apart the sides to get a good look at the contents.

Smackkk!

The sound of the wrench hitting Grimes' head made a sickening thud before the man collapsed to the floor. Bryant looked across at Jimmy, and for a brief moment, their eyes met, both wide with panic. For a split second, nobody moved. Everyone watched in shock as Grimes's body crumpled to the floor, the life sucked out of it. The three Rangers who had been closest to him exchanged shocked looks before reaching for their tasers. Realising what he had done, the man with the snake tattoo charged, his eyes wide with anger. He took down the first Ranger before he had a chance to remove his taser. Then for the ensuing moments' chaos rang out in hanger six. Some other miners joined in the melee and in what became an epic face-off—brains against brawn, privilege against poverty.

Bryant and Jimmy stood frozen in their spots. Panicked, unsure what to do. In the distance, someone hit a switch on the wall. Red lights flashed, and an alarm sounded. Amid the lights and the sounds, Bryant surveyed the scene before him. It was like a war zone. He couldn't fathom what was happening. He watched on, unable to believe his eyes. The man with the snake neck throttled a Ranger on the floor. Some others had their tasers withdrawn and were facing off

126

against a group of miners. Bryant looked at Jimmy, who stared back at him. What was even happening? He became a Ranger to go to space, not get involved in a hamfisted bar brawl. None of this made any sense. With his focus back in the room, he looked at Grimes, who was now face down in a pool of his blood, and it was then it hit him. "Mia," he thought to himself. Scanning the area, he watched on in horror as she approached the man with the snake tattoo. She pulled her weapon, but something alerted him. He looked up from whomever his current victim was, and as she approached, he swatted the weapon from her hands before she had the chance to use it.

There were lights, noise, shouting. It was chaos. But Mia was undeterred as she jumped onto the back of snake neck, desperate to remove him from the stricken Ranger. He stood with her wrapped around his shoulders still, violently shaking to remove this pest, but she clung on, steadfast, what a woman. The man with the tattoo turned and swung her into the boxes of mineral current sat on the weighing pad. She let out a wail, but still, she hung on. Bryant still hadn't moved, frozen in his spot. Something was dreadfully wrong about all of this. His thoughts raced, each one competing with the other. He needed an analysis, and he needed to understand it. Finally, he shook off the cowardice. He couldn't watch anymore. He barely knew this woman, but he had to help; he needed to do something.

Reacting, he glanced down at his belt and removed his taser. When his eyes returned to Mia, he saw Jimmy's father Butch already making his way towards Mia and snake neck. Butch hated the Academy. That was an absolute truth. Surely he, too, wouldn't attack a Ranger? With his taser shaking nervously in hand, Bryant swallowed. If he was going to act, it needed to be now. Darting across the room, he arrived just as Butch did. Taser out, arm raised, there was no time to hesitate. Amidst the bright flashing lights, the yells, the thuds, he could just about make out faint screams of "No Bryant, don't, he's trying to hel…"

The words fell on deaf or distracted ears. Bryant wrapped his finger around the small trigger and squeezed it as hard as he could. The aim was misguided, and the projectile landed on Butch, shooting 50,000 vaults into the side of Jimmy's father. Butch stood frozen for a moment. A shocked look filled his eyes before he slumped to the floor, shaking, convulsing. He just lay there, eyes wide in horror. But there was no time to think about it. The still unknown man with the tattoo had shaken Mia loose, and she too lay in a crumpled mess on the ground, bodies strewn everywhere, like a poetic battle reenactment, but this was no drill. The mad man then stood, frenzy in his eyes, he turned his attention to Bryant, who was frantically trying to re-arm his taser, but there was no time. The crazed man beat it from his grasp like swatting a bug. Bryant took a step back, away from him, but as he did so, he stumbled and fell onto a pile of boxes. Time then slowed down as his assailant grabbed him by the neck and began to squeeze the very life out of him, oxygen failing.

Bryant tried to fight back, but he could muster little in response. His vision blurred now. Over the man's shoulders, he could see bodies laid out everywhere. In his periphery, he saw Mia writhing on the floor in pain. "Mia!" He tried to call out, but it was no use. Large hands were clamped firmly around his neck. He couldn't breathe. He blinked as he tried to inhale but, it was no use. He'd come this far. Was this it? With no fight left to give and no help coming, his hands fell to his sides and finally, he closed his eyes and waited for death.

The grip loosened from his neck as his assailant slowly recoiled and slumped to the floor. Eyes were opening wider now, oxygen returning. He saw the figure of Jimmy stood above him, bloody wrench in hand. Jimmy dropped the wrench and knelt next to him.

"Bryant, Bryant," Jimmy said, shaking him. "Are you alright?"

"Jimmy," he gasped, "you saved me."

"Not for the first time, if we're keeping score," Jimmy joked.

"But your dad," said Bryant, "I tasered"-

"He'll be fine," replied Jimmy.

Bang!

The pair barely had time to look up as a second team of Rangers entered the hanger, gas masks adorning their faces. Smoke grenades rolled in with them, and the air turned a hazy shade of grey. Jimmy slumped to the ground next to Bryant, breathing in the dense fog that travelled through their airways and into their lungs.

"Jimmy," Bryant managed, "you're a good friend."

Bryant turned to look at his comrade wilting next to him; his eyes were shut. He felt his own eyes failing now as he watched the new Ranger team secure the building. Through the fog, he could just about make out the figure of Mia. He stood desperately to go in her aid. He managed just two steps before crashing back to the earth, taking larger gulps as he did so, the toxic air consuming his lungs. His eyes failing once again, he glanced at Jimmy. Then back at Mia once more before his eyes closed, and he was gone.

Divide and conquer.

In the days that followed the incident, Bryant had been confined to the med bay. He was free to leave but urged not to. For his health, his safety.

He had given reports, detailed accounts, written statements, signed documents, and been questioned repeatedly. He'd not been allowed contact with anybody from the day, anyone at all. Sitting in his hospital bed, another form in hand. It didn't quite add up. They were desperate to understand something, discover the truth.

As odd as the questions were. The first few days in medical had been outstanding. He reeled from his near-death experience. A man tried to strangle him, and the nurses were all delightful. They fed him, and he slept, then he ate again; it was very relaxing. But bit by bit, he felt much better. He just wanted to leave. He grew tired of the questions. They kept telling him otherwise, but it was as though he was stuck here. He needed to know what had transpired. Wanted to speak to anyone, to understand what had happened to Butch, Jimmy, Mia? All he knew was that they were unharmed. Injured Rangers were in the med bay and the civilians, the District hospital. The questions continued. He was forced to recount every detail over and over. By the end of it, he questioned his recollection of it, of reality in general. It had been days, maybe a week, since it happened. Whenever he asked about leaving, the response was the same. "It would be better for you if you didn't." Any member of staff uttered the same line. When they left, he would peak through the door as it opened. The same armed guard hovered outside.

Someone was responsible. Whoever it was would pay the price.

There had been fourteen miners in total on the day in question. The foreman, a 'Hector Niles', would escape severe punishment, but he would face public humiliation for failing to control his crew. A day in the stockade in the centre of the District. Citizens were invited to heckle and throw rotten fruit at the man. The same fate nearly befell Jimmy's father,

130

Butch. But a fierce defence from Bryant spared him the indignity. The other miners in question would be subject to a year of curfew and monitoring. They would also be accompanied by a member of the Authorities on all future mining endeavours. But there was no mention of the man with the tattoo, however.

Aside from being stuck in his room for five, six, maybe seven days. Plus the endless series of questions and forms to sign. Bryant's time in the med bay hadn't been terrible. He had been well fed; he enjoyed plenty of time watching films, and the medical staff were all excellent. Whenever he remonstrated, another reward would come. Not only would he be on full pay the whole time, but there would be a bonus for his actions. What were his actions?

Somewhere across the District, still haunted by what had happened. Jimmy sat propped against the wall in his room. He was losing his mind. He'd spent seven days in the white space. Maybe it was six. He didn't know anymore. The area was about eight feet by eight feet, with barely room to swing an e-dog. He remembered nothing after the incident. He was with Bryant and then woke up here. The white walls were padded; it was empty save for a metal bed bolted to the floor and a receptacle that doubled and both toilet and sink. Jimmy was dressed in a white boiler suit. He had zero possessions and had seen or heard from no one he knew. The days rolled by as he was questioned, poked, and physically prodded. There were medical examinations. Seemingly ordinary at first, but they grew weirder as the days passed. Forms, questions, forms, questions. His concept of time was the first to go, with no sunlight, no point of reference. He had no idea how much time had elapsed. He was angry initially, then grief, followed swiftly by doubt and despair. Hours and days drifted by; minutes and seconds ceased to exist entirely. He wondered if he had died, and this was hell, purgatory, or something even worse. There had been whole days when no one had entered. Not a word uttered, silence except for the crunch of the floor or the noise his suite made when it rubbed against itself. It was soul-destroying. The questions when they came were incessant. Then they would stop, only to continue. He was questioned repeatedly. His version of what happened became blurry. What he remembered became a doubt.

Finally, day eight, nine, seven? A man appeared with some more forms. Thrust under his nose, he hastily signed—anything to get out of here. More time faded away, then just like that, finally. The door clicked open. At first, he was sure it was a trap, poking his head from the room several times before retreating. Were they testing him? When he gathered what remained of his courage, he departed the white space and found himself in a bright corridor. One end was just a wall, opposite it a door. Creeping gently along the passage, he arrived at the exit, drew a deep breath before hesitantly stepping through it.

In a flash, he was back to normality. He looked around him, surprised, shocked. People were buzzing about, some sat waiting on chairs, and there was a reception desk to his left. There were food vending machines and in front of him a double automatic sliding door. He stopped and turned. The door he had just walked through seemed to no longer exist. Behind him now, he saw only a notice board. He blinked, rubbed his face. Was he going mad? Going in search of answers, Jimmy approached the reception desk.

"Where am I?" he inquired.

"Why, sweetie, you're in the District hospital." was the reply from the friendly middle-aged lady behind the desk. "You've been with us all week," she glanced down at the screen in front of her. "It seems you're all clear to go home."

Jimmy was in disbelief. He nodded and thanked the lady, "Had he just been in hospital?"

It didn't matter; he wanted to be anywhere but here. He turned and made swiftly for the exit.

"Hold it there," said a security guard who appeared and blocked off his path.

Jimmy swallowed, "No," he thought, "no one was stopping him getting out of here." He grabbed a ball-point pen that was on a nearby table and put it between his knuckles. He took a step forward and readied himself to do whatever was necessary.

"I can't let you leave," said the guard.

"Move," said Jimmy, "I'm leaving whether you like it or not."

"But you'll be wanting your belongings back," chuckled the man.

Jimmy shook his head. He looked down at himself. He was still dressed in the awful white suit. He glanced up at the man in his way. He was probably early sixties, slightly rotund and balding. His uniform was faded and fit where it touched. His cap was worn, and the stitching on the sewn-on 'Security' badge was unravelling.

"We can't have you wandering the streets like that," the man spoke again. "Come on, young man. Let's go find your clothes."

Jimmy cooled his rage. He relaxed his fist and glanced down at the pen in his hand, trembling at the reality of what he was prepared to do. He slid the pen into his back pocket and set off after the man.

After several days of isolation, Bryant was discharged. He didn't know what had changed, but he wasn't questioning it. He stepped from the building. *Crunch* back to reality as his boots touched down on the dirt in the quad. The sunlight hit his face, warming him instantly, how he had missed the daylight. He stood momentarily, eyes closed, basking in the glow, opening them again, blinking fiercely to remove the black dots. He stood and watched on. Across the quad, he could see a platoon marching in the distance. The man who led them looked just like the man with the tattoo! Surely it couldn't be? He was too far away to be sure, and he couldn't see any tattoos. He took some steps towards the platoon to get a better look.

"Fisher!" barked a familiar voice, halting him in his tracks.

Spinning around so fast, he almost gave himself a concussion. Bryant found himself face to face with Sergeant Himinez.

"Yes, Sgt," replied Bryant.

"Fisher," she ordered, "get yourself over to HQ. It's your initiation today."

"Today?" gulped Bryant.

"Is that a problem, Fisher?"

"No, sergeant," Bryant bumbled, "not at all."

Confused but excited, Bryant set off toward the headquarters. "Fisher," Himinez called after him. "It's a global event. We can't have you dressed in a tracksuit."

Realising his attire, Bryant smiled. "Yes, boss," he replied before eagerly setting off towards his quarters. His heart pounded. This was his day. It had been a long time coming, the thought balloon distracting him entirely from the last week. Excitement splashed all over him. He dashed off towards his quarters—time to get dressed. The world would finally get to hear the name Bryant Fisher!

To the world.

TV crews had gathered at the public access section of the Academy. For Bryant, the tension was now palpable. There was a section of the Academy which he now knew to be a 'front.' It could be accessed and viewed by public and media alike, but it wasn't real. Bryant had taken a tour of the place with his father as a child. It was like being able to attend a working museum. You could read about the history of the Academy whilst watching scientists develop rocket engines behind plexiglass. Something Bryant now knew to be just for show. What the scientists were working on, if anything at all, he had no idea. There was also a dedicated media section since the Academy issued regular global updates. Press conferences, speeches, and public events were all delivered from here.

The tour couldn't be taken by just anyone. It was handed out to competition winners (of which there were many). The vast walls of the camp would also broadcast images. They allowed the adoring public to turn up and sit around the fences to watch events. On occasions such as this, all non-essential workers were given a mandatory break to attend.

After taking light years to dress, a time that featured several different hairstyles. Bryant finally reported to HQ, ordered to arrive one hour before the address for makeup and 'preparation.' Upon entrance. He was escorted to the public side. Sitting behind the scenes now, he could see the stage and podium through a curtain. Makeup was applied to his face, and despite his protests, he was brushed, hovered, and polished to within an inch of his life.

Looking at himself in the mirror now, he looked like an action figurine. His chosen hairstyle had been opted against, and his hair had been glued down, shined into a side parting. It almost looked like plastic. He hated it; he raised his hands to rub it all off, but while contemplating doing so, he heard the sweetest of sounds behind him.

"Bryant?"

Rising from his seat and shrugging off the apron, he turned to see Mia standing behind him. They were both dressed and made up for the show. But with one notable difference. She looked fantastic, her hair neatly arranged in a shiny plait. Her eyes shone out of the makeup. He watched on, spellbound as her bold lips opened as shut, enunciating every sound. He knew she was talking, but he heard no words.

"Mia," he managed. Clueless to anything she might have said. He made his way towards her, stretching out his hand. Before he could do so, she rushed him and threw her arms around him in a warm embrace.

Bryant's excitement grew. He felt feelings he had never experienced before. He could feel her warm skin against his, the feel of her chest pushed up against him. He could feel a vigour rising inside him. Then, in a mild panic, he broke free from the embrace.

"That glad to see me?" he said coyly.

"You saved my life, Bryant."

Bryant chuckled, "Well, I'm not sure I'd call..."

Mia abruptly put her finger to his mouth and shook her head. "Oh, you're too modest, Bryant." Her sentence was interrupted by a woman who appeared. She had a tablet in hand and a headset bolted to her temple.

"Ah, the heroes of Hanger six, we're ready for you," she beamed.

The pair herded out onto the stage. Before they knew what was happening Bryant, found himself stood on the platform. Mia by his side a room filled with cameras, bright lights, microphones, and reporters. There were large screens on all the walls, capturing the live feed of the vast audience that had gathered outside. It was eerie. There were watching people watching them. So many individuals gathered to watch the pair as they embarked across the stage. He suddenly felt nervous. Panic spread over him as the lights hit. His stomach rumbled under pressure, and his body forced up some cold sweat on his forehead. He almost froze. He wanted to stop, but as he did so, he felt something grab his hand. It was warm and comforting. Studying his fingers, he saw Mia's hand meet his, her touch gentle. Glancing back up at her, she smiled, and they walked hand in hand to the centre of the stage.

The rear of the platform was packed out with dignitaries of the Academy past and present. There were serving officers mixed in with retired men in uniforms, festooned with medals and ribbons. All of whom featured the look of people who had been forcibly dragged from their homes—doing their best to convey their excitement. Bryant looked at the faces that stood before them. He recognised almost none of them except for Colonel Brooks, still no sign of their illustrious leader Commander Steele.

Bryant had pictured, dreamt, and even rehearsed this moment many times in his bedroom, lining up all of his toys, who cheered on as he accepted his fate. The fantasy was always fantastic. The reality, however, was awash with mixed emotions. This was it, the dream moment. But yet thoughts lingered in his brain, nagging away at him. Until the event in the hanger, he had been the perfect Academy man. But the last week had taken an expected turn, and something didn't quite add up anymore. What happened? Where was Jimmy? Why was everything moving on as though nothing took place? He felt as though he was awakening, starting to see things. Comforting was creepy once more; normal was unconventional.

Suddenly Bryant yearned to see his family. He wished they were here. That his mother, Julie, and Jimmy were sat in this crowd. He wanted to speak to his father or anyone he knew well. There were too many thoughts, and his brain was racing out of control.

The room was packed wall to wall with people. Yet, he felt so alone. He knew almost no one, and here they were, thousands of people inside and out, all here for him. None of them knowing the truth. Nobody knew about DeVore and the cheated test. Clueless about the miners who risked their lives to get underpaid by those who were supposed to provide for them. His eyes darted about the room. He was desperately looking for an exit. He wanted to run; he wished he could just flee.

Amid his panic, he felt the warm grip on his hand tighten. His fear turned to comfort. He looked Mia in the eyes as she moved closer to him.

"Together," she said.

Ushered forward, they traversed the stage hand in hand. The wild audience grew and roared into a crescendo. Forced towards the oddly welcoming, outstretched arms of Brooks, who stood at the podium. He greeted them like long-lost relatives. His grin beaming wider still. Brooks stopped, turned, and, using his arms, motioned to the crowd to silence. The noise gradually petered out. When it ceased, Brooks mounted the podium opening his jaw to speak.

"My fellow citizens, welcome and thank you for joining us for this momentous occasion. Today gives us two reasons to celebrate. But first, as always, please join me in giving thanks and remembrance to the legendary Hector Rosario. The man who gave his life so we could survive."

The noise rose once more. The audience inside and out went crazy. People were jumping and shouting, and strangers were hugging each other. Watching people maniacally celebrate nothing on cue was a strange sight. The considerable gathered noise then stopped before hushed silence ensued. Brooks spoke again.

"We are here today to welcome our recruit to the Academy. Today we unveil the man who passed the 2369 entrance exam."

The crowd roared on once more. Bryant observed curiously as the expectant mob celebrated his inception. It was almost as though they had no memory of taking part in this very event just a few months ago.

"Step forward, Bryant Fisher."

An usher appeared from backstage and almost physically pushed Bryant forward. Forced on, Bryant approached Brooks, who grabbed him. As they met, he held his arms aloft as though they were old friends.

Silence fell, allowing Brooks to ramble on further.

"As promised, today's ceremony is duplicitous. Not only are we welcoming Bryant Fisher to the Academy. But we are here to honour him."

Mia was shoved forwards, joining Brooks and Bryant at the podium.

"Now, before we give you the good news. We must break the bad," Brooks continued. "We had a minor situation last week. Those who seek to derail the space programme. The traitors who would rather see us rot here on Earth snuck on to the base to steal ore from right under our noses."

The crowd piped up once more. Choruses of voracious boos rang out across the world.

"The would-be traitors might have been successful! Were it not for the two heroes you see here. Corporal Evans detected the invaders, only to be savagely attacked by those involved. She might have been severely injured were it not for the heroic actions of Corporal Fisher."

Setting the crowd off once more as they remained planted onstage. Listening, waiting for the audience to finish their moronic catcalls, was sickening.

"But no amount of treachery can defeat love," roared Brooks. "Not the love for our cause, and not their love for each other."

Grabbing them both by the arm, he raised their hands towards the skies. Screaming, "Rangers in arms."

Setting the easily provoked audience off yet again, Brooks spoke once more, "Now, let me assure you. Those directly involved in the attack have been dealt with, but you will find a list of those who conspired in it behind me. They have served punishment for their crimes. But let them feel your fury, let them feel the wrath of the world. Make them know that nothing will disrupt the space programme. Nothing will get in our way!"

Another screen appeared behind the platform. Bryant watched on in horror as it dropped from the sky. It flicked on as it descended and displayed the names and faces of all the miners involved that day.

The hated was real. Objects were thrown as the crowd jeered. For five long, painful moments, it filled the whole world with loathing for those on the screen.

Bryant felt sick. He looked around him in panic; he wanted off the stage. He wished to be anywhere but here. Stuck on display, like a deer in headlights, there was nowhere to run. The video behind was on a loop. The names and faces scrolled past him until there it was! The two at the end, Butch and Jimmy Fletcher. Bryant was mortified, angry. He wanted to run over, throw Brooks off the stage, grab the microphone and tell everyone what really happened. Tell them it was all a lie. He surveyed the room. Armed guards were positioned at every door, every exit. There was nothing he could do, nothing except stand there and smile.

With the façade finally over. The lights dropped, and the two of them were shepherded backstage once more. Furious, Bryant broke free and powered towards Brooks, who was still basking in the audience's glow.

"How could you?" he demanded angrily. "How can you tell these lies? Commander Steele would never allow this to happen."

Brooks stepped away from the podium. Ensuring his microphone was off.

"And who's idea do you think this was, boy?" Brooks replied.

"No," said Bryant, "you can't do this."

Annoyed that the intrusion continued, Brooks took a step towards Bryant, pulling him in tight.

"You're a member of the Academy now, Bryant," he whispered in his ear. "This is the way it has to be. What's more important? Your friend or humanity? Either you're with us or against us Bryant, what's it going to be?"

Shocked, Bryant forced his way out of his grasp. Scuttling off backstage.

"I'd leave it alone if I were you, Bryant," Brooks called after him. Before turning back to his audience.

Once offstage, Bryant kicked out at a chair in frustration and smashed his hand hard against one of the mirrors sending cracks running through it.

"Bryant, I'm sorry," Mia said, walking up to him.

"Did you know about that," he scolded, "were you part of the lies?"

Bryant stormed around the room furiously. Mia frozen in her spot. He picked up a chair and threw it hard against the wall, letting his frustrations gush out, angrily pacing as Mia stood frozen in panic still. Her face was white with fear, and tears were forming in her eyes.

Bryant caught sight of himself in the cracked mirror. Blood from his hand running down it. He looked at his face between the cracks; he was red with anger, and veins popped venomously from his head. His reflection was a terrifying sight. Aware of how intimidating he must look. He cooled his rage. He never meant to scare her. He stopped and composed himself.

She grabbed him firmly and leaned in close to him; the embrace caught him by off-guard. But she held him tight and whispered tenderly in his ear.

"We can't talk here," she said, "they're listening." The words sent a chill across Bryant's skin. She broke from their hug and picked up a paper from a nearby table.

She scribbled something on it, balled it up, and thrust it into Bryant's pocket, "I'm sorry you feel this way, Corporal Fisher, but we have a duty to our planet." She gave him a kindly look before saying, "Now, if you'll excuse me, I have duties to attend to."

The Bunker.

It had been two days since the ceremony of lies. His mother had attempted contact with him. But he just couldn't bear it. He wished they could talk. He didn't know what he would say to anyone he knew. The truth was ugly, not that he was even sure what the truth was. He wasn't sure about anything at the moment.

He had followed Mia's instructions to the letter. Making sure he wasn't followed. He waited now at the edge of a field where it met the forest; it was at the very end of the camp, and there was nothing for miles around. As he waited, he worried. It seemed like an odd spot to meet. Secluded for sure, but very random. He glanced down at the tattered bit of paper; it said to be there at two o'clock. The time was now a quarter past. What was keeping her?

Phewwwwt.

He heard a whistle. Where had it come from? He spun around so fast he almost fell over. He looked up at the sky, then down at the floor. It was then he saw it. There was an old bunker just poking up from the grass. A familiar face was protruding from it.

"Over here, genius," she called, "and keep your head down!"

Bryant grabbed the top of his head as though it would somehow make a difference and darted towards the bunker. As he entered, she slammed the door behind him. They hugged him once more; he liked the hugs.

"Did anyone see you come this way?" she asked.

Bryant shook his head. He took in the sights before him with wonder. It was like they had fallen into a time warp. The bunker was old and a little dusty but fully equipped. It looked like something from a turn of the millennium disaster movie. It was like being in a museum.

"What is this place?" Bryant quizzed.

"I found it about a year ago," she said, grinning. "It must be an old fallout shelter." The building comprised of solid steel walls, a water recycler, and plenty of old rations. "It isn't on the camp schematics. No one knows it's here."

Bryant was amazed, fascinated. He could spend all week picking things up just to see what they did.

"Bryant," Mia spoke.

He beheld her face. Joy had faded, and she wore a graver look now.

"We have little time," she uttered, "we can't drop off the radar for long without someone noticing."

"What.." – Bryant started.

"I'm sorry," she said, "I know you have many questions, and I hate dropping this on you all at once. But you're not like the others, Bryant. I feel like I can trust you."

Bryant nodded.

"I'm sorry about the other day, Bryant, I am. But that isn't the strangest thing going on here. I need your help," she pleaded.

"But.."–Bryant started

"Please," she said, "just listen. There is a tracker in your arm. They put it there during your medical. Please listen carefully. You need to go to them and tell them you've been having headaches. It is a glitch sometimes caused by the tracker. They'll remove it for a time and run diagnostics on it. They won't replace it until they know that it's not causing your body harm. They want to know where you are, not kill you."

"A tracker," he burbled, "but why?"

"Because Bryant, freedom is a luxury. Please, just do it! It will buy us some time. You want to help your friends and family, don't you?"

Bryant nodded. His mind jumped back to his mum, Jimmy, "Yes, of course, I do. I'd do anything for them."

"Okay," she stated, "do what I said. We'll meet back here again in two weeks. Don't tell anyone about this, Bryant."

He nodded dutifully.

"Not even your family or friends."

"Okay," he replied. Not sure that he still had any friends.

"You're more important than you know, Bryant Fisher."

She kissed him on the forehead, and just like that, she was gone.

Bryant's head was a mash. The last weeks had gone from the sublime to the ridiculous. One minute he was living his dream as an Academy Ranger. Everything was great. Nothing was weird. The next, he was tangled up in something he still didn't understand. All he knew was that he'd let down those who were most dear to him, and he would do anything to make amends.

Losing track.

Their meeting in the bunker felt like a dream, and he'd replayed those minutes on multiple occasions. He recalled the way she looked, the way she smelt. He'd thought about it so many times he questioned now if it was real at all. Was it a dream? He wished he could close his eyes and just wake up a week ago. Better still, just go back to the summer after they finished school. It was mere months. But it seemed like a lifetime. So much had changed.

He was still embarrassed about the events of his initiation. But he felt like he was going mad. He needed to talk to someone; he needed his mum.

Pride swallowed. He activated the screen in his room, placing a call home.

"Mum," he said shyly as the call connected.

"Oh, Bryant," she gushed as the face of her son appeared before her. "It's really you? I've tried so many times."

"I know, mum," he said, "I'm sorry. Sorry for everything."

"I've been worried sick, Bryant! I thought you might have been in an accident or been sent off to space," she ranted.

"I'd tell you if I ever went to space, mum," he replied.

"Would you," she asked. "We even tried you on your birthday. I had a little surprise gathering here for you. It's not quite the same when you can't get a hold of the person whose birthday it is."

"Oh, my," he thought. The revelation shot through him like a dart; it was October. His birthday must have come and gone in the days he spent in the medical centre. How could he forget his birthday? "I'm sorry, mum, I was ill that week, is all."

"Ill, Bryant, are you okay?" Pam asked. "I'm worried about you."

"Oh, don't make a fuss, mum. Please, I'm fine. But mum," he said, changing the subject. "Have you spoken to Jimmy?"

She shook her head apologetically. "That was quite a shock Bryant, what happened? One minute we're celebrating

145

you. The next, we're making villains of our friends. Surely it's not true? I mean, Butch can be rash, but I just can't see him doing that."

Bryant shifted awkwardly in his chair. Despite being alone in his room, he didn't know who might be listening.

"Mum," he replied, "I can't talk about that now. I'll tell you more when I see you next."

Pam spoke again, but Bryant made sure he cut her off.

"Mum, just leave it."

As a mother, she had become adept at knowing when she wasn't being told something. Eager to sort this out but knowing he would only tell her when he was ready. She moved on.

"Have you seen Jimmy, though?" Bryant asked again.

"I'm sorry, bunny, no. I've tried getting in touch with Butch, I have. I went around their house as soon as I heard the news. But no one answered. You know how busy the miners are. They are probably at sea."

"Have you rung them?" he pleaded.

"I did, yes, honey, but I've had no luck."

"Then try again," Bryant demanded!

"Bryant," Pam exclaimed, shocked, "what do you want me to do? You don't talk to us. We don't know what's going on. I mean, I swear the only way we know you are still alive is by reading news updates. Something is going on with you at the moment, and I don't like it."

Bryant paused. He was studying the screen in front of him. His mum looked tired, gaunt. He observed the figure in front of him. She was wearing her uniform. But there was a name tag on her chest. It read 'Pam Fisher Deputy Manager.'

"Deputy Manager?" he asked.

"Yes, Bryant," she said, "you remember the audit, don't you? I mean, you'd know what was going on here if you bothered to speak to us."

Bryant wept a little, "I'm so sorry, mum. There's just so much to do and…"

There was so much he wanted to tell her. He just wanted her to hold him in her arms, tell him it would all be okay. He opened his mouth to continue, but something stopped him. It seemed idiotic, paranoid even. But the words of Mia saying, "They're listening," filled his brain. He realised he could say no more.

Adjusting himself in his chair. He wiped the tears from his eyes. "I'll come and see you soon, mum," he said assuredly. Changing the subject, he asked, "How's Julie?"

His mum might have replied. Any response drowned out by a knock at the door.

"In a minute," Bryant called out.

The door knocked again and again. Finally, a voice called through it.

"You're needed in medical Fisher," barked the voice.

"Yeah, I said in a minute," he replied.

"Now, Fisher."

This was important. The idea that he was physically tracked gave him nightmares.

"I've got to go, mum," he said. "I love you." He switched the screen off, grabbed his jacket, and set off in the direction of the med bay.

Revelations.

"Were you followed?" she asked.

"No," chuckled Bryant. The 'were you followed' greeting was still odd. He felt like he was in an espionage movie.

"This is serious, Bryant," Mia said.

"I'm certain," Bryant scoffed, "I wasn't followed."

Having the tracker removed was far less painful than he imagined. A little sedation, some scans, and that was it. They had requested to see him again in a fortnight. Which presumably meant that's when it would be re-inserted. He shuddered. People putting things in him really got under his skin.

They met at the bunker once more; it was evening, meaning they had crept there under cover of darkness. They weren't followed, and they weren't tracked. Time was theirs today.

Safe in the bunker door locked. Bryant spoke,

"So, what's the big conspiracy? Wait, don't tell me. Dragons run the Academy," he said jokingly.

"Hey, this is serious, Bryant," she scolded. "If you're not interested, you are free to leave."

Sensing that he had upset her. He apologised, sitting down next to her.

"Okay," he said earnestly, "I'm listening."

"Well," she said, "let's start with the man you replaced. DeVore."

Bryant rolled his eyes at the word 'replaced', which Mia met by a cold stare.

"Okay," said Bryant, "say your right. Let's assume he had help to cheat the tests. Why would they go to all that trouble just to wind up getting expelled?"

"Expelled Bryant! He's dead. They killed him!"

"What," Bryant blurted out, "that's extreme for a bit of cheating."

"Oh, Bryant," she said, "open your eyes. Look at what happened at your initiation? Think about what Brooks said to you. Think about the fact that they have been tracking you."

Bryant's face grew pale.

"Think about it, Bryant. We're both Rangers."

"So?"

"So," she said, "how many Rangers do you know have been to space?"

"Well, none. But I don't know that many Rangers," Bryant responded.

"Have you been to space?"

"No, but I'm new."

"That's what I thought," she said. "I'm still waiting." She went on, "When was the last space mission?"

"I remember reading about one at the start of the year," Bryant protested.

"That's right," she said, "you read about it. But I was here. I don't remember any launch."

Bryant paused, "Then I guess they take place in secret? I've heard people talk about space," he remonstrated.

"Talk, Bryant, it's cheap, that's all it is. Talk!"

Bryant shook his head. This couldn't be possible.

"No," he said, "this is a joke, right? Ha-ha, hilarious."

Her face was as serious as ever.

"Bryant," she said, "I knew DeVore. I know why he wanted to get into the Academy."

"This will be good," he laughed nervously.

"I know this is heavy, Bryant. But DeVore was on to something. He was working with a group called the 'Uprising.' He was going to show me, tell me what was happening. But they got to him first."

Bryant had long since realised that Mia wasn't kidding. Everything she was saying made sense. He'd been living in denial for weeks. Something about the Academy seriously didn't add up. He panicked. He thought about how he'd never seen Commander Steele, the posters, the wild celebrations, the brainwashing. He thought about the life they had and its stark comparison to others. He'd been desperately trying to forget about what he'd seen, about what had happened. But now, the words of Brooks rang out in his brain.

"Either you're with us or against us, Bryant! Either you're with us or against us, Bryant!"

"But.. buh," he tried to talk, tried to comprehend. But his body was riddled with panic, fear, realisation.

"Breathe, Bryant, breathe," she said.

He drew longer breaths, sucking in wild gasps of air, "If this is true, we need to tell everyone. We have to let everyone know." he started, talking louder, burbling, motioning wildly.

"Bryant," she grabbed his arms, pulling them to his side. "Look at me, Bryant. Look at me."

"No, Mia, we have to…"

The kiss took him by surprise! She grabbed his head with her hands and pulled him in tight, and they stood there connected, locked in a moment. Everything ceased, his world stopped spinning, and suddenly nothing mattered but the two of them. She gradually moved her lips from his. They stood face to face, inches apart, their chests heaving. He could feel her breath on his face. He could taste her lips. He threw his arms around her face and pulled her lips towards his passionately once more. The emotions were overriding. Falling apart had brought them together. The hormones of the young pair sprayed all over the walls.

Moving towards the old bed, they paused for a second as she removed her top. Bryant stood motionless. He watched her breasts move up and down with each breath she took. He'd never seen this much of the female figure in the flesh before. Sensing his hesitance, she grabbed his hands and placed them on her chest. He gasped in disbelief. She moved away from him, towards the bed, removing her trousers as she walked. Bryant's eyes unfaltering, he took a step towards her and then stopped, tentative.

"Come on then," she said. "What are you waiting for?"

Together on the bed, bodies entwined, naked aside from the partial cover of an old quilt. Her head lay on his chest, eyes closed. He watched her as she dozed. He was studying her face. She was beautiful. Her lips were perfect, her eyes

150

exquisite. Bryant was not unattractive, but he'd never considered himself particularly handsome. Despite what his mother said. Only in his wildest dreams had he imagined a girl like this taking an interest in him! He stroked her hair with his hand, and she made a soft purring noise. He had never known a connection like this. Never felt such a closeness. For the first time in months, he no longer felt alone.

"We can't meet here again," she said, breaking from her daze. "We must keep our distance in public."

The words scratched at Bryant's heart, "Why?" he asked, bolting upright.

"I just want to be careful, Bryant. Especially after losing DeVore. I don't want to lose you too," she said. "They probably still think you are angry with me. If we keep them thinking that, then they are less likely to suspect we are working together."

"But," Bryant protested, "I don't want to be apart."

"Oh, I know neither do I, Bryant," she said, sitting up and kissing him delicately on the cheek. "Don't worry. We'll see each other again. But we need to be cautious."

Bryant nodded. He understood, he didn't like it, but it made sense.

"Also," she said, gesturing to his arm. "They'll be putting that tracker back in soon. We need to get it out for good."

"How?" Bryant asked, confused, slightly deflated.

"DeVore took me to a place in the District. There's a guy there who can remove the trackers," she replied.

Hearing the name DeVore again, Bryant wondered. He got jealous.

"So, did you sleep with him too?"

"No, Bryant," she said, "it's not like that."

"But what about him?" Bryant replied.

"What matters, Bryant, is I chose you. I picked you because you are everything good about this world. You're kind and sweet. You're not like other people."

"Bryant," she said, taking his hand, "this isn't a game. DeVore is dead. He was nothing like you. He cared about his ego, about his legacy Bryant. He was shallow."

Bryant nodded, feeling a little better.

"But he was from your District F. If the others trust anyone, it will be you."

"Okay," he said, not entirely satisfied, "we remove the tracker, and then what?"

"Well, then we find the rest of the people he was working with, we make a plan, and then I guess the burden of proof lies with us."

Bryant contemplated it. Just about everyone the world over worked for the Authorities. They all worked long, dangerous days for little to no reward—all towards a common goal, the greater good. But if the people knew they were being lied to, if they knew the truth. They would break free from the shackles of their oppressors. Jimmy would no longer have to risk his life in the mines. His mum wouldn't need to work thirteen-hour days just to put food on the table. He could live a happy life at home. With his mother, sister, friend, lover, civilisation in harmony. Equals that shared, basking in their freedom. Showing their humanity.

"Okay," he said defiantly, "I'm in."

It had been a few weeks since the time they shared in the bunker. He yearned to feel Mia's touch again. Desperate to hold her in his arms once more. Time was on a fast march towards December, and she was all he could think about; their paths had crossed occasionally on camp. The longer it had been, the harder it became. He knew what they were up against, but sometimes he just didn't care.

The weather was turning; it was getting gradually colder. They had seen one dusting of snow, and more was expected in the coming months. Bad weather meant that all space launches were on hold indefinitely—something Bryant would normally have taken as gospel.

December was one of a few merry times. The festive period would soon be upon them. Everyone across the globe got the 25th of December off to spend with family and friends. Because December the 25th was Unification day.

Bryant remembered his father telling him stories from books about 'Christmas.' But the term had long since been removed and branded as 'capitalist propaganda'! Books and or any information pertaining to 'Christmas' were notoriously hard to find. It was part of the old ways of producing, making, and wanting more than they needed. People would push themselves to the brink of debt to show their family how much they loved them—showering them in expensive goods. It was a constant stream of having to outdo yourself, buying bigger and better gifts each year. The attitude had been one of the most significant factors in the planet's decline. Shiny plastic goods were produced constantly, only to be used for a few months and then branded 'old' or 'obsolete'—many perfectly wonderful objects finding their way into landfills within months.

Bryant had saved most of his leave to use around unification day. It would be nice to spend some of it with his family. Get away from it all. He was also hoping that he could see more of Mia. Everything in his life was a mess, yet somehow together in those small moments. Everything made sense. He would happily give it all up, the money, the glory, the excitement, space, the Uprising, even the truth. He would relinquish it to wake up every morning with her. Go to work at the cinema and come home to her. He dreamt of that now; he yearned for it. Bryant hadn't know Mia long, and he didn't understand how he felt. When they were together, he was no longer alone—the moments they shared connected all the dots. So much stood in his way, but they would never be free to do as they pleased. Not in the current system.

Margery and Reginald.

Bryant looked at his reflection in the window. He barely recognised his own life anymore. It was December the 18th, the last time Bryant took leave from the Academy; he hurried to meet his friend at Planet Pizza. This time he was on his way to get a tracking device removed from within him. Then hopefully, find a revolution. What was happening? He missed the simple decisions involved in what to do after school every evening, what to eat for dinner, he missed being bored. Everything was so complicated.

He left the camp in a taxi. Humans still operated some, but the reality was they were there just to make sure nothing went wrong. Most were automated, and the driver had little to do. Bryant had always preferred the real ones, the human company, but right now, someone asking intrusive questions was not what he needed

On foot now. He followed the instructions Mia had slipped him a week ago; seeing her handwriting made him happy. He'd read the tiny bit of paper dozens of times, playing the words over to himself in her voice.

The directives ended, and he found himself in a run-down part of the old District. There were more independent shops here than anywhere else. She'd led him to an old watch repair shop. Glancing through the window, he looked on in amazement. Citizens had long since been advised against analogue technology due to its ability to fail. An analogue watch could stop or lose time. It was branded as archaic, barbaric almost. His entire life had been digital. As a result, he had never seen an analogue watch before, caught in childlike wonder. He stared on through the window as the hands glided around the face at the command of the cogs behind them.

Being early, he found a dry step and took a seat. Academy members were some of the select few who were allowed to cross the boundaries between Districts. Despite not being from his District, Mia would have no trouble getting here.

Mia arrived roughly twenty minutes later. He stood excitedly as she came; it had been so long since they had been together. He went to hug her, but she didn't break her stride. Instead, she grabbed his hand and led him swiftly inside. The interior of the shop was even more remarkable than the exterior. There were projects everywhere. Broken watches lying about, everything so mechanical. The man behind the counter didn't look up as they entered. He was probably mid-seventies, tall, thin, with a whisper of hair left on his head. He studied a device in front of him through a magnifying glass. His hands were moving, slow and meticulous.

Approaching the man, Mia Spoke, "Hi, we need help. My friend has a strap that is too tight. Are you able to help us loosen it?"

The man paused, looked up from what he was doing, and opened his mouth to speak.

"Analogue or digital?" he asked curtly.

"Digital," replied Mia.

"Then I'm afraid you've come to the wrong place," said the man.

"But I was told..." Mia protested.

"Then you were told wrong!" he replied.

Bryant stepped forward, "Now wait…"

The man flicked a switch near to him, and the door to the shop swung open automatically.

"If I press it again. It sends a distress signal to the Authorities," said the man. "So, I suggest you leave."

Mia froze for a moment in disbelief. Bryant grabbed at her arm, "Come on, let's go," he said. "He won't help us."

He continued at her arm until she conceded. Fleeing the shop, they rounded the corner, stopping in the alley behind.

"I'm sorry," she said, "I'm sure that was the place."

He pulled her in close, holding her for the first time in weeks. Bryant breathed it all in as they stood alone together in the dark alley.

A figure appeared almost from nowhere, turned the corner of the alley and walked straight past them. The words he uttered were so stealthy, so silent. It was haunting. Bryant felt the words hit the back of his ears like a ghost entering his soul. "Follow me," reverberated down his spine. At first, he thought he might have imagined it. But Mia looked up too. Together their eyes darted to the source of the noise. The figure barely visible against the backdrop made its way hastily towards the end of the alley, turned to the left before ghosting from sight.

Mia grabbed Bryant's arm, "Come on," she begged. "We have to go."

"But we," he began. "What if it's a trap?"

"Well, there's one way to find out." She pulled his arm so hard he was sure it might dislocate. "Come on!"

Bryant paused and took a deep breath before the slack on his arm gave, yanked forward. Together, they darted down the alley, hanging a left at the end. They caught sight of the man's boots departing the end of the next. Speeding up, they followed him through the labyrinth of back alleys. Twisting and turning through the maze until finally, they caught up with him. It was a dead-end; the man faced them. He wore a dark full-length coat, his face masked, gun in hand. He motioned at the two of them with the gun pointing to a drain in the floor. The cover was off, and they could see a ladder that descended into darkness.

"In there!" he ordered.

Neither of them moved, frozen in fear. The man stepped towards them with the gun, "I said in there."

Bryant went first. He climbed down the ladder as slowly as he dared, confident he was descending to his demise.

"Please," he yelled up as he climbed down. "You don't need to do this. We were just looking for some help. Please, we have credits."

"Shut it!" shouted the man as he entered the drain. He slid the top closed, cutting off what little light there was, "Just keep climbing."

As he scaled, Bryant noticed a small amount of light appear near the bottom. Looking up, he glanced at Mia. Above her, he could see the man climbing down, gun in hand trained on them both still.

Bryant reached the base first. He looked at his surroundings; it was damp and dimly lit. Tunnels led off in multiple directions. They could try to run for it, but where? They might never find their way out of this maze. The man dismounted the ladder and motioned to the first tunnel on the right, "That way," he said.

Mia spoke now, "Please, we are not looking for trouble."

"Walking, not talking!" he said. He was pointing down the tunnel once more with his gun.

The two strolled silently to the end of the tunnel. The man shone a torch ahead of them, and they walked until they could finally see a large metal door. As he arrived, the man rapped on the door with his knuckles, a coded message to whoever was inside. The large metal entrance opened, and they were forced in.

The sight that greeted them was far from what they had expected. An elderly lady opened the door, but she was far from frail. Bryant had expected to see a creepy lair or some headquarters. Instead, the inside was like an old-fashioned cottage. A freshly brewed teapot sat on the table, and a record player warbled away in the background. There was a fabric stitched sofa with actual patterns on, a chunky white fridge, and posters on the wall.

"Sit," said the man as he removed his mask. The gentleman sat down on the chair in front of the two of them. He was probably late fifties but well built; he had a large scar that ran across his neck and down his shoulder.

"Tell me why I shouldn't kill you both," he beseeched them. "Leave your bodies out for the rats?"

"Please," Mia sobbed, "we're after the same thing. We need your help, please."

"And what would that be?" he asked. "You both wreak of the Academy."

His wife, who had been unmoving, set her cup of tea down and spoke. "Reginald," she scorned, "what are you bringing Academy down here?"

"Had to," he said, looking at her. "They were asking questions in Winston's shop. I needed to find out what they were after."

Reginald gesticulated as he spoke, the gun-waving about with each word. Bryant and Mia sat still, silent, terrified.

Reginald's wife, Margery, stood, pulling a gun from under the table. She walked across to Mia, putting the weapon to her head.

"Not so fast!" Reginald waved his gun at Bryant as he looked to stand. Two pistols trained on them now.

"Now," said Reginald, "empty your pockets slowly and explain to us what you're doing here."

"Okay, okay," trembled Bryant. He started unloading his pockets onto the floor. "Please let us explain."

"Now you," said Reginald, looking at Mia.

She carefully unloaded the contents of her pockets onto the floor. Margery then stepped back a pace, aiming her gun at both of them, "Stand!" she ordered.

The pair stood gingerly and were immediately patted down rigorously by Reginald. "They're clear," he said. Satisfied, they had nothing else on them.

"Now, what are you doing here?" asked Margery as Reginald set about rummaging through the contents of their pockets.

"We are from the Academy," said Bryant boldly. "But it's not what you think. We need your help. We can help each other."

"We need nothing from you," scolded Reginald coldly. As he sorted through the pair's belongings, "Why would we help you, anyway? Do you know the only useful Academy member?"

"No," replied Bryant.

"A dead one," answered Reginald.

"Anything?" Margery asked, growing impatient at the time he spent examining their belongings.

"Nah, nutin useful, my sweet," he mused. "Just phones and some academy ID's!"

"Fine," she said, "they've been here too long already. Take them outside and shoot them."

"Come on then, outside," Reginald said with their ID's in hand still. "It was nice knowing you, Mia Evans and Bryant Fisher." Grabbing Bryant by the scruff, he hauled him to his feet, motioning to the door with his gun.

Margery had been unusually silent. She pondered as she watched her husband usher the two terrified faces back to the metal door.

"Wait," she stammered, "did you say Bryan Fisher?"

"Nah, Bryant," replied Reginald. "With a 'T.'"

Margery thought a while longer. "Okay," she said, "take them to the tunnel. Shoot them, then burn their belongings."

Bryant looked at Mia as she was forced to the door. Panic covered her face.

"Wait, wait," he pleaded. "Why did you ask about my father?"

"Come on, get out," said Reginald.

"My father was Bryan Fisher. I swear," said Bryant. "I'll tell you anything you want to know about him."

"Hold on a second, dear," Margery said to her husband.

"Nah, talking rubbish," said Reginald. "They'll say anything to stay alive, these rats."

"It's true, it's true," wept Bryant, "I can prove it."

"Bollocks," said Reginald, "Bryan had no family."

Margery stepped towards Bryant, face to face now she said, "Go on then, show me."

"My phone," he sobbed, "I need my phone."

"You think I'm stupid?" asked Reginald. "I ain't givin you that."

"Okay, fine, you do it," Bryant said. "The back cover, it comes off. Take it off, and you'll see."

Margery nodded towards her husband, "Do it."

Reginald picked the phone up, taking a knife from his boot. He cautiously prised open the phone and slid off the back cover. Pressed inside between the cover and the battery was a tattered, folded bit of paper. Reginald removed it and handed it to his wife. She unfolded the paper and studied the picture in front of her.

"Lower your gun," she said to her husband. Reginald looked back across at his wife.

"Now!" she commanded.

"I don't understand," he said.

Lowering her gun, she handed the photo across to her husband, who stared at in disbelief.

"Well, I'll be dammed," he babbled.

"So then," Margery spoke. "To what do we owe this honour?"

Revelations.

The words, "Shoot them," reverberated around his brain. The entire experience had been terrifying. He had never even seen a gun before, and having one pointed at him had been a horrific experience. One that he wasn't in a hurry to repeat. His life had flashed before his eyes in those moments as he stared death in the face. It was as though time stood still. He saw his Mum, Julie, Jimmy, and sweet Mia. Part of him wished he'd never stepped foot in the Academy. When they made their plans in the bunker, it had all seemed so easy. He'd never once imagined that the Uprising, or anyone, would want to kill them.

Reginald and his wife Margery were not active members of the Uprising. Nobody was anymore. At one point, they were in the thick of it. But the revolution wasn't quite the beating heart that they had imagined. They were still loyal to the cause, but there wasn't much of one. Knowing the reality of the world, the pair liked to spend most of their time underground. Enjoying creature comforts, each other, and the simple pleasure of not being monitored.

The revelation that his father had somehow been a part of all this came as a real shock. Stories of his dad were short in supply. Bryant much preferred his father as a radical than a drunk gambler, and he was desperate to know more. Margery was suspicious by nature, despite him being the son of a great revolutionary. They were keeping their cards close to their chests until they knew where everyone stood.

Reginald and Margery had agreed to contact the others: if they were interested in what they had to say, then they would be in touch. It wasn't quite the warm welcome Bryant had expected, but it was a start. Reginald had at least removed Bryant's tracker before leading them back up through the tunnels.

"Apologies again," said Reginald Gruffly. "We can't take any chances. You must understand?"

"You mean for nearly killing us?" Mia said flippantly.

Reginald shrugged, "Nature of the beast, I'm afraid."

"What do we do now?" Bryant asked.

"They'll be in touch," said Reginald. "Just relax, act normal, and try not to anything else stupid."

Mia climbed the ladder ahead of him. Bryant went to begin the ascent before the arm of Reginald grabbed his shoulder, stopping him. Bryant turned to see Reginald stood before him. His eyes were red, almost tearful.

"I can't believe it's true," he said happily.

He looked Bryant up and down before pulling him in for a hug.

"Stay safe," he said.

Mia had paused halfway up the ladder, Bryant nodded at her, and they both climbed.

Safe back on the surface, they ducked under an old archway, huddled together.

"I'd better get going," she said to him.

"Already?" he replied sadly.

"Yes, Bryant, I have to go back to the Academy."

"But the revolution?" Bryant pleaded.

"Say it louder, if you like," she joked. "I'm not sure everyone heard you? I'll see you at yours for Unification."

"Really?" said Bryant, his face lighting up.

"Yes," she said.

She took his hands and looked him straight in the eye.

"Promise me you'll be careful; they might contact you in the next few days."

"I'll be fine," he said casually.

"Promise me," she demanded. "You're very important to me, Bryant."

"I promise."

They stood just holding each other for what seemed like years before Mia pulled herself away from the embrace.

"Sorry, Bryant, I have to go."

He nodded sadly as he watched her disappear down the alley. As she approached the end, she stopped and turned back his way.

"I love you, Bryant Fisher," she shouted.

162

History lessens.

It was December the 20th. Bryant had been home two days. His mum was busy at work, and Julie only got the days off either side of unification day. Meaning he's spent the two days alone in a vacancy.

He could still hear Mia's words in his head. He'd played them again and again. The time he'd had in the last two days had afforded him that much. She'd told him she loved him. He couldn't believe it. The words had caught him by surprise. He'd managed nothing as a reply. He wanted to open his window and yell, "I love you, Mia Evans," to the world.

He tried Jimmy's phone the minute he got home. Desperate to get in touch with his friend, he needed to know if he was okay; he still had no idea what had happened to him! Alone once more and now frustrated, he required his buddy. His mum had begged him not to go to Jimmy's house. She warned him it wasn't a good idea. Butch Fisher had a short fuse, and she worried how he might react if Bryant turned up at his home given what had happened.

He told her he wouldn't go, but there was nothing in the world that could keep him away from his friend. Especially not now. They had so much to discuss.

The taxi stopped. This one was automated. He paid the robot and hopped out. It was about half a mile still, but he thought it prudent to walk the last bit. As he bore down on Jimmy's house, he wondered what he might say when he arrived. Nervous, he rounded the corner at the end of the joining street. He'd prepared himself mentally for many things during his walk, but what he saw upon arrival came as a shock. Jimmy's house was still there. He knew and loved the place before him, but it was a blackened husk, a stain on what used to be. Bryant upped his pace, jogging, then sprinting, until he finally stood in front of the house and looked on in horror. This family home was now startling. The windows were smashed, missing, or boarded up. It was dark, abandoned, and graffiti adorned the walls.

Bryant's eyes scanned the building, 'Die traitors,' 'Scum', 'Rats,' Bryant read some graffiti, then looked away. He'd seen enough.

Bryant looked about. A solitary man strolled casually nearby with his e-dog.

"Excuse me, sir," Bryant called out to him. "Do you know what happened here?"

The man paused, set his e-dog to 'sit', and walked over to Bryant. "Sad story that," he lamented, "hard-working family, that one. I never had a bad word to say about them."

"But what happened?" Bryant begged.

"Ah, not much at first," said the man, "but it were after the news came out. You know about the lads stealing and whatnot. It started with some graffiti. Someone came in the night must of done the spraying. It were gradual, but then one night a brick was thrown, shattered one them windows, and it went from there."

"What happened to the family?" asked Bryant.

"Ah, oo knows," spoke the man. "Ear they got moved away."

"Any idea where?" pleaded Bryant.

"Dunno," he said, shrugging. "Other District, perhaps."

Bryant barely believed his eyes, his ears, even less. This was a nightmare, surely? He thanked the man as he departed. Bryant stood there in disbelief, wondering where his friend was. Some more people appeared, and he realised he'd been foolish. After the TV ceremony, he'd be a recognisable face. He threw his hood up, shoved his hand in pockets, hunched over, and started back towards his house.

Arriving home, he hung up his coat. There was a chill in the air, and the forecast was for snow. Since he'd been back, no one had tried to kill him, he'd not had to taser anyone, and he hadn't been threatened. Life almost felt normal. He was torn straight down the middle; he wanted to discover the truth, the dark underbelly of the world. Then he wanted to show it to the people, but he felt burdened. He hadn't asked for this. As much as he cared, one side of him just wanted to eat, drink, play, and be around those he loved. He had been nineteen for just a matter of months. He wasn't yet out of his teens, and suddenly he had the weight of the world bearing down on his shoulders.

Unification day approached slowly. It was Thursday the 22nd of December. Jules was out with a friend for the night. His mum would be home late. For the first time in a long time, Bryant found himself with nothing to do. He was bored. Sat on the sofa, clutching the book his mother gave him; it had greater significance now that he knew his father was involved with the Uprising. It was an ancient history book, and the truth was he'd never really read any of it. History bored him. But since there was nothing to do when you're locked in a vacancy, Bryant decided he would give it a read.

He opened the first page of Chapter 1: The 22nd century, 'Yawn,' he thought to himself. That was so long ago. He skipped forward to the 23rd century. He settled down on the sofa and started to read.

Reading and absorbing knowledge was hungry work. He glanced up from his book towards the kitchen. Knowing what he knew had put him off 'Planet Rings.' With his book in hand still, he awkwardly shuffled his position on the sofa to slide his phone from his pocket without moving. Finally, he got it, the screen illuminated, no messages. Typing with one hand was difficult, so he opted for voice recognition.

"Dial Planet Pizza," he commanded.

"Dialling Janet Rita!" came the automated response.

"No, no, no!" Bryant said out loud.

Janet Rita was an old friend of his mothers, a lovely lady, but she would talk his ear off. Panicked, he set the book down and cancelled the call. Abandoning the voice dial, using the keypad, he dialled the number he knew so well.

By the time the pizza arrived, he was famished. The smell of the pepperoni pizza filled the room, permeating his nostrils. Without so much as a second glance, he grabbed a slice from the box, sat back down to his book, turning page after page intently. He was fascinated. There was much he didn't know about the beginning of the last century, so much he hadn't heard about before. He digested chapter after chapter. Everything he read made so much sense, connected the dots. That was until he got to about halfway through the century. He was reading about a period in time of more than a hundred years ago. The section was about the last great military commanders, in particular about 'General Steele.' The man who would become the founder of the Space Academy! It made no sense. It must be an ancestor, a relative, surely? He scrolled furiously through the pages to the end, but the book barely got past the first years of the current century. It was as though it just stopped abruptly. He looked at the back cover. The book had been published in 2336, so why did it go no further.

Confused but having eaten eight slices of pepperoni pizza far too fast, he found himself parched. Bryant rolled off the couch and into the kitchen to search for something to drink. He opened the fridge and saw the golden glow of the lagers staring back at him. He grabbed the nearest one, twisted off the cap, throwing a large gulp down his throat. He wandered back into the living room, leaving greasy handprints everywhere he went. He got two steps into the lounge when he saw it. With the pizza gone, hidden amongst the grease, the inside of the box carried a message, it read:

"The old docks, tomorrow, noon sharp, come alone!"

Bryant smiled at the irony of the words. Going 'alone' was the only choice he had.

Bryant returned to the kitchen once more. He took a bunch of beers from the fridge to save himself getting up again, returned to the sofa, and sprawled out. He set the TV to some mindless soap drama and let his mind drift away.

Contact.

Painfully awake, Bryant opened his eyes. It had been a dreamless sleep last night. Sitting up, he surveyed his surroundings. He was on the sofa still, with a blanket delicately tucked around him. On the table, he saw a note:

'Didn't want to wake you. Have a lovely day, sweetie. Xoxo Mum.
    P.S. Please clean up the greasy handprints you've left all over the kitchen.
    P.P.S. Don't forget to recycle the beer bottles.'

He liked that she'd signed it 'Mum' in case he wasn't sure who wrote it. Still, she had come and gone, and he'd slept through all of it. He stood gingerly. His head was fuzzy, his throat dry. He looked across at his phone. It was 0945, "Phew," he guessed that the Uprising weren't people you kept waiting. Bryant stood, took a large stretch before hauling himself up the stairs for a shower.

Sitting in the back of a taxi, he felt much better. His initial plan was to use his e-board, but even the thought of all that movement made him feel sick. The combination of the shower, coffee, and toast had made him feel better quickly. He still didn't understand the fuss behind hangovers. He took the first taxi to the District centre, from there, a second that was almost back to his. He walked a while before finding another taxi rank, making one last journey. Having left the last cab, he waited about for a bit to check for anything suspicious. Nothing, he set off on the walk to the old docks; he was short of time now, but it was better to be safe. He couldn't afford to lead anyone straight to them.

Despite his casual nature, Bryant forced himself to jog the last quarter mile. He approached the old docks with six minutes to spare. Upon arrival, he stopped, looked around, and saw no one. He propped himself casually against a wall and waited.

These docks had once been a great hub. Import and export had been a vast industry. Such was the world's fascination with consumerism. Now it was a creepy, abandoned area filled with creaky clunking cranes, corroded containers, and withering warehouses. He had never been here before in his life. He now knew why.

A creature scuttled near his feet, causing him to jump. Looking down, it was just a rodent, but this seemed different, robotic even. It persisted near his toes, bumping into him a few times before it zoomed off towards an empty warehouse. Relieved that it wasn't a real rat but fearful of what might come next. He set off anxiously after it. The robot rat stopped near a grate on the floor. It beeped at him a few times before disappearing back into the docks. Bryant took a deep breath, reminiscent of what happened last time he ascended down a drain. He gathered his courage and began his descent.

Unification.

Unification day was all but upon them. The cinema had kept Pam tremendously busy this year. In the past, she would close the place for at least a week, allowing everyone time with their family. This year was chaos. The Authorities had introduced mandatory showings for teenagers, forcing them into the cinema to watch brainwashing videos about their duties and obligations. The extra films required Pam and her staff to work right until the end of the 24th. She could feel the hatred in the eyes of those around her when she ordered them about, she was just the messenger, but they despised her for it.

At precisely five-thirty, Pam closed the grand, old doors to the cinema. She was underprepared for the days to come. Unification day had always meant a lot to her, and she was disappointed not to be ready. The District had many conveniently placed stores throughout it. The one nearest to her house also was one of the biggest, which meant it would heave with people last-minute shopping.

Having fought her way through the gathered masses, ashamed at having to be one of the many who had to fight for what was still available on the eve of Unification day. Pam waited for what seemed years for a taxi to arrive. There was real demand, meaning she had to settle for a surly gentleman who was equally unimpressed at having to work. She bustled her way into it with her bags, the morose driver offering little in the form of conversation until the car pulled up outside her house.

"That will be forty credits," he said.

"Forty?" Pam said, shocked. "It's never been forty."

"It's unification tomorrow! That's the rate," said the driver unapologetically.

Pam pulled her phone and tapped it on the reader. She gathered her belongings and climbed from the vehicle.

"That's been declined," said the driver.

"What," replied Pam, horrified, "can you try it again?"

"I can try it a thousand times," said cabbie angrily. "And it will be declined every time. They don't make mistakes."

Pam's rage turned apologetic. Failing to pay for a service was a criminal offence.

"I'm sorry," she said, "just let me go inside, and I'll get my son to pay."

The drive gave her a suspicious look, "You've got five minutes before I call this in."

"No, don't, please," she begged. "I'll be right back, I promise."

Pam shot out of the taxi and into the house, bustling through the door yelling, "Bryant," as she entered.

Mia stood as Pam entered the house, "Hi," she beamed, jumping from the sofa. "You must be Mrs Fisher. It's lovely to meet you."

"Hi," said Pam awkwardly, "it's Mia, isn't it? I've heard so much about you."

Mia stood back from her, nodding as she did so. Sensing something amiss, she asked, "Is everything okay, Mrs Fisher?"

"Yes, I'll be fine," said the flustered Pam. "Is Bryant about?"

Her eyes scanned the room. Mia was alone.

"No," answered Mia, "you just missed him. We didn't think you'd be back yet. He took Julie out on his e-board. What a character she is."

"Yes, yes," said Pam in desperation, "Mia, I'm sorry to put this on you. But I need your help."

Mia paid the driver forty credits, plus the extra five for the inconvenience. Wishing him a "Happy unification" before joining Pam back in the house.

"I'm so sorry to force that on you," said Pam, mortified as Mia joined her in the kitchen.

"It's fine, Mrs Fisher," said Mia. "It was only forty-five credits."

"I'll pay you back, don't worry," said Pam.

"Honestly, Mrs Fisher, you were kind enough to welcome me to your home for unification. It's the least I can do."

"Okay, fine," she said, "but at least call me Pam."

They looked at each other and smiled, "So," said Pam, recovering her pride, "tell me about yourself. What District are you from?"

Unification day itself was everything Bryant had never fantasised about; it had almost been perfect. He figured that if his friend had been in attendance, then it might just have been. It had been a day to remember, one he didn't want to end. But as much as he tried to hold on to it, Unification day slipped through his grasp. Pam was now back to work, Julie back to school, leaving Bryant and Mia alone in the house. It was the first moment they had alone together in aeons, so they made the most of it.

As they lay together on his bed, bodies entwined, starring up at the fake stars on his ceiling. Mia broke the silence as she spoke.

"I wish we could spend every day like this," she said.

Bryant pulled her in closer, "Me too."

"Bryant," said Mia now that they were alone, "what happened the other day?"

"Not a lot, I'm afraid."

"Did you meet them?"

"I suppose," he shrugged. "It was very dark. I think there were three, maybe four of them."

"Did you get any names, see any faces?" Mia asked.

"No, sadly," he replied. "They told me some more about my father. About what he meant to them, what he was planning. Not much else. They seem very cautious. They were very interested in some books."

"Books," she laughed. "What are we going to do with books, bore people to death?"

He looked at her seriously now, "I think there's something in it."

Mia sat up, suddenly more interested. "Go on," she said.

"Well, I have one book," said Bryant. "It's a history book. I thought it might have been a mistake at first, but the book says Commander Steele founded the Academy in the 23rd century."

"That's impossible," Mia replied. "Surely it's a fake or a joke?"

"I thought so too," said Bryant. "But it's a government-issued book. They were the ones in charge before the Authorities. It wouldn't make sense for them to lie."

"But, if it's true," said Mia, "Steele would have to be nearly two hundred years old. That's ridiculous."

"I know," he muttered.

"Then maybe a descendant, grandson perhaps?"

"I've looked," he said, "according to the public records, Steele's father was a miner. He had no siblings. What's also strange is that there is no mention of Rosario or anything about light speed engines."

"And you have this book?" she asked earnestly.

"Yes," he replied.

Mia rose from the bed and stood, gathering her clothes. He studied her for a moment, admiring her naked figure. She noticed his glare and playfully threw a sock at him.

"Creep," she joked.

"Just admiring," he replied.

Pulling on her trousers and changing the subject as she did, Mia spoke, "So, when do we meet them again?"

Old friends.

Bryant still had a few more days of leave before he had to return to the Academy. The euphoria of the last few days, the company he had enjoyed, the thrill and fear of meeting the Uprising, and the words "I love you" all bounced about inside his head. He had felt on top of the world. But being alone, accompanied by the impending return to reality, had sent him crashing back down.

There were so many questions, so few answers with only one place for a time like this; he took a trip to the old stadium.

Lying on his back, staring up at the sky. He closed his eyes and basked in the winter sun's glow. As he drifted off into a daydream, he heard a noise. Sitting up, he scanned the area in search of the source.

"Bryant," came the voice, "Bryant."

"Who's there?" Bryant called out. It took him a second, but it was a voice he would recognise anywhere.

"Jimmy?" he exclaimed as he stood.

"Bryant," Jimmy called back excitedly, "I hoped I'd find you here."

The two friends jogged towards each other, finding the other's arms, sharing the warmest of embraces.

"It's you, it's really you," Bryant said as he held him. "I've been so worried."

"I've been coming here every day since I've been back," replied Jimmy. "I knew I'd find you, eventually. It was meant to be."

"Oh, I'm sorry, buddy," Bryant spoke. "I couldn't find you. I thought they'd moved you to another District."

"They might have," said Jimmy, "but they still want us to mine."

"But your house?" said Bryant.

"This is going to sound crazy, Bryant," Jimmy said, lowering his voice to a whisper. "That wasn't done by the people, Bry. I think it was organised."

Bryant nodded.

"It wasn't there when they moved us," Jimmy spoke, pulling Bryant into him as he did. "Dad thinks they did it themselves, try to make out the public did it. But they didn't."

Jimmy looked at Bryant, "You don't seem shocked by that," he said.

"It's not the craziest thing I've heard recently," Bryant replied.

"What do you mean?" Jimmy asked.

"For now, the less you know, the better Jim."

Jimmy nodded, confused. He went to speak but then thought better of it.

"How's your dad," asked Bryant, "he must hate me?"

"He was angry at first," said Jimmy. "I mean, you did taser him. I tried to tell you, Bry, he was trying to help you out."

"Is he still mad?" Bryant asked anxiously.

"Nah, not really. Not anymore, the new house is better. It's further up the District. Closer to the sea," said Jimmy. "He's convinced there's some conspiracy. The guy with the wrench was a late addition to our crew. We'd never seen him before that day."

Bryant went to speak as he considered his options. "Do you trust me, Jimmy?" he asked.

"Always, Bry."

"You're right. A lot is going on that you don't know about, but it's very dangerous."

"What do you mean?" Jimmy asked, alarmed.

"Just trust me," said Bryant, "the more you know. The more danger it puts you in. I'm working on a plan, and when it happens, it will blow a hole right through the world. Everything will change, Jim. Everything will be better, I promise."

Jimmy nodded confused, "Okay," he said.

"Promise me," Bryant said, "Promise you'll stay out of it?" He took his friend by the face and looked him straight in the eye, "I've got this."

Bryant wished he could confide in Jimmy. Not doing so hurt so much, especially after everything they had been through, but he couldn't risk telling him the truth just yet. Especially as he wasn't sure what the truth was himself.

Laying side by side on the field, they talked the sun into submission. As it set, the cold settled in, snow began trickling from the sky, and the field was soon dusted with a light covering. The two of them moved towards the shelter of the tattered old bleachers. They sat and watched the snow lay thicker and faster. As it settled, the boy's eyes met, both thinking the same thing.

   They chased each other out onto the field, the footsteps disturbing the freshly laid snow like the first steps on a new planet. Forging their way out into the middle, they collapsed on the floor, making angels. Bryant's movement sent a drift of snow cascading over Jimmy, and he laughed, "Hey," said Jimmy, who stood. He shovelled some snow up in his arms and threw it over Bryant, who was on the floor still. Bryant let out a "Yelp," in shock at the cold. Pulling himself from the floor, he balled a sizeable chunk of snow, throwing it at Jimmy. Hitting him square in the chin.

   "That's it," said Jimmy menacingly as he dusted the snow from his face. He bent and picked up as much snow as he could physically manage.

   "This is going down your back," he said, moving towards Bryant.

   Bryant snorted, "You'll have to catch me first." He bolted off, shrieking as he ran.

   The pair chased each other around the field until Jimmy finally caught up with Bryant, and they met in a snowy collision. The light was fading fast as they collapsed to the floor in a heap. The two lay on the floor once more, giggling furiously.

   "Brrr," said Bryant as the snow seeped through his coat.

   "I know, right," said Jimmy, "I'm bloody freezing." They stood and dusted themselves down.

   "Pizza?" Bryant said hopefully.

   "Love to, can't," said Jimmy. "I have to get home. We have a curfew after the incident."

Bryant nodded ruefully. How had it come to this?

"When are you back to the Academy?" Jimmy asked.

A knot formed in Bryant's stomach at the thought.

"Tomorrow," he said glumly.

"I'll swap you," Jimmy said. "We start a two-week rotation tomorrow. We still have to take this Authority guy with us. He follows us about like an unpleasant smell. I mean, he's made a shit job even shitter."

"That good, huh?" Bryant said, patting his friend on the shoulder.

Bryant conceded on paper he had the better deal, but he'd gladly swap places given what he was up against.

They hugged as though they may never see each other again. As they released, Bryant grabbed Jimmy by the shoulders, looking him dead in the eye as he said.

"Remember, don't do anything stupid."

Jimmy nodded.

"I'll see you soon, Jim," Bryant said.

He then watched on as his best friend trudged off into the snowy night. Seeing Jimmy had always been a formality. But as he watched him leave, it occurred to him. It could be months before they saw each other again, if at all.

Helping hands.

Returning to the Academy had been especially difficult! Leaving behind a real-life to return to one that probably wasn't had been tough on his soul. It is one thing to discover a new or shocking reality. It is another one entirely to digest it. Take it on board, but all the while acting as though everything is fine, normal. He'd been forced to question everything he knew about his father, space, the Academy, even the Authorities. Having to make small talk around a mess table, learn about different engines, practice space launches, and zero gravity walks, all while remaining numb inside but positive on the out, was a thankless task.

The curious thing with the Academy was that there always seemed to be a scheduled space launch. But the closer the date got, the further away it appeared to be. There was always a reason, inclement weather, a shortage of Orbitium, and then presumably, if they ran out of reasons, it would be sabotage. The perpetrators would be found quickly and their punishment swift. The public would be outraged and then rejoiced, and the cycle would continue. Occasionally there would be news, talk of a successful launch. But it would always be recent history. History being something he had never thought to question until now.

The next few months flew by uneventfully. Bryant's heightened sense of suspicion diminished somewhat, and he enjoyed things once more. As ever, though, he missed Mia. They exchanged secret notes and found different hiding places to spend time together. But it grew more and more tiresome. He sometimes wondered why they shouldn't just drop the pretence, but he knew they were both safer this way. Plus, if they did, they would have to go through the dreaded Academy relationship protocols.

It was now February, and the evenings were getting lighter. He'd been home a few times. His mum worked harder than ever, and his sister seemed to change bit by bit every time he saw her. He'd not seen Jimmy since their snowy encounter, and he'd heard nothing from the Uprising. Much of it sat in the back of his mind as a hazy dream. He sometimes found himself hoping that was all it ever was.

He had more pressing issues at hand today, though; he needed some new uniform. All the training had seen his body fill out significantly. The uniform he was issued was now far too tight. As great as his connection was with Phil, the quartermaster, he searched for a missing vest. Returning without out would not be a good idea. Finding it, at last, he bundled it up with the rest of his items and strolled towards the storeroom.

His relationship with Phil had been a real plus point at the Academy. He'd devoted many of his evenings to helping the old man out about the storeroom, and he knew the place intimately. Phil would often offer him an alcoholic drink, something not generally permitted on camp. They would drink and talk after hours. It was refreshingly real in a place of lies and something he looked forward to with fondness.

As he arrived at the stores, it started to rain. He carried his unwanted uniform awkwardly bundled in his arms. It had seemed like an intelligent plan until he arrived. The rain was falling faster now, and it was making muddy puddles with the remnants of some dirty snow on the floor. He looked around him. There was nowhere to set his clothes down without getting them either dirty or wet. Not wanting to hand back wet, muddy clothes to Phil, he backed into the door to open it. The door was typically heavy and refused to budge. Taking a small backwards run-up, he set about trying the door again. But as he approached the door backwards, ready to force it open, someone on the opposite side opened it inwards. Unable to stop his momentum, he went sailing through the open door, clothes in hand still, unable to see. Powerless to stop himself bundling into the person who opened it.

Falling back, the two of them crashing to the floor. A tangled mess of bodies and clothes.

"Oh my gosh, I'm so sorry," said Bryant. Desperately hoping he hadn't flattened a superior.

Bryant fought his way to his feet. As he moved the clothes from his view, a familiar scent met his nostrils. As he extended his arm to aid his victim, he instantly knew who it was.

He pulled Mia to her feet. She was still reeling from the unexpected attack, but as she stood, their eyes met.

"Corporal Evans," he said. "Sorry I didn't see you there."

In his excitement to see her, Bryant almost forgot where he was.

She looked back at him, grinning slightly.

"No, it's fine, Corporal Fisher. Everyone enters buildings backwards."

Bryant smirked back at her, and the two stood there for a moment, locked in the other's stare.

"Well, I'd better be going," she said.

"Yes, yes, of course," Bryant replied.

He pushed the door open for her to leave, watching on longingly as she departed.

Stooping to retrieve his belongings, he stood and moved towards the counter. His attention now back in the room, he noticed Phil stood at the desk. His eyes were wide, and his face beamed with a grin.

"Well, that's the cat out of the bag," Phil said.

"How long have you been stood there?" Bryant asked.

"Long enough to know who the mysterious lady is," Phil smirked.

"What, no!" Bryant bumbled.

"Oh, come on," Phil quipped. "I saw the way you looked at her."

"No, it's not what.."- Bryant started.

"Hey," said Phil, putting his hands in the air. "No need to justify yourself to me. I get it. I know how complicated Academy relationships can be."

Bryant grinned bashfully. It was a relief to unburden his mind, even if only a little.

"You know what, actually," said Phil. "There might be a way we can help each other out."

Bryant was intrigued, "But don't you care?"

"Pfft," replied Phil, "like it matters to me what two people do in their free time."

"So, you won't tell anyone?" Bryant asked hopefully.

"I can go one better than that," replied Phil. "I have an old stock room. Full of returned uniform. Needs a good sort out."

Bryant nodded, listening intently.

"The problem is, it's in an old part of the camp, very dark and lonely down there. Few people pass by. There are tonnes of returns there, and it needs a good organise. I'd say it's a two-person job if you know anyone that might be interested?"

"I might have someone in mind," Bryant said, catching on.

"It's all locked up at the moment, so I'd have to give you the keys. Probably best to keep it locked while you in there, you know, in case anyone wants to steal something."

"Quite," Bryant nodded, "I understand."

"Well then, let me get you the keys," said Phil. He walked towards his office, shouting as he did so, "There are two provisos, though. I do need the stock sorting, and you might have to put up with an old man dropping by now and again."

"Not a problem," said Bryant excitedly. "When do you need it done by?"

"Well, I mean, it's a big job," said Phil. "Probably take you months. Maybe longer." Bryant grinned as he heard Phil rummaging about his office before returning with an old set of keys, setting them down on the counter in front of Bryant.

"Now," said the quartermaster, "what can I do for you? From the looks of you, I'd say bigger shirts are the first order of the day."

The insider.

Having the keys to the old storeroom was a dream come true. A weird twisted dream, but a dream, nonetheless. It meant they had somewhere to go, someplace far from the madding crowd. They could do whatever they wanted down there, and the times they had spent had been bliss. The more time they spent together, the more he yearned for this kind of normality. He hadn't realised that normal could be so exciting. His head lived in the stars as he grew up. He'd never longed for this world or ordinary life, yet now he couldn't stop thinking about how great it would be.

Bryant frequented the place even if he was alone. He would sort through the old gear and spend some time unaccompanied with his head. The selfish side of him no longer cared for the truth, for the Uprising, or whatever was going on at the Academy. He would happily leave today, give it up all for an ordinary life with Mia, his family, friends. He thought if it were at all possible, he would probably take that pill. Wake up free of burden and just live a carefree, love-filled life. It was when he went home that reality bit back at him. The District changed bit by bit. Independent shops disappeared overnight. The older he got, the more people he knew from school would be reported dead from the mines. He rarely saw his mum even when he was home, and his sister grew more troublesome. She was starved of guidance or attention.

People had no money, worked just to survive. Or, in the miner's case, not at all. Back in the actual world, he would realise then that things had to change. The euphoria he felt during unification was a one-off, short-lived. The bubble burst fast as soon as those days ended. He'd found himself at home, alone. At face value, it was all the same but completely different at the same time. Watching his friend carted off to sea with a master in toe, risking his life to line the pockets of others. His mother work all day for a place that was no longer her own, and his sister so full of wonder still. She had just six more years, and then she would be off to work like everyone else. It was during these thoughts he remembered what he was fighting for; it was tough.

The old stores had two large rooms at either end of a long corridor. Bryant worked away, neatly sorting old uniforms. Alone in his thoughts, he heard a noise from the other room. It was too early to be Mia, and Phil would make his presence known upon entry. Dropping the tunic in his hand, he went in search of the sound.

"Mia?" he called out inquisitively.

Getting no response, Bryant continued down the corridor, entering the room at the end. It was dark and eerie. Having no voice activation, he slid his hand blindly along the wall in search of the switch.

"Please don't do that." A voice emerged from the darkness.

Bryant stopped dead in his tracks, his eyes squinting hard against the dark. He didn't recognise the voice. Who could it be?

As his eyes adjusted, he saw a figure sat alone in a chair in the corner. One leg casually resting on the other. The moonlight peeked through the window and partially illuminated the area in front of him. The man's face was shrouded in shadows, and Bryant couldn't help but think what a beautiful picture it painted.

"Can I help you?" Bryant asked nervously.

Through the shadows, he could see highly polished shoes leading up to trousers with precision creases. He didn't need to see any more to know that this was an Academy officer. What did this man want, who could it be?

The man stood from the chair and started towards Bryant. He crossed into the light for just long enough for Bryant to catch a glimpse of his face. Bryant's head scrambled as he realised who it was. He recognised the man as the officer who shouted at him on his first day.

Unwavering, Bryant stood tall as the man approached him. "How did you know I'd be here?" asked Bryant.

"I know many things, Bryant," said the man. "I know you probably think you're in some kind of trouble. You're probably wondering how long you have until Mia arrives, and you're probably trying to work out what I want."

Bryant nodded. The man had just listed his foremost thoughts.

"I also know about the Uprising Bryant."

Bryant's heart pounded, sweating. He panicked, before realising this man was here alone, in the dark. He must have his own angle.

"And what makes you think that?" Bryant asked.

"I don't think it," said the man, "I Know." He approached fast now. Bryant took a few steps back, only to find himself pressed up against the wall.

With the man inches from him, Bryant shut his eyes and braced for what was to come. Suddenly he felt warm, comforted. Cautiously, he opened his eyes. Bryant glanced down and couldn't believe his senses. The officer had his arms wrapped about him. His head rested on Bryant's shoulder. He wasn't being attacked; he was being hugged.

"Did you think I wouldn't recognise the son of my best friend?"

Still wrapped in the hug, he continued, "You're the spitting image of him, you know that?"

Bryan's head was in a spin, "You knew my father?"

"Oh, Bryant," he said, "your father meant everything to me. I wouldn't be the man I am today without him."

Removing himself from the hug, the man stepped back into the shadows. There were a table and two chairs. Pulling out the chairs, he said, "Come on, sit, we haven't much time."

Bryant joined him at the table, wearing a look of shock and confusion still.

"You don't have a clue, do you?" The man said, astounded.

Bryant shook his head, the look on his face confirming as much.

"Then we have much to discuss."

Bryant sat, listened, and watched on, his mouth agape as the man who introduced himself as Major Michael Stein explained everything.

"So, my father?" Bryant started trying to comprehend.

"Yes, Bryant, your father was the man who started the rebellion. He had a lot of secrets. Even I'm not entirely sure how he knew what he did. I know that he found out that the Orbitium wasn't being used for the space programme. He discovered that someone had been tinkering with history, tailoring it to suit the narrative. He worked hard in the shadows, convinced others, including me, to join him. He was a light in the dark, Bryant. Hope when we needed it most. He was working on something huge, and we were all so excited. But then, one night, he didn't show up. We looked, we waited, we hoped. But he never returned Bryant. Our cause suffered a tremendous blow the day your father disappeared."

"But, if he knew all of this, why didn't he expose the truth? Why didn't you," asked Bryant, "if everyone knew the reality, there would surely be a huge uprising?"

"Because Bryant, the sad fact is people won't take the raw truth. Without being able to show the world, putting this information out there would do nothing. Some people might believe it, sure. But then you've got the others who wouldn't see the truth, even if they walked by it every day. Too many people are only interested in their own lives, and worst of all, some go with the flow. You also have to consider that people will think you've gone mad. Conspiracies are for lunatics, Bryant. Without serious proof, whatever happens, whatever is said, they will do it.

"Your father thought we needed more free minds; the more people who were on board, the better. He did a good job, showing people the truth, one by one, recruiting as many people into it as possible until he had an army. He wanted facts, undeniable proof. Then, using those who were already free, he wanted to show it to the world. It needed to be synchronised. It needed to happen everywhere, all at once.

There was no room for error. He didn't want drips of truth being handed out; anything small would be squashed or ridiculed before it had any impact. It had to be that way, give them no time to respond. All or nothing, Bryant. That's what your father started, and it's what you'll finish."

Bryant nodded. This was so much to take in, "Why me," he asked, "why now?"

"Bryant, the day you arrived, the moment you walked out of headquarters, I couldn't believe my eyes. The prodigal son, here in the Academy. It's no coincidence our paths crossed, Bryant, don't you see? It's a sign."

"But what can I do," Bryant asked glumly, "I'm not my father."

"No," said Stein. "But you are his son! Bryant, when we lost your father, the Uprising floundered. We tried to carry on, but we lost hope. Your father's army is still there, just waiting to be inspired. I had no idea you even existed until a few months ago, Bryant. Neither did the rest of them."

"How is that possible?" Bryant asked.

"The Uprising is close-knit, Bryant. Nobody knows more than they need to. Most members keep their identity and even their lives secret Bryant. It helps limit the damage if one of us is caught. To most of the Uprising, they simply knew your father as 'Snowball.' Very few people knew his actual name. Take me, for example. I don't know any of the others other than by code name. It's an efficient operation your father built."

Bryant put his head in his hands. He was shaking his head in disbelief.

"Word of your existence has already travelled, Bryant. There's hope again."

Stein knelt on the floor in front of him. Their eyes met. Taking him by the hand, Stein spoke once more. "Bryant, this is your destiny."

Bryant nodded. He'd dreamt of many things in his life. Being the son of a revolutionary, with the hopes of a planet weighed down upon him, wasn't one of them.

"Bryant, are you okay?"

Bryant managed another nod, "I think so."

"Bryant," Stein spoke. "I fear I have been here too long." Standing to leave, he put his arm on his shoulder, "You're not alone, Bryant. But promise me something?"

Bryant nodded again.

"You can't tell anyone who I am. No matter who you meet, how involved they are, how much you trust them. You cannot tell a soul."

"What about Mia?" Bryant asked. Keen to share the burden of what he'd just learned.

"Especially not Mia," Stein replied. "They are ruthless, Bryant. They will take the easiest way to truth, no matter the cost. The more you care about someone, the more at risk they are."

"But," Bryant started.

"No, Bryant," Stein spoke with a real seriousness in his voice. "I've been hiding here in plain sight for years, Bryant. I haven't stayed alive all this time by being careless. Keep this a secret."

"I understand," said Bryant, "I promise."

Stein nodded and went to leave. He stopped in his tracks, grabbing Bryant, pulling him in close.

"I loved your father," Stein whispered in his ear.

And just like that, he was gone. Bryant slumped to the floor against the wall. This was so much to absorb. Mia might arrive at any minute. He needed to clear his head; he had to be ready to lie to the one person he wanted to tell the truth to the most.

Underground network.

Mia lay against Bryant as they sat by the river, watching the world pass them by, it had been four days since his meeting with Stein, and it was like she could sense him holding something back. It was a beautiful day, so the pair had taken a trip to town.

It was mid-afternoon, and the sun was already starting to leave. As much as he enjoyed the simplicity of what they were doing, it was starting to get cold.

He lifted his cup and finished the rest of the hot chocolate the vendor had almost forced him to buy. As he removed the cup from his face, something caught his eye. Hidden at the bottom of the container, partially covered by the remnants of hot chocolate. He noticed something. At first, he considered maybe it was a logo. But it was handwritten. There was a message at the bottom of his cup.

Bryant stood, "Come on, let's go," he said to Mia, almost dragging her up from the floor.

"Geez, someone's in a hurry to get dinner," she said as she stood. "I'll eat anything but pizza."

"Just walk with me," Bryant chided. They linked arms as they powered away from the riverbank.

As soon as they were alone, Bryant stopped. Anxiously looking over his shoulder to make sure they weren't followed.

"What's going on, Bryant?" Mia asked. "You're unusually fidgety today."

He held out his hand, thrusting the empty cup upon her.

"Look," he said.

Peering inside, making out the words amidst the remains of hot chocolate, she read,

"The old docks. Blue shipping container, 6 PM sharp."

"What time is it?" he asked.

"About half four, we don't have long."

Bryant nodded. She was right. They would need to hurry across town if they were to make it. Then he shuddered.

"You okay?" Mia asked.

"Just cold," he replied.

Uprising or not, the truth was the knowledge that someone followed them, knew what they were going to do today, knew where they would be to get a message to them was an unsettling thought.

"Do your jacket up then. It has a zip for a reason."

Bryant grinned, zipped up his coat, and said, "Ok, let's do this."

The journey through town had been an arduous one. Bryant hated the monorail. But it was the fastest route from where they were. The heights made him uneasy. His mother often quipped how he would manage space when he was terrified of the monorail. But they were different. Space was another dimension, whereas the monorail was a high-speed train that dangled in the air.

They arrived with just minutes to spare. There were several blue containers, but only one had a raised fist spray-painted on it. They went inside, through another hatch, another tunnel and down into darkness.

Having descended the dark, wet shaft. Bryant and Mia now found themselves face to face with five people. Two of whom they recognised. The man who appeared to lead them introduced himself as 'Alpha,' he was flanked by another man and a woman. He introduced the man as 'Bravo' and the lady as 'Charlie.'

"And you have already met Reginald and Margery," said Alpha. "But please refer to Margery as Delta and Reginald as Echo."

Bryant and Mia nodded simultaneously. They were slightly dumbstruck. Was this is? Were these five people the Uprising? In his head, Bryant had pictured armies of highly trained, heavily armed men and women. Maybe a high-tech lair, lots of equipment. Instead, he now found himself face to face with people that resembled his teachers, shopkeepers, mechanics.

"Is this it?" Bryant asked.

"Yes and no," said Alpha. "I gather from the look on your face this isn't what you were expecting. But let me tell you, this is now the largest collective meeting of the Uprising since we lost your father."

"So, what have you been doing since then?" Bryant asked.

"Honestly, Bryant," said Alpha, "not much. It's true many lost their way, became disillusioned. Between us, we've just been working to keep the fire lit. But I assure you, Bryant, it is there. We just need the spark."

"And you think I'm that spark?" asked Bryant.

"Come, you two. Sit if you will," Alpha continued, "let me tell you a story."

Looking at each other, Bryant and Mia found the least grimy looking patch, and sat ready, listening.

"Bryant," Alpha began, "your father founded this revolution. One by one, he freed all of us, showed us the world for how it is. He used to work for the Authorities behind the scenes, making things happen. They promised him a good life in exchange for the work he did. But the knowledge he had ate away at him. The more he saw, the less he could keep it to himself. The night we lost him, we were on the verge of something huge. When he went, we all feared for our lives. I would go to sleep each night, terrified that they would come for us, but they never did. Whatever they did to him, whatever happened, he never gave them anything Bryant. We were lost, it's true, but now he's given us you. There's hope again, Bryant, and that's what has been missing, hope."

Bryant did his best to look shocked. Stein had told him as much a few days ago. But it was clear even Alpha didn't know about Stein. He didn't know that he'd already told him most of this.

"Is… is he dead?" asked Bryant.

He felt Mia take his hand, squeezing it gently. He could feel her warmth. He was so glad she was here.

Alpha took a step towards Bryant, "We don't know," he said. Putting his hand on Bryant's shoulder. "Probably."

Charlie stepped forward and spoke, "But we know how proud he would be of you," she added.

"Bryant," said Charlie. "I know this is a lot to take in. But we think your father's plan hinges on you. He knew we would find each other. He had an inside man in the Academy. They were working together. They had proof, something tangible we could use. We were getting ready to show the world the truth."

"What is the truth?" Mia asked.

"The truth," said Alpha, "everything we know is probably a lie. Since they moved everything online, we have no idea how many times history has been altered. We are drip-fed information. It's always vague, usually basic, and regularly updated. For all we know, it might not even be 2370."

"That's not an enormous surprise," said Mia. "Governments have manipulated the truth for centuries."

"True," said Charlie, "but what about space? We know that Orbitium isn't rocket fuel. It's a mineral of some sort, but we aren't sure what it does."

"Does that mean we haven't been to space at all?" said Bryant.

"Who knows," replied Alpha, "probably at some point. But it doesn't seem like we're on the cusp of developing Mars."

"What about DeVore," asked Bryant, "where did he fit into this?"

"DeVore was arrogant," said Alpha. "He was impatient, and it got him killed. He was one of us, yes. But he was determined to be the poster boy of the revolution. We warned him. But he didn't listen. We're lucky he didn't cause us more harm."

"So, what now?" queried Bryant. "I have a history book hidden at home. Can we not take that public?"

"One isn't enough, Bryant, sure. It might convince a few people, but we need more than that. Your father had quite the library. No doubt he hid them well. But we don't have a clue where they are." said Alpha.

He continued. "No, what we need is to take away the restraints. Think about it, the lure of space, all the talk of a new life on another planet, I don't think it's coming. It's the system that keeps the people trapped, trusting, hoping. If we can destroy that, then we have a chance."

"Consider this," said Charlie, "who's in charge? Who really knows what's going on? There is a brilliant system in place that keeps everything working. But it has to be working for someone. Look at how much you two get paid compared to everyone else. We are all supposed to be equal. Beyond the Academy, how many others get their pockets lined and do nothing? I'll bet there's many."

"But what about the natural resources? What about the planet?" asked Bryant.

"Who knows," said Beta, "but it could all be part of the illusion. Humanity has been destroying the planet since we arrived. But no one knows what is beyond the Districts. I'll bet that Earth has recovered fairly well since we were all herded into cages, even if it hasn't. I'd rather die free on my feet than live-trapped on my knees."

The thought that Earth may be a perfectly viable place to live had never even crossed Bryant's mind. All he'd ever known was a shortage of space and resources. But what if it were true? What if the masses had been shoved into Districts whilst the elite roamed free? Never bothered, never questioned.

"But why would they do this?" he asked.

"The people who run the world, Bryant," said Charlie. "They have created a loop. One where we all work and toil in vain to give them what they need. A loop that constantly resets and then continues serving them."

Bryant felt sick. He looked at Mia, who was pale. The world they had known was crumbling before their eyes. If this was true, it changed everything.

Bryant stopped the cogs spinning in his head long enough to speak.

"So, what do you need from us?"

"Bryant," spoke Alpha, "we need you to get a sample of Orbitium. Try to find some proof that the space missions have been falsified or that they never actually happened. Locate your father's missing books and finally, track down the inside man."

"So not much then?" Bryant chuckled, only half-joking.

Alpha put his hand on Bryant's shoulder once more, "I'm sorry, I know it's a lot to ask. You do that, get us what we need, and we'll do the rest."

Alpha went to continue, but Bryant cut him off.

"I know who my father's contact is in the Academy."

All exchanged shocked looks as the words rang out, bouncing off the confined walls.

Mia grabbed Bryant's arm, "Wait!" she said. "You do?"

"Sorry," he mumbled, "I'll explain later." He continued, "But I cannot tell anyone who it is."

Alpha nodded understandingly, "See," he said, "there's that hope I've been talking about; we would never have found him if we lived to be a thousand years old."

"What about the books," Charlie demanded, "you said you had one?"

"Hey," said Beta, "we've put enough on his plate already."

"No, it's fine," said Bryant, butting in. "As you said. I have one. If it's as fated as everyone says, I'm sure I'll find the rest."

"Well, alright then," said Charlie.

Margery and Reginald, who had been silent, rose, and Margery spoke.

"We should go now," she said urgently. "It's not good for us all to spend this long together."

"Agreed," said Alpha reasserting control. "This will be the last time we all meet, for now."

Bryant and Mia stood. He motioned towards the ladder, and she started to climb.

"Best not to come back here," Alpha said, grabbing Bryant by the shoulders. "And as always."

"You'll be in touch?" Bryant cut him off cheekily. Shaking hands with Alpha, Bryant made his goodbyes and cursory nods to the others before following Mia back up the ladder and into the fresh air.

They walked silently, briskly, for ten minutes. Putting as much distance between them and the docks before Mia stopped abruptly, grabbing Bryant by the arm.

"Hold up," she said. "I thought we were in this together?"

"Mia. We shouldn't stop here," he said. Walking on.

"Don't you trust me?" she continued. "I'm not going any further until you talk to me, Bryant."

Realising he had no choice, Bryant stopped and walked back to her. Taking her by the hands, he said,

"I trust you more than anyone else on this planet." She sighed and tried to pull her hands away from him.

"Look, I'm sorry. Not being able to tell you this has been the hardest thing I've ever had to do."
She relented slightly as he pulled her in, stroking her hair.

"This guy came to me, a touch of the dramatics, but he made me promise I wouldn't tell anyone who he is. I gave him my word Mia. What am I if my word means nothing?"

"You're right," she said. "That's one of the reasons why I love you."

Tears started to form in her eyes now.

"I guess it's just all overwhelming. I'm miles from home in a strange District. I don't know who is good, who is bad. I don't know what is real anymore. My father was in the Academy Bryant. Can I trust him? I'm scared, Bryant, frightened of what we're up against, I fear what's coming, and I'm terrified of losing you. You're all I have," she said. Letting the tears flow freely from her eyes. He held her tighter now.

"Don't worry," he said. "Trust me. Everything will work out exactly the way it's supposed to. I'll die before I let anything happen to you, and I'm not planning on dying anytime soon."

What goes up?

Given what he knew about the Academy, about Orbitium meant working there made him feel sick. He looked at everyone he encountered with disgust. Did they know, were they all a part of this? It was like he was stuck in some odd reality show. Everyone knowing it to be fake, except him.

It had been a month since they met with Alpha and the others, and he was still no closer to the truth.

He had yet to be cleared for active duty since the incident in hanger six. In another life, it would have been something that angered him. But for now, he was happy not to be in the spotlight. His days comprised of training, running, medicals, and lengthy talks with councillors. The official line was that they wanted to make sure there were no lingering mental health problems after such a traumatic event. But he suspected, in reality, they just wanted to make sure there was nothing wrong with their property. Rangers going off the rails was bad for business.

Not having the shine on him had given Bryant plenty of opportunity for observations. In the last month, there had been five scheduled space missions. Two were cancelled due to bad weather, one due to technical difficulties and another because of staff sickness. The last did launch, only to return early due to mechanical issues, at least that's what the records showed. All launches were televised events, this one included, but if it did launch, it wasn't from the Academy.

Being a ranger did at least make it easier to sneak access to flight plans. If he knew who had been on the aborted flight, then he might be able to work out what, if anything, had happened. Maybe someone would talk to him. Perhaps they could help each other.

Bryant sat down in his new room. Making sure the door was locked, he shut the blinds before he pulled the folded piece of paper that he'd hidden deep inside him. Convincing one of the cleaning bots that he'd left his hat in the control room had been relatively easy. Sneaking into a room he'd only ever seen in movies had been a genuine thrill. The adrenaline boost was sensational, and he was still riding high. The records unsurprisingly existed only on paper. He'd swiftly made a copy before slipping back out.

His eyes scanned the page in front of him. Most of the names meant nothing to him. The Academy was a big place. Tracking one of these people down would be impossible. But just as he was about to screw the paper up, a name jumped off the page, catching his eye. 'John Murphy' was written clear as day. He wondered how on earth Murphy had passed the Ranger course? It might be someone else. But it seemed like too much of a coincidence. Tossing the paper in the bin, he grabbed his cap and set off to find Murphy.

Stood outside Murphy's room, Bryant paused for a moment, composing himself before knocking.

"Come in," came the voice at the sound of his knuckles.

Bryant opened the door gingerly, sticking his head around it as he did so.

"Fisher," came the friendly voice. "To what do I owe this honour?"

"Can I come in?" Bryant asked.

"Sure, why not," said Murphy, "it's been forever. How's your mum, still hot?"

Bryant picked a pen off the desk and chucked it towards Murphy, hitting him in the nose.

"Hey," said Murphy.

Bryant chuckled as Murphy rubbed at his face.

"Guess I deserved that," he said. "So, what's happening?"

Bryant sat, and they talked. As they spoke, it became clear that Murphy was far more intelligent than he let on.

"Yeah," said Murphy, "I figured it would be easier to fit in here if I acted like a bit of a Jackass."

"Well, you did a good job," Bryant joked.

Murphy chuckled, "Always better to have people underestimate than overestimate you, Bryant."

"So, Bryant," Murphy continued, "I'm guessing you didn't come over here just to insult me. What do you really want?"

"Space," said Bryant. "Rumour has it you were on the last launch."

Murphy chuckled, "Yeah, I guess you could say that."

"What do you mean?" Bryant asked. "You went right; how was it?"

"Hazy man," said Murphy, "I've only just started to feel normal again. I mean, I know we train for the g-force, but it's nothing until you experience it. That and the drugs, it's all there, but it feels like a lucid dream."

"What do you remember?" asked Bryant.

"I remember how beautiful the world looked from above, Bryant. I passed out on take-off, I'm afraid, and I was a bit of a mess when we landed. But I'm scheduled for the next one too! I hear you might have been in with a chance had you not tasered a miner."

Bryant nodded. It wasn't quite the revelation he was after.

"Sorry I can't tell you anything else. Maybe I'll remember more the next time."

"What about the others? Maybe I can talk to them?"

"Woah," said Murphy, "someone is keen on a space story."

"I've just always wanted to go, Murphy. I'm desperate to know what it's like. Do you remember who else was with you?"

"Erm," said Murphy, "I think my assignment schedule had a list of names. Let me see if I…"-

Bryant cut him off, "Names are no good, John, tell me about the people, was there anyone you knew, anyone that stood out?"

"Nah, not really," said Murphy.

"Think, please," implored Bryant, "there has to be something."

"Since you mention it, there was one guy. A real a-hole, had a horrible tattoo of a snake on his neck?"

"Cheers, Murphy," said Bryant, kissing him on the head.

"Yeah, anytime."

Bryant stood.

"I gotta go."

Phil.

It seemed whenever something unpleasant happened, any dirty deed. This guy with the tattoo would be right there, always in the thick of it; what was his role? Bryant needed to think, wanted space. So, heading straight to the storeroom. He entered to find himself alone. He paced up and down the long corridor as he contemplated. How was this guy part of everything? Who was he? Who did he work for?

Time vanished as Bryant lost himself in his mind until finally, he heard the familiar click of the door amidst his pacing.

"Mia," he said excitedly, bounding up to her like a dog reunited with its owner.

"Woah," she said. "Someone is excited to see me!"

"Mia," he said, "I think I'm on to something."
The last few letters of his sentence trailed off as he noticed another figure enter the building behind her.

"And I've brought Phil."

"Hey Phil," said Bryant, "I didn't know you'd be joining us tonight."

"I just thought I'd check in on my team," the Quartermaster spoke. "Pay my intrepid workers a visit." He stepped inside, shutting the door behind him. "And," he said, bringing his hands from behind his back. "I brought whiskey. I don't know about anyone else, but I could sure use a drink."

He sat the bottle down on one of the old tables. The impact of it physically threw some dust into the air.

"Well, don't just stand there," he said to Bryant. "We need cups."

With Bryant having retrieved and rinsed three old mugs. Phil poured a glass for each of them and motioned to the other two, who eyed the mugs hesitantly.

"Come on," he said. "It's an eighty-year-old single malt. Don't let an old man drink by himself."

Mia didn't need a third invitation. She grabbed the cup from the table, sending yet more dust flying. Pouring the contents down her neck, "Oh, that's smooth."

The three sat and drank. It was good to enjoy a small dose of normality, better still enjoying a drink.

"Phil, you see a lot of what goes on around here," Bryant started brimming with Dutch courage. "You don't know a guy with a tattoo of a snake on his neck, do you?"

"I might," replied Phil.

"What does he do," asked Bryant, "who is he?"

"Well, Bryant, you can't make an omelette without breaking a few eggs. Institutions such as this don't survive as long as they do without adopting the same principle."

"So, what? He's a spy, internal affairs?" Bryant asked, slightly confused.

"Something like that Bryant, he's someone who does whatever is needed of him," Phil replied.

"And you're ok with this?" asked Bryant. "I mean, he was with the miners. He attacked Grimes."

"Oh Bryant, you ask too many questions, you know that?" said Phil, pouring another round of drinks.

"But he attacked Grimes!"

"Oh Bryant, from what I hear, Grimes had been skimming profits from the deals for years. Him and his crew. But that's beyond your pay grade."

"But, the miners?" Bryant started.

"Some of them got what they deserved, Bryant."

Bryant was in disbelief now. This guy sure didn't seem like one of the good guys.

"But how do you know all this?" Mia asked.

"I'm the Quartermaster. As you said, there is very little that gets by me. Now, if you'll excuse me," Phil said as he stood. "This old man needs to use the bathroom."

Phil made his way down the old hallway to the toilet, closing the door behind him. With the door safely closed, Mia turned to Bryant and spoke.

"What are you doing?" she quizzed. "You do ask too many questions."

"It's Phil," said Bryant, "we can trust him."

Mia conceded, Phil didn't care much for what went on.

"Anyway," said Bryant, "I don't buy it. I think there's more to this than Phil knows."

"What do you mean?" Mia asked.

"The guy with the snake tattoo," Bryant said, "you remember him, right?"

Mia shuddered, recalling the sickening thud made by the wrench.

"Well, he was on a space mission last week. Or at least that's what we're supposed to think."

"So, what does it mean, should we find him?" Mia asked.

"I don't imagine he's the sort of guy you find that easily," said Bryant. "It doesn't matter. If he's involved, you can be sure there is something dodgy going on."

"Euch, this all seems impossible Bryant, I mean, what do we do now, what do we even know?"

"We know what we need to do, Mia," Bryant reassured her. "We just need to have faith. Everything will happen the way it's supposed to."

His story.

It was now April, and the evenings continued late on into the day. It hadn't stopped there being a heavy snowfall recently. But the warming sun coupled with the long days had quickly laid waste to most of the lingering remains. Stood alone at the stadium. Bryant watched the sun setting over the field and the dirty remains of the snow casually lying in the extremities. Admiring the beauty in the world as he watched on. Jimmy would be here today, he hoped. He was sure of it. He had come here for the last six weekends on the bounce, with no luck. Surely today would be the day. It was cold for April, so he moved from the open field and took shelter in the old stands. Many of the seats were missing, broken, or rusted. But some parts still had old-fashioned, very uncomfortable looking chairs that folded down to let the spectators sit and cheer their favourite team on in cold agony. "What an odd way to enjoy yourself," he thought. Walking along the bleachers, he approached the first pew that still looked operational. Looking down at it, he noted the seat number '1984'. He attempted to move it to sit, but the hinges were rusted in place. Several failed attempts later, he acknowledged that there were, in fact, other seats. So he moved on. He had to move across to the next section to find a place that didn't look like it would crumble under his weight. Finally, this one looked good, seat '2100'. As he pulled it, a noise akin to a demonic wail escaped from its hinges. He sat, threw up his hood, rubbed his hands together before thrusting them into his pockets. In his seat, he imagined himself waiting for his favourite team to take the field.

The seat he had chosen was even more wretched than it looked. Unable to bear this amount of discomfort, he stood up. He considered that even the floor would be a better option. But as he stood, the seat attempted to fold itself back into place, but it struggled almost as though it was too heavy for its design. Bryant walked away from it rubbing his back. But something made him look again, and it was then he saw it. From this angle, the padding on the seat looked out of shape. It was curious, and something didn't add up.

Returning to the torture chair, he bent, dropping to his knees alongside it. As he studied it, he realised that was something inside this seat. It made sense, given how uncomfortable it was. Looking over his shoulder to make sure no one was watching. He removed his pocket knife and made a small incision in the fabric.

The stadium had been classified as a heritage site many years ago. But unlike some buildings, that remained to be celebrated. Ones like this were supposed to rot and die. They were lingering as a reminder of the greed, the capitalistic ways that created this situation. Overpaid men and women would arrive here and put on a show, a display of gluttony and corruption. Its withering corpse was to serve as a reminder of what was.

Bryant was careful not to put a big hole in the seat. Damaging any property, even ones condemned to rot, was an offence. With a cut just big enough for his hand, Bryant reluctantly stuck his arm in, desperately hoping he wouldn't find rotten foam, rusty springs or worse. Wriggling his hand inside, he soon discovered what he was after. It was a solid oblong object that had been vacuum wrapped. He pulled it out slowly, "Clever Dad," he thought to himself. What he had in his hand was another book, a concise history of the 2100s, the date correlating with the seat number. His father had created an alfresco library. It was the perfect place. Few people came here other than him. It wouldn't be destroyed, and it would be years before it rotted away completely. Darting around the old seats like a field mouse, he patted down the surrounding seats. He scuttled up a few rows and found seat number '2000', another slight cut and, sure enough, another book. He repeated the trick for '1900', gathering all three books together. There were countless tomes hidden here. His curiosity wanted to rip them all from their hiding places, sit and just absorb the knowledge. But he knew better. There was no sense removing more than he needed to just yet.

Jimmy arrived at the stadium to the sight of his friend doing star jumps in the field's corner.

"Am I late for try-outs?" Jimmy asked.

"I'm cold, Jim," said Bryant

"It's April! You baby," Jimmy joked. "Try waiting here all day in the snow."

"Yeah, but you're a miner. You should be used to the cold."

Jimmy chuckled, grabbing his friend for a hug, "Where do you think we mine, Bryant?"

"Oh, who cares," said Bryant. "It's good to see you. You lump."

"So, you still remember me now that you have your fancy Academy friends?" Jimmy joked.

The pair laughed, and Bryant changed the subject, jumping up and down still as he spoke.

"Hey Jim, did you know they didn't invent the first mobile phone until 1973?"

"Cheers Bry, I was literally just wondering when that was on my way over?"

"Were you?" Bryant asked innocently.

"No, you goon," Jimmy said, punching him playfully on the shoulder. "Why would I care about old irrelevant boring facts? Why would anyone? It's history, Bry, just that history."

Bryant stopped his jumping, looking his friend in the eye.

"But do you not think it's a little interesting?" Bryant asked.

"I guess," replied Jimmy. "I suppose that was only a few hundred years ago. How did people stay in touch, pay for things?"

"I dunno," said Bryant, "apparently all phones used to have a massive wire attached to them."

Jimmy laughed, "What was the point in that?"

"Wanna know something else interesting?" Bryant asked.

"Not really," replied Jimmy. "But I sense you're going to tell me, anyway."

"So, they had no available mobile technology. But get this right, the first space flight was a decade before they had mobile phones."

"That's weird," said Jimmy. "The people couldn't communicate when they were out. But they could go to space."

"Yeah," chuckled Bryant, "do you reckon the spaceship was on a really long wire?"

They both laughed.

"So, where did you get all these random facts from?" Jimmy asked.

"Come with me," Bryant said excitedly, "I'll show you."

"So, let me get this straight," said Jimmy, having been regaled with yet more history. "You want me to take these books down a mine and hide them?"

"Just the three of them," said Bryant.

"Have you gone mental?"

"Please," begged Bryant, "it's more important than you know."

"But they are so big and heavy, Bryant! They'll literally fill one of my bags. What will I tell everyone? Oh, I'm just bringing a sack of bricks down the mine with me?"

"You trust me, right?"

"Always," replied Jimmy.

"Then please just do it," said Bryant. "It will all make sense, eventually. I promise you. You're..."-

"Yeah yeah," Jimmy cut him off, "I'm better off not knowing!"

The two talked long past the setting sun. It was refreshing like old times. Finally, as it got dark, Jimmy stood and motioned to leave.

"Better get going," he said, "got a bag of bricks to hide."

Bryant laughed. "Don't tell..."-

"Yeah, yeah, don't tell anyone," Jimmy cut him off, "pain of death yadar yadar."

The smile dropped from Bryant's face, "Jim, if you knew how serious this was...?"-

"But I don't, Bryant, because you won't tell me."

"Hey, look," Bryant said, taking his friend by the shoulders. "Believe me, in a few months. Everything is going to be different. The world will wear a very different face."

Jimmy nodded, "I preferred when we met at Planet Pizza."

"So do I, Jim," Bryant conceded, "I promise, the next time we meet. There will be pizza."

The two then said their long goodbyes before trudging off separately into the night.

Orbitium.

The next part of their plan was relatively simple to concoct. However far from easy to execute. Orbitium was brought to the base daily, in vast amounts. They just needed a tiny sample. But there was only one way to get it. The plan was this. Stake out a hanger, wait for a trade, then follow it to its destination. It would surely lead to where it was kept.

Orbitium poured into the Academy daily, but there had been just one recorded space flight in the last six months. The ratio was well off. Were the Orbitium to be used for flight, they surely had enough to fly to the sun and back millions of times.

Hanger seventeen was the only one scheduled for use that day, and boy had it had been a walk. So many hangers. What were they all for? By the time the two of them arrived, the outer doors were already closed. It was a good sign as it meant trade was in progress. They knew that the Orbitium would be loaded into trucks, which would then depart the hanger. The last vehicle always stopping to secure the door before catching up with the others. That would be their opportunity.

"Bryant," said Mia, "get back here. The shutter is coming up."

"Of all the moments?" They had been hiding outside for hours. It had to be the moment he chose to urinate.

"I'm coming," Bryant whispered back. He hurriedly zipped up his trousers and darted back into position.

"What did I tell you?" said Mia.

"I could never have stayed hidden holding that in," he said. "I would have given myself up so I could pee."

Mia chuckled silently.

They watched the shutter rise and the trucks pour out. Bryant readied himself for the dash, but Mia put her hand out and stopped him.

"What is it?" he asked.

"Look," she said, pointing to the door.

Bryant glanced across. There he was, the guy with the tattoo, clear as day. He departed the hanger. But instead of joining the others, he stopped. Lit a cigarette and wandered away into the shadows.

"Change of plans," she said. "You go after the ore. I'll try to follow him. See where he goes."

"But," Bryant protested.

"We've been given an opportunity here, Bryant. We have to take it."

He nodded; he knew she was right.

"Be careful," he said. "Who knows what that man is capable of?"

"I'm just going to follow him, but you need to go now." Three trucks poured out of the hanger. The first two made off straight away. The last one stopped. The driver jumped from the cab and set about securing the large door.

Bryant stood and prepared to dash before her hand dragged him back again.

"What is it now?" he asked.
She didn't reply. Instead, she kissed him longingly on the lips before pulling herself away.

"Now go."

Bryant ran as fast as he could. His heart pounded as he reached the truck. With one swift motion, he climbed inside, dug himself in amongst the boxes and old sheets that covered them—settling in for the ride.

The truck drove on and on seemingly forever, making him very glad he'd emptied his bladder. They assumed it would be a brief journey across the Academy. But wherever it was going, it wasn't close. He was concerned that he might not even be in his District anymore. He'd never left before. He had no idea how he might get back. But that was a problem for future Bryant. The hum of the truck was very soporific. He felt as though he could easily drift off here. But right as it seemed the truck might never stop. It abruptly ground to a halt, sending him sliding hard into one box. As he rubbed his head, he heard the driver step out and slam the door. He could just about make out an exchange of words. It seemed that maybe it was a discussion. The voices were muffled. Bryant lay motionless in the truck. He waited for maybe ten minutes, but there were no other noises. Peeking his head out from under the tarpaulin slowly at first, he looked around. There was no one here at all, totally deserted. Taking a deep breath, he stood silently and carefully lowered himself from the truck.

The sight that greeted him was like nothing like he imagined. In his mind, he'd pictured a secure vault just piled high with gold, gems, trinkets. He'd imagined it this way because he'd never seen Orbitium, not in the flesh. He wouldn't recognise it if he walked past some. Carefully surveying the area, he glanced around, taking in his surroundings. The trucks were under a shelter; it was like one of the hangers. Except it had large openings at either end. He counted the lorries. There were fourteen, including the one he travelled in. The hollow room was empty aside from the trucks, a train track, and some cranes. This wasn't the Academy. It wasn't anywhere. He guessed that a train must come through, load the ore, and repeat the trick somewhere else. If this happened elsewhere, then they were collecting vast amounts every day. What was it all for, where did it go? He could wait and sneak aboard the train, but who knows where it would take him.

"Stick to the plan, Bryant."

Climbing cautiously back into the truck, he found a crowbar and forcibly opened a crate. Silently opening a wooden box with a crowbar was difficult. But eventually, he got the lid open. He'd envisioned shiny gold, diamonds, or even some luminous, glowing substance—anything but what met his eyes. The first thing that he noticed was the smell. It had an oily musky fishy smell. It wasn't unpleasant, but he didn't much care for it. Reaching in, he cautiously pulled out a handful. The texture was consistent with hard, dry mud. Although if you looked deeper, it was crystalline in texture. So much fuss for smelly dry soil. Undeterred, he broke off a fair-sized chunk, wrapped it in a strip of torn cloth before disembarking the truck. He was amazed at the lack of security here. It was utterly deserted.

Darting between the trucks, he checked the coast was clear before scuttling towards one of the open ends of the building. It was curious that he hadn't seen a soul. Stood safely at the exit, he peaked out. He saw nothing he recognised, nothing of anything except open land. It didn't matter. He had the ore, and now he needed to put as much distance between himself and this place as he could. Standing, he peered around the end of the doors. There was no one for miles. He limbered up and prepared himself for the run.

"Don't move, Fisher," barked a voice from behind him. "Put your hands where I can see them."

Bryant's heart sank. His eyes scanned the landscape in front of him. It was unforgiving. There was nowhere to run, nowhere to hide.

"Don't even think about it, Fisher," came the voice again. His back to his assailant still, he heard the now familiar *click* of a pistol.

Bryant raised his hands. They must be on to him, but as long as he was still alive, there was hope. "Buy yourself some time, Bryant", he thought to himself. He wasn't about to go gently into that goodnight.

"Now," said the voice, "carefully set the ore down on the floor. Step away from it and walk over to me. Try anything, and I will shoot!"

Bryant gently reached into his pocket, removed the Orbitium, and knelt, setting it down on the floor.

"Carefully does it," barked the man.

Bryant laid the Orbitium to rest but paused before standing upright once more.

"What's taking long? Stand up, Fisher."

"Just tying my lace," said Bryant nervously.

He finished fiddling with his shoe. Standing once more, he stepped back two paces and turned about.

He spun to find himself face to face with Colonel Brooks.

"Sir," he managed, surprised. "What are you doing here?"

"I ask the questions," said Brooks.

Keeping the gun trained on Bryant, Brooks crabbed past him. Maintaining his focus as he knelt. Brooks bent awkwardly, carefully picking up the ore. Once he'd done so, he climbed into the truck. Gently tipped over the broken box, returning the missing ore to the rest of its contents, spilling it out over the bed of the truck. Using his sleeve, he wiped down all the surfaces that had been touched and jumped back to the floor.

"What are you doing?" asked Bryant.

"Clearing up your mess, Fisher." As he approached Bryant, he shoved the gun into his ribs, "Move."

Brooks prodded Bryant towards a parked car that was hidden just behind one of the large doors.

"Can you drive?" Brooks asked him.

"I guess we'll find out," replied Bryant.

They got into the vehicle. Brooks sat in the passenger seat, gun in hand still.

"Drive!" he said.

Misdirection.

Bryant drove on it to the night, very awkwardly at first. The only driving he'd ever done had been the school simulator lessons. The basic proficiency test was a formality. Most people would be unlikely to drive in their lifetime, never mind own a car. Operating it was complicated at first. But he soon got to grips with it. Just point and steer. It would have been an enjoyable occasion was it not for the armed lunatic sat across from him.

They drove for an hour in weird silence. The only words muttered had been the odd direction, usually followed by a jab of the gun. The barrel alone really hurt. Looking at it each time, Bryant shuddered to think of the damage that could be caused by one of its bullets. It was rare to see an actual gun, but he'd seen his fair share recently. Tasers were the official weapons. Guns were usually reserved for criminals, used by those who didn't want to be traced.

"Please don't kill me," Bryant uttered, breaking the silence.

"Kill you?" laughed Brooks. "I've just saved your life."

Bryant looked at him, confused.

Another jab of the gun, "Eyes on the road."

"I… I don't get it," Bryant continued.

"I know what you're up to," said Brooks. "I've seen people go down this road before Bryant. It never ends well."

"You do," asked Bryant nervously, "how?"

"I can see it in your eyes," said Brooks. "I know what you want to do with it. But I assure you it isn't worth it."

"But you don't know what it's worth," replied Bryant.

"Oh, trust me," said Brooks. "I know exactly what a chunk of ore that size is worth! That will fetch you at least a million credits on the black market. Your family would never need to work again."

Bryant swung his gaze across to Brooks, something that was met by another jab in the ribs.

"Arrggh," screamed Bryant, "enough with the jabbing."

"You might not realise it now," said Brooks. "But the payday isn't worth it. I mean, what are you even thinking? You make more than enough at the Academy. I wasn't going to let you throw it all away. They would catch you eventually. I had to stop you from getting yourself into serious trouble."

"Wait," said Bryant, "you followed me to stop me from taking the ore? Then you made the box look like it had fallen over?"

"Yes," said Brooks, "what else would I be doing?"

Bryant kept his mouth shut. It was clear Brooks didn't know what he was really doing.

"Look," remonstrated Brooks. "I know things might not be perfect at the Academy. But you can't steal from them. Trust me. Bad things happen to those who do. Do you understand me?"

Bryant nodded, "You're right," he said. "I guess I just wanted it so badly."

"Well, then you're welcome," said Brooks.

"Why did you help me?"

"We're Academy Bryant," he said, slapping him on the arm. "We look out for each other. Now promise me you won't try this again?"

Bryant conceded, "I promise."

"If nothing else, you don't know how unstable that stuff can be."

Bryant was confused, "What do you mean?"

"Eugh," said Brooks. "Me and my big mouth. Look, Bryant, the Orbitium works, but some of it is unstable. Why do you think we need so much of it? We take it miles off-site, test it in the middle of nowhere. If it works, we use it for flight. If it doesn't, well, there is a big bang. It's why there is so much security around it. Subject it to the wrong conditions; a bad batch can blow up right in your face. It's what's slowed down the missions, Bryant. But we'll sort it. We always do."

"No," said Bryant, "this can't be true. I've heard that…"

"You heard what, Bryant? That there is some kind of conspiracy? God damn it, this is all his fault, bloody DeVore!"

A chill shot through Bryant's bones, "What about him?" he asked anxiously.

"Oh, the lunatic was working with some fanatics. Determined to prove that the Orbitium was useless."

"So…so you killed him?"

Brooks roared with laughter, "Good god Bryant, listen to yourself. This isn't the mafia. No, the fool stole some ore. Blew himself up trying to prove some crackpot conspiracy."

"But you knew he cheated the test," said Bryant.

"And he would have been punished accordingly, Bryant. We're not murders. Where do you think you are?"

Bryant's head was in a spin; Brooks spoke with such conviction. If he was lying, he was damn good at it. Nothing made sense anymore.

"But, I've been told.."

"Look, Bryant," said Brooks lowering the gun. "Whatever you've been told is just nonsense by people jealous of what we have. I know the Academy isn't perfect. But it works Bryant, the system works. I mean, come on, do you really think we are the bad guys?"

"But," said Bryant, "what about the man with the snake tattoo?"

"Oh, you mean Miguel?" asked Brooks. "He's a sweetheart if you get to know him. I'd rather we didn't need people like him, Bryant, but he's a necessary evil. I'm sorry you had to see that nasty business in hanger six. But we'd been on to Grimes and his crew for a while. We had to catch him in the act. We needed you two there as a witness."

Bryant pulled the car to the side of the road, putting his head in his hands. Everything Brooks said made sense. It tied up with what Phil had said about Grimes. Maybe it was all a lie, and perhaps he was just being used? Brooks' story about the ore was far more likely than the idea that space missions were fake. That space didn't exist, or that the ore wasn't used to power rockets. He didn't know who to believe anymore?

Brooks readjusted in his seat. Leaned over to Bryant and patted him on the shoulder, "I'm sorry, I know growing up can be hard. We are forced to go from boy to man in a flash. But we need to keep working Bryant together for the people."

Bryant wiped at his eyes. Maybe his father was just a reckless drunk? He'd latched on to the idea of him being a revolutionary. Anything was better than an ignorant man who'd abandoned him. He needed to be smarter, only believe what he could prove.

"Now," said Brooks as he raised the gun once more. "I'm sorry to have to do this. But I need you to get in the boot!"

"What?" said Bryant. "No, wait! I'm sorry, I won't do it again. I promise."

"Just get out of the car Bryant."

Bryant saw the gun barrel come his way again. He couldn't take another jab in the ribs.

"Okay, okay," he pleaded. "I'm getting out."

Bryant exited the car. He looked around him. Running wasn't an option. They were in a refuge area in the middle of an electric highway. Getting to safety would involve crossing several lanes, dodging high-speed silent vehicles, and live electric charging grids. None of which seemed like a good way to die.

Brooks opened the boot.

"In."

Climbing in reluctantly. Bryant's protests continued, "Please, Brooks, you don't have to do this."

Brooks sighed and stretched out an arm to help him into the boot. With Bryant finally inside. Brooks stood above him. Gun in hand, the other clutching the boot lid. He looked down at Bryant and said, "I apologise for this."

"No wai"- Was all Bryant managed before the gun barrel came crashing towards his head, and everything went black.

Medical leave.

Bryant stared intensely at the small chunk of Orbitium he'd smuggled out in his sock. So much fuss over such an insignificant-looking chunk of mud. His head hurt, both from the blow and knowing so much and so little despite knocking him out with the butt of his gun and the incessant jabbing. Brooks had appeared to have been genuine. Much to his surprise, when he awoke wasn't dead. He found himself back on base in the medical centre. Apparently, he'd knocked his head during training. Being in the med centre had been an excellent place to hide, avoiding everything and everyone, including Mia. The knock bought him some medical leave, so he discharged himself and fled home. He had no idea what to do now, what was real, what wasn't?

Sat alone on his bed, door locked, Orbitium in hand. He looked at it in wonder.

"If only you could talk," he said to himself.

Knock Knock.

The rap on the door startled him. The door handle moved as if to open. But the lock did its job, repelling any would-be invaders.

"Bryant, are you okay," came the voice of his mum, "how's your head?"

"Er, I'm fine, mum," Bryant said, springing up from his bed.

"And why's your door locked?" she called through the shut door.

"Erm, er, I'm naked, mum," he shot back.

"Okay," said Pam, "well, if you feel like getting dressed. Dinner's ready."

All this thinking had been exhausting. His stomach rumbled, confirming the hunger. Bryant wrapped the Orbitium back up, but he paused; there was a feeling that nagged at him. So, he delicately split the Orbitium in two, wrapping both bits up separately, hastily stuffing one between his mattress and the other in the gap in the floorboards, the place he used to hide magazines from his mother. With his stashes safe, he threw on a jumper and opened his door.

He arrived downstairs to a pleasant aroma but an ugly sight. "Mum," Bryant yelled, "why did you order pizza?"

As much as he loved his pizza, the memory of the last time he ordered was fresh in his head. He didn't want to think about the Uprising or anything associated with it until he knew what to believe.

"Since when do you not like pizza?" Pam asked.

"Just had a lot of it recently, that's all."

"Well, excuse me for not keeping up with your dietary preferences Bryant, maybe if you stayed in touch more..."

"Sorry, mum, I've been busy," Bryant said. Shrugging.

"I'm sorry, honey," replied Pam. "I've been crabby lately; so much has happened. But, it's good to have you here. If you want, I can make you something else?"

Bryant looked at the fresh pizza on the table. She'd even ordered the garlic bread. It stared back at him, and his mouth watered.

"No sense in letting it go to waste, mum," he said, tucking in.

They were both interrupted by the sound of the door opening. Julie bustled in. Sat down, grabbed a slice, and said, "Ooh, Pizza."

Pam turned her attention away from her son.

"Hey, young lady," she said. "Where on earth have you been?"

"Out!" Julie replied nonchalantly.

"Julie Maria Fisher!" Pam said, hands atop hips. "It's 9:30 at night."

"So," she shrugged, "it's not like you're ever home! Anyway, Bryant's here now. You can go back to giving him all your attention."

Julie had a big brain for someone her age, a big brain that came with a sizeable amount of sass.

"How dar..?"- Flabbergasted Pam tried to speak.

Bryant put his hand on his mother's shoulder. "It's okay, mum. I've got this."

Flustered, Pam walked off, disappearing up the stairs, shaking her head.

Bryant grabbed a slice of pizza and then crashed down on the sofa next to his sister.

"Hey, trouble," he said. Julie murmured pizza in one hand, phone in the other. She munched, scrolling absent-mindedly through the feed in front of her.

With her attention fixed on the device. Bryant licked his pinkie. Ensuring it was dripping wet, before ramming it deep into his sisters' ear.

"Eww, gross," she said. Spitting out mouthfuls of pizza, desperately trying to defend her ear using her shoulder. Bryant's aim had been true. He wet his finger well and sunk his saliva deep into her ear, forcing her to put down her belongings. She wrestled away from her brother and, using her free hand, desperately clawed spit out of her ear.

Bryant sat there laughing hysterically.

"You're disgusting," she said. Punching at him playfully. "Why would you do that?"

Bryant shrugged. "Got your attention, didn't it?"

"Eugh, couldn't you have just asked me something? You know, like a normal person!"

"Ok, so why are you so hard on mum?" he asked.

"Course you're on her side," she groaned.

"Hey," he said, "I'm not on anyone's side. I'm just asking."

"You're not here, Bryant," she said. "Mum's never here. No one is. Everything has changed, and everyone's stupid!"

Bryant had spent the last year thinking about how much everything was different for him. It had never really occurred to him how that might affect others.

"I'm sorry, Jules," he whispered. "I wish everything was different too. I could happily spend all my time here with you, mum and Mia."

"But what about space? Don't you want to be there," she quizzed.

"Yeah, I did," he said wistfully. "I guess sometimes you have to lose what you had to realise how important it was.

"Does this mean you're gonna stay?" she asked. Eyes wide with hope, "I mean, I can hit you on the head some more if you like?"

Bryant chuckled, recalling the initial bump on the head, "Please don't."

He looked at his sister, then around the room. He leaned in close to her. Bryant had spent the last few days mulling over and over the words of Brooks. He was wondering what was true, what wasn't, whether the Uprising was real. But looking around him, he saw how life was for his family, how every family must live.

He watched his mother work herself into the ground for little reward. He saw how his sister might grow up with no one around to steady her, and he knew his friend risked his life to provide for a system that saw him as expendable. Whatever was going on, he was going to find the truth. He would blow this world wide open, make a hole big enough for everyone to see.

"I'm working on something, Jules. I can change everything. We can have a life that we have always dreamed of."

"You sound just like dad," she groaned.

"Wait," asked Bryant, "what do you mean?"
Julie was just a child when their father left. There was no way she could remember things he'd said.

"Dad, you remember dad?" she inquired. "You sound like him."

"Julie," Bryant stammered, "how do you know what Dad sounded like?"

"From watching the videos," she said casually.

Messages from beyond.

Bryant stood by his door. He waited until he could hear the snores coming from his mother's room. Then, he snuck silently across the hall into his sister's.

"Julie," he said, shaking her gently. "I need to see those videos."

"You're so annoying," groaned his sister as she stirred.

"Please," he begged.

Julie rose begrudgingly, "I changed my mind," she said. "I preferred it when you weren't here."

The pair snuck silently out of the house. Bryant following her lead as they slipped into the garage.

"How did you get so good at being sneaky?" he whispered.

She shrugged, "You're good at being a nerd. I'm good at sneaking."

"So, tell me again," Bryant asked. "Where did you get these videos?"

Julie shrugged again. "Someone delivered them?"

"And you're sure they are real?" he asked sceptically.

"You'll see," she said.

Julie removed some bricks from the rear of the garage wall. Behind it was something Bryant had never seen before. She reached in and pulled out the odd-looking device. Set it down on the workbench. She removed a bunch of strange small oblong-shaped objects, placing them all down together.

"Okay," she said. Pointing to the video camera sat on the side, "this pulls out. It's like a small phone screen. But the quality is awful. These go in here." She pointed to the oblongs. "Then this button makes it play."

Bryant looked at the camera. It was so old, "What's with all the shapes?" he asked.

"Dunno," said Julie, "but you need the triangle to make it go. The square to stop, and the sideways triangles to go backwards or forwards. Got it?" Bryant picked up the small black device, surveying the thing in his hands.

"I guess," he said.

"Oh," said Jules, "but if you watch all of it. Once it gets to the end, you have to use the sideways triangles to make it go back to the beginning. It takes forever. And whatever you do. Don't press either of the triangles whilst it's playing because it eats itself."

She looked at her older brother, "Understand?"

Bryant nodded, "I think so."

"Good," she said and then started towards the garage door.

"Wait," Bryant whispered, "where are you going?"

She yawned, "Bed Bryant."

"But don't you want to watch with me?" he asked.

"I've watched mine, and I know what to do," she said, motioning to the small cassettes in Bryant's hands. "They're yours."

"So, you've not watched these?" he said, stunned.

She shook her head, "Nope, dad said not to." She took a pace to the garage door and opened it, stepped outside but stuck her head back inside before leaving. "I enjoy sneaking about with you, Bry," she whispered.

He chuckled quietly, "Go to bed," he said. And like that, she was gone.

Bryant put his videos in the machine. He now had so many more questions. Desperate for answers, he sat and pressed play, watching them on a loop. He watched on, tears filling his eyes. The first two tapes were just home movies. The memories he had of the times he spent with his father were old, hazy. Reliving it was pure. It was beautiful.

The digital age in which they lived meant that everyone had a substantial online profile. Masses of cloud storage filled with photos, videos, selfies, social media accounts. Endless amounts of online data. The Authorities had put such an onus on the future, not the past. This meant that thirty days after you died, your online presence would be deleted. There was no sense having gigabytes of obsolete historical data floating about. Providing you named a legacy contact, they could keep up to a gigabyte. His father had named no one. Meaning there was nothing left online of the man at all. Bryant kept the photo of the two of them close to him because it was the only visual representation he had of the man who was once his father. Being able to watch, listen, and rewind his words was wonderfully cathartic. He thought he knew this man, but his memories were sparse, and his photograph didn't tell a thousand words. The videos did.

The last tape was very different, no memories this time. Instead, his father sat behind the camera. Alone in the dark. He wore a sincere expression as he adjusted the lens and spoke.

"Hi, Bryant," he said, "I hope it's you watching this. But if it is, then it means I've failed, and they got to me first. Please listen carefully. They act fast, and so must you. We haven't much time."

Bryant shifted for comfort in his seat. This was going to be intense.

"Bryant, I'm sure you've realised that the world is not quite the place it seems? I don't have all the answers for you, but I can tell you this. The planet is run by an organisation called 'The Order.' I don't mean the Authorities or the governments. The Order controls everything they always have. They used to lurk in the shadows, give power to puppets and let rich and powerful rule the world at their command. It was an excellent system. The world used to be split into continents, and within those continents, smaller zones called countries. Each one under its own rule, each passionate about what it had. Unable to cooperate with even its closest neighbour. They ensured that patriotism, language, national pride, and prejudice would keep everyone divided. It was rare that any two neighbouring nations even spoke the same language. The Order gave power to despots and crooks.

Knowing that they were under their control. It was a system that worked for thousands of years.

"All that changed at the end of the 21st century. The people who were given the roles of Presidents, Prime Ministers, Dictators abused their powers, ignored the instructions. Power corrupted even to the highest level. The people, given power, turned on their masters. The system had worked well for so long. But the advancement of technology, the wealth of riches available spiralled out of control. There had been a time when The Order would put someone on a throne and tell him how he had to rule in exchange for a better life. But counties overthrew their Kings and Queens, replaced them with elected officials. This worked, too, because only the elite, a select few, could even be considered for the roles. However, it reached a stage where people could make millions from video channels. Reality TV stars could become presidents, and scientists could privatise government space programs. It was chaos! Presidents ignored their orders, chasing after personal fame and riches, starting wars just to stroke their egos. Life on earth worked until the people did whatever they wanted. Individuals could get rich just by exploiting the land, ravaging natural resources, or posting images of themselves online. The Order has always worked in the planet's best interest, and it was clear they were failing. They took away the freedom, the rulers. Removed the greed and the corruption, blinding the world, governing through a mixture of fear and hope. A select few roam free while the others are enslaved. Toiling, working for what they believe is a common goal.

"It's true. Humanity was destroying the planet, and the population was vast. But not to the extent it was claimed. The Districts and the hope of a new world were meant to be a short-term fix. The initial plan was a reset. Remove the corruption, decadence, and greed, reorganise and get everyone working as one. But The Order realised that humanity would always default back to that. I don't know how

many are in the Order, but they live beyond the Districts, Bryant. The rest of us are trapped, blind, working away for a future that will never come.

"Bryant, I don't know everything, but what I know is we need not abandon our planet. People don't need to work their entire lives for someone else's goal. There is power within the people. Suppose we can remove the blindfolds. Show them they have a choice. Everything can be different. I have no doubt that you will have found the Uprising. But be careful of red herrings, Bryant; misdirection and misinformation are rife. Believe in me, Bryant, believe in the Uprising.

"I dedicated my life to this cause, Bryant. There is a world beyond the Districts, I'm sure of it. This is our destiny. I gave my life for this cause, and if it comes to it, so must you. My only regret was that I didn't get to see the man you've become."

The video stopped. The garage was dark except for the small light of the video screen, which partially illuminated his face. Tears had rolled down his cheek and formed in his lap. The tapes were hard to watch. But he was clear in his mind now. Destiny called, and he knew what he needed to do.

The last of the walls fell, sending cheers ringing out across the globe. The divisions were gone. The people were no longer blind. The Academy had been exposed, and the hoarded riches divided out. What was left of The Order had gone into the shadows. They had been chased down like dogs, rolling over on each other. The Uprising was here now, taking control. They were led by its gallant hero Bryant Fisher, the man who freed humanity.

People could come and go as they pleased. Elections would be held, and committees would decide the fate of the world. That was all to come. Bryant stood on the smoking pile of rubble that used to be the walls of the Academy. He had his

224

rifle in hand, and blood streamed from a wound on his head.
Smoke filled the air. The scene was epic. He was flanked by
his love on the right and his faithful friend on the left. The
adoring crowd watched on as single-handed he tore down the
last of the walls brick by brick. They were vociferous. He
raised his hands in the air, bringing them down to silence the
crowd. A hush fell on the assembled mass, and Bryant opened
his mouth to speak.

"My Friends, today will go down as one of the greatest
days in history. Everyone here today will be remembered.
Because today truth, freedom, and equality won. No more
shall we be controlled. We have shown that the people united
we can never be divided."

The crowd roared on. Bryant raised his rifle to the sky and
fired some celebratory shots into the air. Once the group
settled, he spoke again.

"Tomorrow marks a new chapter for humanity. We start
again. We rebuild, bigger, better, fairer than before."

The adoring masses cheered furiously still.

"Tomorrow will go down in history as the day the people
were unified. But you know what?" he asked the masses.
"That is for another day! We must celebrate. For tonight we
dance!"

His words sent the crowd delirious. They screeched and
yelled, extolling his name as loud as they could. Cheered to
the heavens, bellowing to the hells.

"Bryant, Bryant Bryant, Bryant."

"Bryant, sweetie," his mum shook him gently. "Your cab is
outside to take you back to the Academy."
Bryant opened his eyes and looked at his phone.

"Eugh," he said, "can you tell them to wait, mum?"
She went to speak but thought better of it.

"It's your money," she said, bending to kiss him on the
head. "I've got to get to work, darling. I'll see you again
soon."
She walked towards the door, but before she left, Bryant
called after her.

"I love you, mum," he said. Pam stopped short of the door. Paused for a second before turning.

"I love you too, Bryant," she said with a smile on her face. She departed his room and descended the stairs; how nice it was to have normality back. She grabbed her coat and dashed out of the door. Pam smiled at the waiting driver, his eyes wide as he watched the meter run-up. She nodded at him as she went, "This will be a lovely month," she thought to herself.

Bryant was flustered; he knew the taxi was outside waiting. But he wasn't ready to go back to the Academy. The Orbitium was still at home. He needed to get in touch with Alpha. But pressingly, he needed a coffee, a shower, and breakfast in that order.

He threw his dressing gown on, donned a pair of his mum's slippers, and dashed out to the waiting car. He paid the man for his time, plus the journey he didn't take and darted back into the house, poured a strong coffee and jumped into the shower. Once in the spray, the warm water hit his skin. The room steam up, and he stood there soaking it all in. He wondered what his father had said to Julie in the video? He'd forgotten to ask, and it irked him now. Surely, he can't have told her what was going on. Maybe he had. Perhaps she'd watched all videos. Did his sister know? His brain ran wild. He needed to focus. Everything else could wait. During his vacillation, he'd lost precious time. He needed to get the Orbitium into the hands of the Uprising before he returned to the Academy.

"Think Bryant, think! Margery and Reginald."
He knew how to find them, and it would be a journey. But it was his best shot.

Freshly showered and with a stomach full of leftover pizza, Bryant swapped taxis for the third time. The final one pulled up near the watch shop, back in the old town. He paid the driver, thanked him, got out, and walked as he approached the shop. He noticed how dark it was. The shutters were still down, and there were no lights on. The sign on the door said it opened at nine. Bryant checked the time. It was just gone eleven, "Weird," he thought to himself. He had no time to waste walking on by without so much as peering in. He navigated the maze of alleyways before finding himself back at the drain, quivering when he reached it. The memory of that gun still fresh in his mind.

Once down, he fought his way through the damp tunnels arriving at the metal door. It was ajar when he arrived. Knocking and getting no answer, he thrust his head around the corner. The lights were on, but there was no one inside. It seemed odd for the two of them to leave it like this. But it didn't matter, setting the ore down on their table. He scribbled a brief note, complete with a smiley face, before swiftly departing.

Bryant travelled back through the damp tunnels, up the rusty ladder, down the alley maze, and past the watch shop. The door was closed still. But light now peeped out from inside. "Lazy morning," he considered. He kept going, round the next corner and out of sight.

The plan.

Sat alone on his bed at the Academy, Bryant desperately tried to think. Things were progressing faster than he would like. But they were on the verge of something huge; he could feel it. Hopefully, by now, Margery or Reginald had got the Orbitium to someone who could analyse it. Presumably, they would be some way towards working out what the smelly mud did. His brain was working overtime, retracing all his steps, thinking about everyone involved. Had they missed anything?

An awful noise rang out from the room next door. All he could hear was the eerie soundtrack to one of the ridiculous Academy films. They dared to make dramas about real life that was yet to happen. This was the movie about exploring Saturn. He'd loved these films once, but the heresy angered him now. He couldn't think with the noise of this drivel. Donning his boots, he made straight for the one place he knew would be quiet.

The old store was empty when he arrived. He'd run the entire way there, catching his breath before entering. He knew Mia would probably be here later. He'd ignored her the last week, and he'd need to deal with that at some point. But she'd understand, he hoped.

There was an old desk in the room's corner. Desperate to sit and plan, he dragged it out from the wall. The bureau was solid wood and weighed a ton. He couldn't lift it himself, instead choosing to drag it across the floor. The noise was deafening as it screeched its way into the middle of the room. Happy with its new position, he turned to grab a chair. As he did so, a male figure appeared right in front of him. Bryant let out a "Yelp!" Jumping completely from his skin. He fell back onto the dusty desk. Helplessly gasping for breath as he examined the man stood before him.

"Do you want to make any more noise?" Stein asked. "I don't think they could quite hear you in the centre of the District."

"Oh my gosh, Stein, it's you?" Bryant said. "You scared me half to death." Any lingering suspicions had vanished, as much as Stein had terrified him yet again. He was delighted to see him.

They sat, and Bryant burbled on about everything that had happened, the videos, his father, the Orbitium, Alpha, the Uprising. It was such a relief to get it all out.

Stein listened on intently as Bryant recounted his week at light speed.

"Well, you have been busy," he said. "Just slow down, take a breather."

"But what about Brooks," asked Bryant, "does he know?"

Stein chuckled, "He's an idiot Bryant, harmless really, but an idiot. He thinks of himself as a father figure around here. But he has no idea what's going on."

"So, he"-

"He just thinks he's looking out for you, Bryant. Trying to protect your career, that's all."

Bryant nodded, relieved. He felt better.

"So, you know about The Order now, Bryant?"

"Yes," said Bryant, "I know everything."

"Well," said Stein, "not quite everything. Your father and I spent a lot of time together before his disappearance. We had been working on a plan together."

Bryant looked at him with intrigue.

"You see, Bryant, I loved your father, and he loved me too. We were working for a different world, one where everyone could be free."

"But my mother?" said Bryant.

"He loved her too, Bryant. Just as much as he loved you and your sister, it was complicated. Bryant, I know this is hard to take in. But everything will make sense one day. Please, just listen to me."

Bryant nodded.

"I came here to give you this," said Stein holding out a flash drive.

"What is it?" Bryant asked, glancing at the item in his hand.

"Proof Bryant! Everything you'll need. This will shock you, Bryant, but every space mission since the first Moon landings have been faked. As technology's improved, so has the footage. I don't know if we have ever been to space or not, Bryant. But every public exhibition, every moon landing, every launch, all fake. Everything shown to us a lie. They give us exactly what they want us to see." Stein motioned to the item in his hands. "This drive is essential. It has behind-the-scenes footage of all of them, Bryant." Stein pushed the device into his hands, "Take it."

"But what do I do with it?" asked Bryant.

"You wait," said Stein. "When the time is right. When you are prepared, plug that into any networked device, and it will do the rest. It's programmed ready, Bryant. Whatever is being shown anywhere in the world. Every screen will burst into life, and those videos will play on a loop. It's heavily encrypted. It will play several times before they shut it down."

"But why now, why me?" asked Bryant.

"I'm sorry I wasn't more forthcoming with you, Bryant. But I had to be certain. Sure that you could do it, sure that I could trust you, definite, you were ready."

Bryant nodded. He understood. He'd been through a crucible of his own recently.

"I have to keep my hands clean, Bryant. Whatever happens, I can never be a part of this. I have to remain anonymous to everyone. Should you fail, there needs to be a backup."

"What do I do now?" Bryant asked.

"It's your revolution, kiddo," replied Stein. "This is where my involvement ends. I hope we see each other again because if we do. It will be in the new world."

They hugged once more, sharing a lasting embrace. Bryant reluctant to let go. Knowing how close this man was to his father, he barely knew Stein, but the man felt like family.

"I must go," said Stein.

"We'll meet again soon," said Bryant.

"I hope we do. Take care of yourself, Bryant Fisher."

Stein stepped back into the shadows, disappearing from sight.

Bryant wasn't alone for long before he heard the door click at the far end of the corridor. He took a moment, composing himself.

"Bryant, are you in here?" Mia whispered. Wiping away the tears that had formed on his cheeks, he centred himself and whispered back.

"Yeah, I'm in here." She closed the door and dashed down the corridor towards him, jumping into his arms on arrival.

"I thought I heard voices," she said as they hugged.

"Oh, probably just me talking to myself," he replied.

"Oh my god, where have you been?" she probed. "I'm so glad you're okay. I heard you hit your head? Bryant, I've been worried sick."

"It's alright," he said, "I'm fine, really."

"When you didn't return, I feared the worst."

"Ah, it takes more than a bump on the head to keep me down." he beamed.

"The Orbitium, did you get it?"

"Yes and taken care of."

"Yess," she shrieked. Hugging him tightly. "What on earth happened to you?"

"Trust me," he said, "it's a long story. I'll explain later. Right now, we have bigger things to attend to." He waved the flash drive in front of her.

"What is it?" she asked.

"This Mia," he said smugly, "this is freedom."

Action.

This time last year, Jimmy and Bryant were planning how to skip their last ever school lessons. Life was simple. Fast forward a year, and he was planning a revolution, how things change. They had most of the pieces in place to set their plan in motion. Word had spread through the channels, and the Uprising was awaking. Timing would be critical. The end of the month saw the next scheduled rocket launch. It was mandatory viewing, and they planned to hijack it, commandeering the airwaves. They would play the video. Show the world the farce, the lies, the fakes. After the film, it would cut to Bryant. He would read some history, forcing out the truth about the planet. Show them they were trapped by invisible shackles, expose the Order, the Orbitium. They would encourage the people to rise, to join the revolution. There would be one, and it would be televised.

It was ambitious, but he had hope, faith. Fate was on their side. There was no fighting destiny.

The last part of their plan hinged on the Orbitium. It didn't matter what it did; what they used it for as long as they could show that it was not rocket fuel. Their scientists had easily worked out that the muddy substance couldn't power a kettle, never mind a rocket. But what it did remained a mystery still.

Despite knowing, feeling that this was his destiny. Bryant wanted to spend just one more weekend being normal before it happened. Whatever transpired when the truth came out, things would undoubtedly change. He yearned for just one more weekend at home playing the role of Bryant Fisher. Son, brother, lover, as much as he was keen for everyone to know the truth. He'd never asked for any of this. Heavy lies the crown of the reluctant hero.

"Bryant!" exclaimed Julie, entering the kitchen to find her brother.

"Hey, trouble," he said, stooping to hug her. Pam shut the front door. Bags of shopping still in hand, hearing the commotion. She chased after her daughter and entered the kitchen.

"Hi, sweetie," she said, genuinely amazed. "We didn't know you'd be home this weekend."

"I thought I would surprise you," he said, smiling.

Pam set her shopping down and extended her arms. "Well, you did," she managed pleasantly surprised. "Aww, bring it in both of you." The three of them shared a warm embrace in the kitchen before Julie broke the silence.

"Mum, can I show Bryant my science project?"

"Sure, honey," Pam replied.

Julie took Bryant's hand and almost physically dragged him out of the kitchen. With an arm half out of the room, Bryant looked at his mother, who was surrounded by piles of shopping. She smiled at him before mouthing the words, "Go," with her lips.

Bryant gave in to his sister's determination and followed her out of the kitchen. They entered Julie's bedroom, and she shut the door. Diving under her bed, she dragged out a cardboard box that had the word's 'Science Project' scrappily drawn on it.

"Bryant," she whispered, "I finished the rocket!."

Caught slightly off-guard, Bryant said, "The rocket?"

"Yeah, duh," she said. "We made them in science. You even helped me with some of it. Remember? You said it would never get to space. So I altered it."

He remembered; that seemed like another lifetime. With a heightened sense of intrigue, he watched her remove the box's lid before taking the rocket from the container.

"Julie, that looks amazing!" he exclaimed.

"Cheers," she said, "I've added a camera and some nitrous to it. Wanna see how high it will go?"

"Julie," Bryant gasped. "How do you know how to do all of this? I mean, that's pretty extreme for an elementary science project."

Julie shrugged. "I can't tell you without lying to you, Bryant."

Bryant chuckled. His sister never ceased to amaze him. "Fair," he said. Knowing it would be useless to enquire further. "We'll take it out next time I'm home."

"You promise?"

"I promise," he said, "I know just the place to take it."

Together.

Alone in the dark. Bryant paced up and down the old corridor. His mind was going through every detail, each person; it raced at a million miles per hour. Was there a weak link, was anything suspicious, had they missed anything? Tomorrow was the day everything came down to this. What they did next would change everything. The people would be free, or so he hoped. He would rewrite history, that or die trying.

He was monumentally excited but incredibly nervous, in desperate need of a stiff drink. They had a plan, and everything was in place. He fretted about meeting at the watch shop again. Something felt odd the last time he was there. He couldn't quite describe it, but he felt uneasy. Alpha had assured him it would be fine, that he had a plan. But it didn't cease his stressed brain. This was too important an opportunity to miss. Tomorrow they would find out the secret behind the Orbitium. He often speculated about what it might be, each idea more absurd than the last. Was it valuable, did it have superpowers? Strangely, his mind enjoyed the mystery. Although he was glad, it was being laid to rest.

His greatest fear, though, wasn't something going wrong. It wasn't getting caught. What if they showed the people the truth, but they didn't care? What if they had been slaves for too long? Would the change be too much? What if all they did was for nothing? The door opened softly; it was Mia.

"Hey, you okay?" she asked, sensing Bryant's anxiety.

"What if it's all pointless?" he asked. "What if we risk everything. Expose the truth and change nothing? What then, Mia?"

She grabbed him by the arm, looking him straight in the eyes.

"Where's all this coming from?" she asked. "Have faith, Bryant. You know this is your destiny."

"Do I?" he demanded. "A year ago, I lived in blissful ignorance. I didn't know any different, and I didn't care. What if this is just the way the world needs to be?"

"Hey, hey," she said, stroking his hair, "I know this is a lot. I know you didn't ask for this. But you can't fight destiny. You're Bryant Fisher, and we need you; the world needs you. Anyway, think about all the people you care for, think about Pam, the world your sister will grow up in. If to live you have to be numb, would you not rather know the pain?"

He looked at her eyes. They sparkled brightly at him. "You're right," he said. Mia pulled him in tight and squeezed him hard.

"I couldn't do this without you," he said.

"And you won't," she replied. "We do this together."

There hadn't been a gathering this size involving the critical members of the Uprising ever. The risk of them all being together was vast—a chance they wouldn't usually take. Today was different. After this, they would no longer need to meet in secret.

The televised launch was at eight, and there was still much to discuss beyond this moment. It was bigger than just tonight. They needed a plan for the future. The world would look very different in a few hours. They had to be ready for the unknown.

The meeting was scheduled, and everyone had individual instructions for how to arrive. Bryant had his, and he finally arrived in the old part of town, but he still felt uneasy. He'd jogged some of the way, and his heartbeat so fast he worried he might not last the evening. He'd barely kept any food down all day up. He was pale, sweaty, anxious, and tired.

His dreams of saving humanity had always been orthodox; he would be leading his planet to space. Never once had he dreamt that he would be on the other side of the fence, taking it all down, leading a revolution.

The meeting was well planned. Alpha was a master of misdirection. Fortunately, they weren't staying in the old town. The downside was the actual location was a secret. One he would need to decipher to get there.

The instructions were hidden ever so subtly in posters, signs, even graffiti. Almost too well for Bryant's liking as it had taken him a while to figure it out. Stood outside the watch shop; he worried that he might have missed something. Motionless in front of the dim storefront. He noticed a brightly lit LED juxtaposed against the dark behind it. The arrow pointed left; it had to be a clue. Following it aimlessly, he saw a poster for a movie, 'Space Academy 9: Jupiter's Moons'. "Eugh," he'd sat through that one at the cinema. Three hours of his life, he would never get back. The poster was covered with graffiti. "Probably because it's awful," he thought to himself. Tutting, he turned to walk on before noting further directions hidden in the paint.

Once in the maze, Bryant deciphered and followed several other concealed clues before he came face to face with a wall. A dead-end! He must have taken a wrong turn, but as he went to leave. He spotted the words, 'Rise Up' written on the wall. It was tall. But he'd run enough assault courses now to know it wasn't insurmountable. Taking a run-up, he jumped and grabbed the top of it, passing over it to find himself on the edge of the river banks. Without warning, an enormous figure appeared from the gloom—Gun in hand.

"Wait," Bryant spoke. But the man cut him off. "Get in." He motioned with the gun towards a small inflatable speed boat that lurked in the shadows. They got in. The man fired up the engine, setting off at pace.

Bryant had never been in a boat before. The trip was exhilarating, and this was fun. Life, too, would soon be fun. The wind blew through his hair as the vessel bounced over the water, sending cool droplets of liquid cascading over him. As it skimmed across the waves, Bryant closed his eyes, drinking it all in.

The noise of the engine relented as the ship slowed. Bryant opened his eyes again to see a gigantic mass in the water ahead of them. As they drew closer, Bryant realised he was looking at several old container ships. From their position in the water. The liners looked down upon them like goliaths. He felt so small as he surveyed the graveyard of

237

rusty boats. As they neared, Bryant heard them creak and groan as they moved in the water. The dying wails of rusted giants. Their small craft pulled up alongside one in the middle. It was in better condition than the rest, with large cables hanging down from a crane. Upon arrival, his companion, the silent brute, stood and connected them to the boat before he could protest or comprehend. The small craft hoisted haphazardly into the air and up towards the deck of the ship.

Safely on board the petrifying ordeal of being dragged through the air over. He was led into the heart of the ship. They passed through several heavy bulkhead doors and finally into a control room. Once inside, the door slammed behind them. Bryant looked around at his new surroundings, amazed at the sights that greeted his eyes.

"Bryant," said Mia bounding up to him.

"Mia," he said, relishing her warm grip.

They broke from their hug, and Bryant looked about the room. There were computers, radars, radios, monitors, and tv screens. The room was full of faces, both new and old.

"Good of you to join us, Bryant!" Alpha said, standing from his station, offering him a warm handshake.

"May have got confused with the directions," Bryant conceded.

"It's fine," said Alpha, "you were the last to arrive. So let us begin."

Bryant beheld the chamber before him. It was a veritable who's who. He recognised Mia, Alpha, Beta, Charlie, Margery, and Reginald. Exultant as he greeted all of them. There were dozens of others here, too. Some he recognised and many he didn't. Still, some of them caught him by surprise.

"Mr Goldstein, Mr Rubinat?" he said. Amazed by the irony that he now led the man he exasperated at the car wash. They both nodded at him. He recognised others, a coffee guy from the park, two familiar pizza guys, and a host of strangers. All of whom were presumably leaders of specific divisions. Bryant shook hands with those he knew and offered a 'nod' to those he didn't. It was an incredible sight, like being at a superhero convention.

"Bryant," spoke Beta, "we don't have time for pleasantries right now. Please, everyone. Take a seat."

Alpha then stood and spoke. "Thank you all for coming. Some of you know each other, and perhaps many of you don't. But we are all here together for the one reason, one cause. We all want the truth. We have many reasons to be excited and much to discuss for those of you who don't know him. I would like to introduce the son of our revered leader. Stand Bryant, please."

Bryant stood as a vocal round of applause rang out. Word had spread, and his presence clearly meant a great deal. Looking around the room, all these people cheering for him was surreal. They had known resistance for aeons. They had toiled and worked at this for years. And yet, after a few months, here he was, sat atop of all this. Somehow the key.

Alpha spoke again, "Today, ladies and gentlemen is also about hope, destiny. Bryant finding the Academy, finding us, was no coincidence. I know our numbers have dwindled. I know many of us have lost faith, lost hope. But today, we rise again from the ashes."

More cheers rang out, bouncing off the enclosed metal walls. The din was magnificent.

"I call on all of you to look inside yourselves. Find that fire that brought you here in the first place. Then take that flame and spread it as far as you can. You all have networks, and you have alliances. We will need all of that, not just today but in the weeks and months to come."

Alpha paused, took a deep breath before continuing.

"For those of you who don't know why you're here. Today is the day we have waited, worked, and planned for; we have everything in place to bring out the truth. Remove the blindfolds. Expose the lies, the corruption. Show the world that they don't have to be afraid. I know it might appear we've been down this road before. But we have all the proof we need. We have each other. Tonight we take the truth to the people. We take over the airways and take the planet back. No longer will the Order blind us with lies, no more will they use our safety to enslave us."

Alpha walked over to a table. Picking up a tablet as he did so.

"It gets better," said Alpha, grinning. He looked down at the device in his hand. "Bryant got us a sample of Orbitium. We have worked hard to analyse the ore. To work out what it really does. We all suspected that it didn't power spaceships, and that is true. But today, I can share with you what it really is!"

Alpha cleared his throat to continue. But something interrupted him before he could.

"I'm afraid I can't let you do that!" exploded a voice from the darkness.

Silence fell as everyone looked around in a panic, searching for the origin of the noise. The man behind the clamour stepped forward brazenly from the darkness.

"Surely not; it couldn't be?" Standing in front of them, clear as day, was the man with the snake tattoo. He was heavily armed. A smug grin was plastering his face. How had he found them? How did he get in here?

Some stood, pulling their weapons, desperately searching the room for their would-be assailants.

Bryant looked at them, then back across the room. The man was gone, no time to react. It was then he spotted the gas canisters and desperately tried to yell out to the others. But it was no use. The gas filled the room faster than he could speak, his words failing amidst the commotion, dropping to the floor, clutching at his throat. They were going out with a whimper.

Through the smoke-filled room, he could see green laser beams cutting through the smog. He was forced to watch on in horror as he saw those who tried to resist getting cut down by the hidden assassins.

Bryant sat on his knees as the smoke filled his lungs. Reaching out, he grabbed Mia's hand. She gripped his fingers tight. They lay there hand in hand. The surrounding noise finally calmed down as armed soldiers appeared from the shadows. He felt the grip on his hand wither. Shifting his eyes across to Mia, he saw that hers were closed. He didn't have long now, his brain using his last breaths to search for answers. He'd run through so many what if's in his head. He'd played out so many scenarios, but not one of them involved them being caught. They'd been so careful. How could they have known? Then it hit him. Everyone was here, everyone except Stein. How could he have been so blind? Of course, he wanted to remain anonymous, hiding in plain sight. Bryant felt betrayed, heartbroken. He'd trusted that man, even considered him family. He'd listened to his lies. His heart rate slowing now, eyes failing. He looked over at Mia one last time. He could just about make out her face through the fog. He studied her face, her lips, those beautiful eyes.

Alone.

Eyes open, he wasn't dead! He blinked furiously, his vision was blurry, and his head pounded. As he tried to focus his vision, he realised he couldn't move. Panicked, he desperately tried to will his limbs into life. It was no use. Was he paralysed? As the blur dissipated, it became more apparent. He could see enough to make out the room. It was all white with just the one lamp that hung from the ceiling. The walls were padded, and there was a solitary solid door at one end of it. No windows, no natural light. He was in a chair. But it was solid metal. His limbs strapped down, including his neck. He couldn't even so much as move his head. He struggled using all his might. But there was no escape. What would happen now? Where was he? His panic quickly gave way to anger, "Mia." He remembered the look on her face, the horror. What had they done with her? If they hurt her, he'd kill them, kill them all.

There was a clunk, and then the heavy door swung open. A bright light filled the room, blinding him momentarily before closing swiftly. Blinking once more, forcing away the spots that filled his eyes, he focussed his vision and looked up and down at the familiar figure stood before him.

"It's you?" uttered Bryant. "Help me out of here. There's been a huge misunderstanding."

"I'm afraid that can't happen!"

"Phil," said Bryant, "what's going on?"

"You just couldn't leave it alone. Could you?" he said. Bryant felt sick. This couldn't be real.

"It's been you all along?"

"You give me too much credit, Bryant," said Phil.

"But I trusted you," he growled.

"I gave you every opportunity to drop it, Bryant. It didn't have to come to this. We could have worked together. I liked you, Bryant."

Bryant spat out at him. Angry, disgusted, hurt, "You scumbag," he said. "You've been behind all of this.

Phil casually removed a handkerchief from his pocket. Gently wiping away the saliva from his face before speaking, "Oh Bryant, you know nothing at all, do you?"

"You'd be surprised," he said defiantly. "I know everything. I know the lies about space. I know that you're controlling the people. Lying to them for your own gain, you're despicable. I mean, did we ever go to space, or is the whole thing just another lie?"

Phil laughed wickedly, "Oh, Bryant," he said, wiping at his eyes. "Thanks. I needed a good laugh."

"What do you mean?" Bryant asked.

"Space Bryant, it's perfectly real. We've been many times. I've even been to Mars twice. I have some fabulous pictures at home! I could have shown you one day."

"You're lying!" Bryant shouted.

"I wish I was Bryant. Mars, Venus, Mercury, and far beyond. We've seen it all, and there's nothing worth having Bryant. No other sustainable life. Not in any relative distance, anyway. Earth is all we have."

"I don't understand," said Bryant. "Why all this charade? Why the Academy, if even the quartermaster has already been to Mars?"

"Because Bryant, our planet has a wealth of riches. Some we've probably not even discovered yet. It's our home. It's all we have. But yet give the people a choice, and they will just tear it down. Keep on destroying it. We have this perfect world. But instead, we ravage it, always looking out instead of in. The Order doesn't enslave humanity, Bryant. It preserves it."

"Protect it? By sending miners off to die. By killing those who rise against you?" Bryant growled.

"All necessary, Bryant. Think about the bigger picture. The few for the many."

"It won't work," said Bryant. "You'll never squash the revolution. The truth will always win. My father was there before me. And there'll be more after me."

Phil moved closer to Bryant, "Ah, your father, I knew him well. We were good friends for a time."

"Bullshit," said Bryant, "just another lie."

"Oh dear, poor Bryant," Phil spoke. "Did daddy not tell you everything?"

Bryant wrestled against his restraints.

"Your father isn't quite who you thought he was, Bryant." Phil continued. "You share the same conscience, though; I'll give you that."

"More lies."

"I wish it were Bryant," said Phil. "I regret what happened to your father. Just as I regret what's going to happen to you."

"Say what you want," said Bryant, "I'm not going to believe you."

Phil moved face to face with Bryant and looked him straight in the eye. "You don't even believe that yourself, Bryant. How about I tell you a little story?"

"Enough already," said Bryant. "Torture me, kill me. Whatever! Just get it over with."

"I admire your fight, Bryant. I do. But it won't last."

"Then why bore me with your stories?" asked Bryant.

"Why?" replied Phil. "Because I need you to understand. I need you to see the world for how it truly is. I need you to see sense in what we're doing here. I mean, you have nowhere to be, and I have all the time in the world, humour me.

"You're half right. I do work for The Order, but I'm not the leader. Call me security if you like. But Bryant, you have to realise that The Order has existed since the beginning of man. We are called The Order not because we trap, kill or enslave. But because we keep order at any cost. If you look back through history, humanity has put itself on the brink of destruction many times. Plagues, wars, famines. They have all be orchestrated by us but for a specific purpose.

" We used to hide in plain sight. Allow people to have the power that we gave them. We owned Kings, Queens, Presidents, and governments. We let them enjoy a better life as long as they kept their people from destroying themselves, and it worked for a time. Giving people the illusion of freedom kept the world spinning.

"However, we reached a point at the beginning of the 21st century when we realised it had to change. The leaders we put in place became corrupted by the power, and they thought they were bigger and better than everyone, including us. I mean, we had reality TV star billionaires who made their way into Presidencies and then denied that they were ruining the planet. So that they could further their economic advantage. We had despots cutting their country off from the rest of the world. Deciding to test nuclear weapons out at sea. Oil companies ravaged the land just to get ahead of their rivals, and anyone could become rich, powerful, and then suddenly join this club."

"I already know this. You're wasting your breath," said Bryant.

"Perhaps. But you must understand Bryant. The planet was heading for collapse, and we no longer had the power to stop it. It didn't matter what we did, how we tried to show the people that they would destroy their only home. They just didn't care. The people became wrapped up in possessions, selfies, social media, food, cars, drugs, and alcohol. We were left with no choice, Bryant. We decided if we changed the narrative. Made the threat real and have everyone believe that the most important thing was working together. Then we could stop the damage from being done."

"It can't have been that easy," Bryant protested.

"You'd be surprised what the people will believe, Bryant. Feed them a lie, and then slowly turn the screw. We started it with a simple virus, a pandemic. We realised people would do whatever you told them if it was for their safety. We put the word out. People did the rest, Bryant. Neighbours turned on each other. Families would cease to communicate, never seeing each other. Bit by bit, we put the walls up. Each community safe behind the barriers. Fearful of the disease and the people on the other side."

"I don't understand what my father has to do with this?" replied Bryant, confused.

"Well, Bryant, it was all his idea."
The words hit the back of Bryant's brain. It felt as though a knife had been plunged deep into his heart. He felt sick.

"I don't believe you," he managed.

"No, of course, you don't. Bryant Fisher, he always knows best," replied Phil.

"Maybe I would. But there's a big flaw in your timeline. There's no way he's old enough," said Bryant.

"Just like Commander Steele isn't old enough to have founded the Academy?" asked Phil
Bryant looked at him.

"I know you've read the history books, Bryant."

"What are you talking about?"

"Steele?" replied Phil. "He's dead now. But we let him live to the ripe old age of 167! But then he outlived his usefulness."

"You're insane," cried Bryant, "why would I believe that?"

"It's like I said, Bryant. This planet has vast untapped riches. Take the Orbitium, for example."

"What about it?" Bryant demanded.

"See Bryant? You want to know," Phil continued, "think about it. The Orbitium comes from the dark reaches of the ocean. It was discovered by a research team studying life at depth and how it survived. They had no idea what they stumbled across Bryant. And we couldn't let them keep it.

"Think about life at the bottom of the ocean. How does it survive? No sunlight, no air, limited food. It's simple. That team discovered the mineral, realised it had fantastic regeneration powers. I remember it quite well, Bryant. It was the early 21st century. That poor crew thought they would go down in history.

"So, you're telling me you are over 300 years old?" asked Bryant.

"367, to be exact."

"No," said Bryant, "doesn't make sense. You still look old."

"Ooft, low blow Bryant! But you're right. It regenerates cells. It doesn't reverse the ageing process. It just preserves life."

"What about my father," asked Bryant, "what does this have to do with him?"

"We were partners, Bryant. We worked in intelligence together, both rookies at the time. We were sent to retrieve the Orbitium when it was discovered. We took out that whole team and the research with them. Made it look like an accident."

"No, it can't be true," said Bryant. "How do I fit into this? My mum, Julie, the Uprising?"

"That's the sad part Bryant," said Phil. "The plan was supposed to be temporary. It was a short-term strategy to preserve the planet. However, most of The Order decided that we could never let the people go back to their old ways. It was obvious they would return to destroying the earth and each other as soon as we did. Can't you see, the people need an incentive to work together, Bryant.

"Your father? Well, he disagreed. Said the people should be given a choice. He grew tired of living a never-ending life and grew weary of The Order. Out of the respect we had for him, we let him leave. Pick a District to live out the rest of his days. I gave him every chance Bryant, I did. But like you, he wouldn't leave it alone. He was determined that humanity should be given a chance, a choice. To know the truth and show that they could work together."

"So you killed him?" Bryant yelled tearfully.

"Yes," said Phil, "I did it myself. But I never wanted it. He just wouldn't listen." Bryant was in floods of tears. It made sense, but he wished it didn't.

"So why tell me all this?" Bryant asked.

"Hope Bryant, hope is dangerous. I'm annoyed at you for letting it come to this. Your father created hope, and I mean to destroy that. He was a clever, meticulous man. He hid the revolution very well. He gave up absolutely nothing. We could have used you and your family to make him talk. But even if he did, hope Bryant, hope would live on. We expected that the revolution would collapse without him. But it didn't."

"So, you used me?" Bryant said tearfully.

"Yes, Bryant, did you think you passed the entrance exam? I mean, come on, you guessed the last questions. Do you really think anyone passes it? We've made it impossible. Nobody passes the test, Bryant. We handpick entrants, people we know will be happy to take a better life and not look too deep into what's going on. The Academy isn't full of the bright-eyed brainy future of tomorrow, Bryant. It's made up of people who will take the money, put on a show, and keep the illusion alive."

Struggling in his seat, Bryant said, "Not all of them."

"See, there's that hope again, Bryant. It's dangerous."

Bryant said, "But what about DeVore, and why fake space missions if you've already been to Mars?"

"DeVore," said Phil gleefully. "I'd almost forgotten about him. To be honest, he kind of fell into our lap. He was rash, a poser. He just liked the idea of being a revolutionary. We knew he cheated the test, and so we thought we'd go with it. See what we could get from him. Sadly though, for you and us, he knew very little. He met no one face to face. He gave up everything before he died. Which wasn't helpful."

"Then you went back to me?" asked Bryant.

"See," said Phil, "you're getting it. As for Space, it's not a constant lie. We just need to keep everyone working, Bryant. Keep the hope of a better life dangling in front of them. One that they can never quite reach. It wouldn't work very well if we told them we'd explored every speck of Mars, and there's nothing there now, would it?

"No, what we do is drag it out. Make them think they are working for their future, then their children's future. Two steps forward and then three steps back."

"You're crazy," said Bryant. "It will never work."

"Ah," said Phil, "this isn't my first rodeo! It has been working for over a century now. Time is very different for us. We can stretch a plan out. This isn't the first time we've pretended to send a mission to Mars Bryant."
Bryant strained his eyes to meet the gaze of Phil.

"Oh, you look surprised," he said. "No, it's easy. We space the big events out. Take today, for example. Today's flight is supposedly going to Mars. We tell everyone today that the craft landed on the planet. That's the statement now. Then we slowly change the narrative. Perhaps there will be a setback, sabotage, shortage of Orbitium. We put things on hold for a while. But the people believe. Then over time, they forget what happened. In ten years, when people look at today, history will say that we got near to Mars. But it didn't land. It's rare anybody notices the change if history says otherwise. Anyone who thinks differently is branded as crazy."

"And if they persist?" asked Bryant.

"We kill them," exactly said Phil.

Bryant was crestfallen. It was utterly insane. But perfectly possible.

"Oh, don't look so glum," said Phil. "You always wanted to be the Space hero."

"I'm going to space?" Bryant asked, confused.

"Well, no, not physically," said Phil. "But in the hearts and minds of everyone, you will be. 'Bryant Fisher' the first man on Mars. That will be your legacy until we change it. I'm afraid it will be tragic, though, Bryant. You'll perish in the process. But tell me what I need to know, and it will be painless. I promise."

"But you know everything. What can I tell you that don't you already know?" asked Bryant.

"Just two things. Your friends have told us everything they know. But you're organised, smart Bryant. None of them has told me where the books are or who the rat is inside my Academy. They haven't told me Bryant because they don't know. But I'm willing to bet you do."

Bryant laughed furiously.

"Something funny about what I said?" asked Phil.

"Yes," Bryant laughed on. "You know who the inside man is. I mean, he led you to us?" He paused, thinking. It suddenly occurred to Bryant that Phil genuinely didn't know who was inside at the Academy. Meaning Stein hadn't given them up. So who had?

"I don't have time for you daydreams, Bryant."

"I won't tell you," said Bryant boldly. "It doesn't matter what you do to me."

"I believe you," said Phil. "You probably even believe you. But the clock is ticking. So I apologise for what I'm about to do."

Phil clicked his fingers. The door opened, and the man with the snake tattoo dragged someone in, tossing them to the floor like a sack of potatoes.

"You," Bryant seethed.

"Oh, don't be mean to him," said Phil. "He was like you once. But he understands what needs to happen." The man nodded dutifully at Phil before departing. Bryant strained his eyes to look down at the person before him. Realising who the dishevelled figure was. His elation at seeing her quickly turned to fear.

"Mia, Mia," he shouted. Her hands and feet were tied. Her mouth gagged, leaving her unable to speak. She was a little roughed up but was otherwise unhurt.

Phil bent and grabbed Mia by the ponytail, forcing her to her knees in front of Bryant. Their eyes met. Tears streamed from her eyes, those beautiful eyes.

"Hey," he said, "look at me. Mia. It's going to be okay."

She shook her head wildly as if trying to speak. The sounds from her mouth were muffled, and Bryant desperately tried to make out what she was saying.

"Okay, reunion over," Phil said. He removed a gun from his belt, placing it firmly against Mia's head. "I'm going to ask you one last time, Bryant. Who is the inside man?"

"You don't have to do this," Bryant pleaded fiercely. "Phil, please?"

"No, Bryant, you're the one making this happen. Tell me, and it stops."

Bryant looked back at Mia, "It's okay he said. Look at me. It's going to be okay." Phil cocked the gun and pushed it hard into the back of Mia's head.

"Ten seconds Bryant. Do you really want her brains splattered all over you?"

"Please. Phil," Bryant begged, "this isn't you."

"Five seconds, Bryant."

Bryant looked down at Mia. Then back at Phil. He had a demonic look in his eyes. He wasn't bluffing.

"Okay, okay," he said. "It's Stein, Major Stein. He's the one you want. Just please don't hurt her." Phil removed the gun from Mia's head.

"See," he said, "that wasn't so difficult, was it? Now since we all know where we stand. I need to know where the books are, Bryant. All of them."

"No, please, please," he pleaded. "I'll take you there. You and me. We can get the books together."

Phil put the gun back against Mia's head. She looked up at him, such a terrified look in her eyes. His world was falling apart in front of him. He couldn't take it.

"Alright," said Bryant, "fine, the old stadium. Hidden in the seats. They're all there."

"Thank you, Bryant. But somehow, I don't believe you would have kept them all in the one place," said Phil. "So tell me. Where are the rest of them?"

"That's all of them, I swear. Don't hurt her, please don't hurt her!" The pressure was too much. He'd given the rest of the books to Jimmy. It was an impossible situation. Mia or Jimmy. He had to choose one of them.

"Okay! We do it my way," said Phil. He raised the gun once more; the world slowed down as he squeezed the trigger and fired!

The noise was deafening, reverberating horribly around the room. Bryant watched on as Mia fell to the floor; muffled screams were coming from her mouth. Tears streamed from her eyes as blood billowed out on the white floor. The sight was sickening. The red splatter went up the walls and even on to Bryant.

As she fell, she struggled against her restraints, desperately trying to clutch at the wound in her leg. Phil bent and grabbed Mia by the throat. He shoved the gun against her skull, saying.

"Next ones in the head, Bryant."

"Okay, don't shoot her, please," he pleaded. "I love her! Don't kill her, please. Please, I'll tell you. I'll tell you anything." Bryant fought passionately against his restraints. Veins burst from his head, snot from his nose, and tears from his eyes.

"I'll tell you anything you want to know," he begged. "Just please don't hurt her again."

"The books, Bryant?"

"The mines, the mines," he yelled. "I gave them to Jimmy. He hid them down the mines. Please, he's not part of this. He doesn't know anything! Please don't hurt him." Phil released Mia, stood and patted him on the shoulder.

"Thank you, Bryant," Phil said. "See, that wasn't so difficult, was it now?" Removing a knife from his pocket. He then crouched down on the floor next to Mia. Bryant yelled and thrashed desperately in his chair.

"Noooo," he begged. "You said you wouldn't hurt her." Unfolding the knife as he knelt. He cut away at the cable ties on her feet, followed by her hands.

"And I won't," he said. Mia stood gingerly and removed the bit from her mouth.

"How's the leg Evans, can you walk?" Phil asked. She nodded.

"Good," he said, "find Stein. Pretend you got away from us and tell him you need his help; if he tells you anything else, then great. If not, kill him."

Bryant looked on in horror, shock, disbelief as she nodded before leaving the room. She didn't turn back. Not once. He couldn't believe it. He didn't believe it. This couldn't be happening. This was a nightmare, surely? He started shaking, convulsing. Wake up, Bryant, please wake up! It was Mia, and it had always been Mia! Mia and Phil, he'd trusted both of them, isolated those whom he held dear, swapping old for new. Jimmy, Julie, Mum. His world crumbled right before his eyes, and he was wide awake. He saw everything now, and he was powerless to stop it. He was helpless, alone and afraid!

"Breathe, Bryant, Breathe," said Phil. "We can't have you dying before the show." A man and a woman entered the room. The woman stepped towards Bryant, syringe in hand.

"No," he said, shaking as hard as he could.

"Relax, Bryant," said Phil. "It's just a light sedative. Calm you down a bit." The man who entered with her was the man with the snake tattoo. Phil grabbed him by the arm, asking, "Is our man still with the miners?"

"Yes, sir!" came the reply

"Excellent," said Phil. "Make sure he finds the books. Then kill them all, destroy the mine. Make it look like an accident."

"But that will destroy the mines," the man with the snake tattoo speaking for the first time. Bryant studied him as he hesitated. Now they were up close. There was a familiarity to both his looks and his voice. But he couldn't work it out; he didn't care, not anymore.

"Did I stutter?" replied Phil.

"No, sir," replied Miguel. "Very good, sir!"Miguel then turned about on the spot, departing the room, leaving Bryant alone with Phil.

"Why?" Bryant croaked in disbelief.

"That look," said Phil, "that look you have on your face now. That realisation that you gave up everything you know, everyone you loved, and for what? I needed you to know Bryant. There is only one way, our way. I needed to stamp out hope once and for all. You had to know you were a minor inconvenience. Nothing can stop us."

"But there will be others!" Bryant managed.

"Oh, I highly doubt that," said Phil. "Thanks to you, we've managed the biggest purge of insurgents in our history. We've dug out every single member of the revolution in every District. That Bryant is your legacy. That was your destiny." Phil stepped in close to Bryant and whispered in his ear,

"But should there be anyone else? If someone else takes us on. I'll be here waiting." Patting Bryant on the head, he continued, "I am sorry it had to come to this. I really am. I had a lot of respect for your father."

Bryant struggled now to muster even a response as the sedative took full effect. In the background, he noticed the door open once more. A nurse bustled in with another trolley. Phil moved towards the door. Before stopping and saying, "Settle in Bryant, enjoy the show. This is the moment you've been waiting for."

The nightmare.

The nurse who entered the room attached a drip to his arm before injecting something into it.

"Don't worry," she said sympathetically. "It will be painless." He wasn't worried. Nothing hurt anymore anyway. Nothing mattered now; he was broken. All that was left was the warm and cosy feeling as the IV drifted into his blood. He'd accepted his fate. It was far from the destiny he'd imagined, but he was ready. Knowing there was no hope, no love, no integrity. This was no longer a world he wanted to be part of.

His breathing slowed now, and his eyes were heavy. His eyelids drooped, and he felt that he could drift away, but suddenly, the wall in front of him burst into life. The inbuilt screen spewed out light and sound into the blood-spattered room. It was an emergency broadcast. Traitors had tried to blow up the Academy. A line of faces paraded across the screen. They were all there, Alpha, Mr Goldstein, even Butch. They'd put this together quickly! The sour note soon ended. There was a reason to rejoice. The narrative continued. They'd know about the attack and had moved their operations. There was excitement in the orator's voice. He spoke about a secret mission to Mars launched the previous day.

It cut to a video. It was a live feed. Bryant was face to face with himself as he watched the version of him on screen. He remembered all the training, the simulations. They had captured all of them on film. The quality of the fake was exceptional. He watched on as the video played out. Watching himself land a craft on Mars, exploring the surface. It was like viewing one of his dreams. The video interrupted, Phil's face filling the screen.

"Do you like my video, Bryant? See, that's you on Mars! Or at least that's what everyone will think. What's left of your friends and family will get to watch you die as a hero. Isn't that what you always wanted, Bryant? That was your dream. To be the hero?"

It made sense; they would use him to hide the truth from the people even further. His death would keep them blind, keep them trapped. It was genius, and he'd fallen right into their hands, given them everything. In a way, he understood. It was a horrible, evil genius, but it didn't matter anymore. Nothing did.

"Don't worry," Phil spoke again, "we've already sent them your goodbye message. They'll understand why you didn't tell them about the mission. I mean, it's not like you've told them much recently anyway, Bryant. You needn't fear for your family, though. I'll have Mia keep them safe."

The screen went black and turned into a wall once more. The whole thing was perfectly staged. A single tear rolled from his eye.

They'd won. The dream had been a nightmare all along, and he'd been too blind to see it.

Across town, Pam got out of her taxi. Finishing work early was always a bonus. There was a curfew tonight for safety, and she felt as though she'd been physically herded back to her house. She opened the door. Julie was sat on the sofa, all available screens blaring away.

"What's going on?" Pam asked her daughter.

Julie shrugged, "I wanted to go out. The dog wouldn't let me."

Pam looked down at Roger. Odd, it had been a while since he'd been remote activated. She took a seat on her sofa with Roger sitting between them and the door.

"I guess they really want us to watch this broadcast," Pam said, snuggling into her daughter on the sofa. "Get Jimmy, will you?"

"Eugh gross," said Julie. "He better not be sick down here." Julie stood and ran up the stairs shouting, "Hey puke boy!"

Jimmy's family had returned to the mines last week. But Jimmy had been violently sick. He'd wanted to go with them. But he was too ill, a burden. His family could ill afford to take him. Meaning he was under Pam's care until they returned.

Having ascended the stairs, Julie burst into her brothers' room. Jimmy was curled up on the bed. "You'd better not puke on that," she said. "This will be my room soon."

"What do you want?" Jimmy groaned. Shrugging, Julie said, "Mum wants you downstairs."

Jimmy stood and awkwardly followed her down the stairs to Pam, who was sitting on the sofa, watching the broadcast begin. Pam's phone rang; noticing it was Bryant, she grabbed it immediately. The screen changed, and she was face to face with her son, "Hey, sweetie," she chirped.

"Hi Mum, Julie, how are you both?"

"Oh," Pam realised sadly. It was a pre-recorded video. Despite how many he'd sent her now. She still wasn't used to them. "Julie, Jimmy, get here. We've got a message from Bryant."

The two appeared, Julie jumping back onto the sofa next to her mother. Jimmy arrived and sat gingerly on the other side of her. Pam pressed play, and the three of them watched on.

"I apologise for sending this a video," said the voice of Bryant. "But time was of the essence, as you are now aware. There was a vicious attack planned on the Academy. Now there's no need to panic. I'm fine. I'm better than that. By the time you get this video, I will be gone, off on a mission. Mum, Julie, I'm going to Mars. It is just a quick trip. I should be back within a few days. But for now, guys, settle in and watch the show. Guys, I'm going to save the world!"

"Eugh," said Julie, "rehearsed much?"
Jimmy looked at Pam. Tears had formed on her cheeks.

"Are you okay, Mrs Fisher?"

"I'm fine, thanks, Jimmy," she said, "I guess I just never expected this day to come."

"It's Bryant," said Jimmy, comforting her. "He'll be fine."

"You're right," she said, "I can't believe it, though. My boy, the first person on Mars." The television grew louder.

"Shh," said Julie, watching on curiously. The cameras were now live at the launch station. The tension was palpable. The entire world watched on as the rocket prepared for lift-off. The three of them sat hand in hand on the sofa as the timer counted down.

5,4,3,2...

Somewhere across the District. Bryant's eyes opened once more. He glanced up at the screen; it was playing again. His eyes opened just enough to see himself climb back into the spaceship from the planet's surface, watching as his ship powered off from the ground. The mission was over a success, back to Earth. The ship roared as it drove up in the atmosphere. Bryant strapped in, helmet on. He lifted his hand, giving a 'thumbs up' to all those watching. He remembered the simulation well. How he wished he hadn't done that. But then tragedy! The world an audience in horror as his craft exploded and burst into flames. A planet overjoyed and distraught simultaneously. United in gratitude for the great Bryant Fisher, the first man on Mars, saviour of the human race. Tributes poured in from around the globe, Earth's hero, Bryant Fisher. A planet rejoiced as it mourned. The drip in his arm increased, drugs coursing through his veins as he drifted away. His eyes glanced at the screen once more. Watching on his ship burnt and fall apart. This was it, and it was all over. They'd won the people would never be free. Bryant Fisher, the first man on Mars. His final thoughts before closing his eyes for the very last time.

Julie Fisher will return in:
Fortis.

Printed in Great Britain
by Amazon